Chaos in the Canyon

A Miranda Marquette Mystery
by J.T. Kunkel
Book 5

Copyright 2021 by J. T. Kunkel
ISBN: 978-1-950613-72-4

Published by Taylor and Seale Publishing, LLC
3408 South Atlantic Avenue
Unit 139
Daytona Beach Shores, FL 32118

All rights reserved. No part of this book may be reproduced, distributed or transmitted in any form or by any means, electronic or mechanical, including photocopying, recording or by any information storage or retrieval system, without permission, in writing, by the author or publisher. This book was printed in the United States of America. For information, contact Taylor and Seale Publishing, LLC.

Cover design and layout by Chris Holmes

Publisher's Note: This is a work of fiction. Names, characters, places, and incidents are a product of the author's imagination or used fictitiously. Locales and public names are sometimes used fictitiously for atmospheric purposes. With the exception of public figures or specific historical references, any resemblance to actual people, living or dead, or to businesses, companies, events, institutions, or locales is completely coincidental. Any historical personages or actual events depicted are completely fictionalized and used only for inspiration. Any opinions expressed are completely those of fictionalized characters and not a reflection of the views of public figures, author, or publisher.

Dedication

To my gorgeous and brilliant wife Susan, the Love of my life, my Marketing Director and endless inspiration. When we met twenty-three years ago, we didn't have a clue the wild ride that we were in for, but we took the 'leap of faith' and jumped in with both feet. I have never had a day of regret. And although occasionally our life is still chaotic, I wouldn't miss a day of it for the world. I look forward to getting old together, although that will be a long, long time from now, and spending eternity together thereafter. I will Love You forever.

Acknowledgments

To Donna Pudick at Parkeast Literary Agency, my literary agent. Thank you for not accepting writing that wasn't up to my potential and continuing to make me a better writer by knowing how to push me to the next level. You have helped me to develop better writing and editing habits which have helped me as a writer and will in years to come. I continue to learn through your feedback and am very thankful to have you as an agent and a mentor.

To Veronica H. (Ronnie) Hart, my editor at Taylor and Seale Publishing. You continue to help me to hone my writing skills, and to help me to understand the subtle differences between an acceptably written dialog and an exceptional one. I continue to learn more as a writer every day with your help and look forward to working with you more on the series as Miranda matures and grows, and I thank you for that.

To Mary Custureri, CEO of Taylor and Seale Publishing. I continue to be amazed at how many authors there are compared to how many published authors. I have been very impressed by the quality of writers and books that you continue to publish. I am thankful that you have chosen to publish the Miranda Marquette Mystery Series and I look forward to a long association.

Chaos in the Canyon

Chapter 1
May 2011

I took a left out of the driveway for the first time since moving in with Jason nine months ago after my friend Patricia's mom took over my apartment lease. It was Saturday late afternoon, and I had already spent a couple of hours tinkering with my motorcycle. I didn't want my bike to feel neglected after spending all that time getting Jason's up and running that morning. Jason, my live-in boyfriend and boss, had taken off to parts unknown after I completed a tune-up of his Kawasaki. Left to my own devices, I grabbed my boots and helmet and set out on an adventure of my own.

A right turn would take me toward the 101 and civilization near Gilroy, California, nearly an hour south of Santa Clara. I had no idea where a left turn would take me, so I turned right. Within several hundred yards, I came to Gilroy Hot Springs Road. I surmised this route might lead to the Gilroy Yamato Hot Springs, which I had heard of but had never ventured to.

The road took me directly to the Hot Springs in a mile or two. I passed one hiking trail and an unnamed road off to my right. Otherwise, there was nothing else in that direction. Reading the historical plaque, I learned that the Yamato Hot Springs had been an active tourist venue from the late 1800s until the 1930s and the depression. World War II dramatically impacted the springs when Japanese citizens, including the owner of the site, were put into internment camps. Attempts had been made over the years to return it to its prior splendor and even make it into an overnight resort, but when the on-site hotel burned to the ground in 1980, the efforts never came to fruition. The site was now a derelict part of California Parks and Recreation, apparently abandoned and forgotten.

I strolled around the grounds and found them deserted. In the middle of the compound, which included several small rooms that looked like changing rooms, was a pool, which I assumed was fed by the natural hot springs located underground. The doors to the changing rooms had all been held open by small pieces of wood. The rooms were immaculate, so clearly, the place was cleaned often.

Not ever shying from an opportunity, I ran back to my bike and grabbed my bathing suit out of my saddlebag. I found it odd that there were no 'No Trespassing' signs, no chains, no gates, no locks, absolutely no deterrents to entering the property. But on the off chance someone in authority discovered me here, I could cite that as an excuse. I could seem pretty innocent when I wanted to.

I picked a changing room and slipped into my bikini. Ten years ago, I might even have attempted it sans suit, but my more modest side was revealing itself since I hit thirty. It was hard to believe that was nearly nine years ago. Not one to waste time, I stuck my foot in the pool. It was perfect, very similar to my old hot tub. I would estimate the temperature at 102 degrees. Without further ado, I stepped into the pool.

Built-in benches lined two sides of the pool. It was probably a thirty-foot square with a painted concrete surface, similar to most pools constructed during that era. It was absolute heaven. I hadn't been in a hot tub since I left Malibu, and since this pool was fed with natural mineral water, it was soothing in a medicinal, Zen sort of way.

That was probably why it was even more disconcerting when I felt a cold gun barrel touch my head as I rested it against the side of the spring-fed pool. I was afraid to open my eyes, so I just froze.

The man, whoever he was, started talking, "So, I finally caught you. You thought you were so smart, a-comin' up here and usin' the place. Well, I outsmarted you now, didn't I? I wonder what the cops are gonna think about that. They ain't gonna be too happy now since they couldn't catch ya. I've got a mind to give them a call and see what they want to do. Maybe we could all have our way with you. What do you think about that? Yeah, you're quite a looker, ain't ya? Yup, quite a looker."

Uh-oh. I was in serious trouble. I was barely dressed, and this psycho had a gun. He also seemed to have a case of mistaken identity, but it didn't seem like a good time to start arguing or calling him a liar. With the gun barrel still grinding into my head, I figured I had to start talking soon before he got trigger happy. "Mr.—"

"Oh, so she can talk. Burt, just call me Burt." I couldn't tell what Burt's horrible smell was, but it was some combination of liniment, sweat, and chewing tobacco.

I squirmed a little under the pressure of his pistol.

He laughed out loud. "Oh, am I hurting you? That's a shame, just a shame, ain't it?" He tsked. "Just a shame."

I tried my best not to move. "Hey, Burt. You seem like a nice guy. And obviously, you've got the gun, and I'm in the pool, so you've got the upper hand, and I'm not going anywhere. Do you think, maybe, you could take the gun from my head so we can have a chat?"

Chaos in the Canyon

He didn't respond, so I didn't know if he was thinking about it or trying to come back with some clever remark. Then, he removed the gun from my head so, I figured we were making progress. "Okay, I removed the gun, now what are you going to do for me?" I couldn't see his face, but I could only imagine it was said with a smirk.

This was getting creepy fast. I had to decide if I would need to take evasive or aggressive action. Nine out of ten times, guys like this were completely harmless and could be talked out of anything with a wink and a flirt, but that tenth guy was a real problem. And identifying them before it was too late was critical. I also needed to decide if I was safer in or out of the water. At this point, I was thinking I was safer where I was because if he tried to get in, I had a tremendous advantage, having been trained in hand-to-hand combat in all depths of water. I wished he would get in and even things up.

I hadn't actually been able to look at my enemy yet because he stood behind me. I wasn't sure how to solve that standoff. Finally, I had a relatively low-risk idea. I figured he could only say No. "Hey, Burt, now that you're not pointing the gun at my head, maybe you could come around the other side of the pool, so I can see who I'm talking to." I pondered being a bit more flirtatious, but you can't take it back once you say it, so I figured I start out safe and slow.

He didn't respond; he just walked slowly to the other side of the pool. He was a big man, mid-fifties. Even with his flannel shirt on, I could see his chest hair between his buttons. He was around six foot five, probably two hundred and eighty pounds, mostly muscle. He was the kind of guy you wanted on your team if you were camping in the woods and a bear was scavenging through your food.

As menacing as he had seemed behind me with a gun, I couldn't look away from his face, which seemed kind, but maybe that was just wishful thinking on my part. I took a chance, "Burt, when you said before that you *finally* caught me, I think you might have me confused with someone else."

He shook his head. "Wait a minute. Are you trying to tell me you haven't been comin' up here, usin' the showers, leaving cigarette butts in the wastebaskets, and clogging up the toilets?"

I smiled. "Burt, do I look like someone who would clog up toilets?"

He couldn't help but laugh in spite of himself. "Okay, you got me there. God, I hate this job. I'm just no good at it. I tried to scare the crap out of you, and in ten minutes, we're already jokin' around. It's a curse."

I gave him an innocent look. "You mean to say you never meant you were going to have your *way* with me?"

He threw his hat down, "God, no! If my wife ever found out she would kill me!" He pulled up an Adirondack chair. "So, what ya doin' up here, anyway? Most people don't even know it exists."

I started to get light-headed from being in hot water too long but still a little too exposed to hang out with Burt in a bikini. "Miranda Marquette. I live down on Roop Road."

He perked up. "Well, how about that—Burt Roop at your service. My family bought this place in the 1860s and ran an upscale resort during its heyday. Then my grandmother took it over, trying to save it during the depression. My dad had a dream of bringing it back to its splendor, which was dashed when the hotel burned on the fourth of July weekend in 1980. We'd have a Class A resort if it weren't for that damned fire." He swore under his breath. "I'm going to catch the guy that burned this place down if it's the last thing I do. I know who it is."

I was surprised. "You do? How come they haven't been caught?"

He stared into my eyes. "We did catch him back when he did it and they let him go, but I'll get him. Wait and see."

I nodded. "I hope you do. What's his name? Maybe I can help. I have an investigation background."

He looked at me for a long time as if he were debating spilling his guts but held back.

I smiled. "Well, if you change your mind, you know where I live."

He said, "Thank you," and re-gathered his thoughts. "Now, we rely on volunteers and the kindness of others to keep the place afloat. My dream, though, is to reopen it to the public someday. This pool is a small concentration of the springs, which are all around this ten-acre area."

I felt safe opening up to this man, "I just moved here about nine months ago. My boyfriend's been here for several years."

He scratched his head. "Jason?"

I nodded and smiled.

"He said he had a hot girlfriend, but I had no idea." I thought I saw him blush. "We're one house up and across the street."

I had to laugh. "What a way to meet your neighbors, right?"

He smiled. "Sally will think it's a hoot, or she'll punch my lights out. Kind of depends on the day." I thought I saw him break a sweat.

I offered, "We'll tell her the G-Rated version, leaving out your obnoxious threat to me."

He looked up at the sky. "Thank you, Jesus."

#

I lost track of time as Burt and I talked about the history of the area, motorcycle riding, him being married to the same woman for thirty years, and loving Northern California. I told him about my childhood in Meraux, my detour to North Carolina and Vegas, my Southern California adventures, and how I ended up here.

Somewhere between stories, I changed back into my street clothes. He seemed way more comfortable talking to me after that. He came across as a gentleman at heart and didn't fit the role he tried to portray at our initial meeting. I thanked my lucky stars for that.

The sun was just disappearing over the canyon when we finally said our goodbyes. He invited me to stop by anytime, especially since the springs weren't yet open to the public. If he was even able to open them, he promised he would give me a deal. We hugged like old friends before I jumped on my motorcycle.

He hummed a song from a seventies band rock opera my parents used to play that I couldn't quite place as I rode away.

Chapter 2

By the time I got home, it was nearly dark. Jason's Kawasaki stood in the driveway, and I could see by the lights in the house that he was in the kitchen. I waltzed through the back door and snuck up behind him. I put my hands over his eyes. "Guess who!"

He thought for a minute. "Wait, oh, I almost had it. No, that's not it. It's been so long I can't actually remember. Maybe if I—" He turned around and kissed me deeply. We both came up for air. "I've almost got it." He kissed me again. "I think it starts with M."

I put my hands on my hips. "That's the best you can do, mister?"

He came up behind me and put his hands around my waist. "And where have you been, young lady?"

I said quietly, "Well, sir, if you must know, I was with Burt Roop."

He pushed me away. "Yeah, and I was with Sally."

I bit my lip. "Hmm, how'd that go? I understand she can be a bit of the jealous type."

He laughed. "Okay, sweetheart, I give up. I know somewhere on your side of the conversation, there's a hint of truth about what you did today, so are you going to tell me, or do I have to guess?"

I put a finger to my lips. "Um, guess?"

He gave me a look, which I took to mean, this was fun, but let's get to the truth before I start to get annoyed.

I took a deep breath. "Okey dokie then. Well, you were gone to places unknown on the motorcycle that I had brought back to life after five years of neglect."

He acknowledged me. "And for that, I will be forever grateful."

I went on. "So, I tuned mine up too, but you still weren't back yet, so I figured I'd take her for a spin. I had never taken a left out of the driveway, so I just thought, what the heck, and I did. Anyway, I took a left and then a right at the end of our road and in a mile or two came to the Hot Springs. Well, you know I'm naturally curious, so I parked the bike and took a look around."

He nodded; knowing me, he wasn't surprised.

"Well, I had no idea this place was even there. A lot of it is quite rundown and in a state of disrepair. It looks like there had been several cabins, some of which are now falling down, some had been restored. Then there were these changing rooms and a pool that was fed by the natural mineral springs. It was heavenly."

He raised his eyebrows in surprise. "You don't mean you actually—"

I protested, "Geez, Jason. What do you think? I keep a bathing suit in my saddlebag just for such eventualities." I glared at him then winked. "So I'm lying back in this heavenly pool, feeling on top of the world, and suddenly I feel a gun to my head."

He shook his head, "Burt."

I nodded. "Evidently, the place has been in and out of his family for a hundred and fifty years, so he's fairly protective." I rolled my eyes, "Well, maybe *fairly protective* is a bit of an understatement. He thought I was someone else who has been giving him a run for his money and abusing the property. At one point, he actually threatened to call the police, so they could all, let's see how did he put it? 'Have their way with me.'"

He didn't seem particularly concerned or surprised. "That will be the day. Sally would kill him. You haven't seen her, have you?"

I gave him a side glance. "No. Why?"

He continued. "Well, if he's pushing 300 pounds, she's a good fifty more at least. I'm sure she could take him. He's scared to death of her, I'm pretty sure. And make no mistake. She's the jealous type. If she even *knew* you two had a conversation, the fur would fly."

I drummed the table with my fingernails. "Well, I guess Burt was taking his life into his own hands then. After that rough start, when I explained that I lived out here and that I'd never been there in my life, we talked most of the afternoon, and a good portion of that I was in my bikini. I was getting chilly so I changed back into my riding gear. Quite honestly, he seemed relieved. Thank God Sally didn't come looking for him. I'd have been a sitting duck."

Jason winked, "That'll teach you to keep your clothes on."

I felt lucky to be with the least jealous guy I had ever met. I guess that came with being secure with himself. He'd often found me talking to guys at work and never questioned me about it like he never gave it a second thought. I wasn't sure I'd be as understanding if one of my co-workers were flirting with him. I guess he was a better boyfriend than I was a girlfriend. I often told him so.

I thought for a minute about the day. "So where'd you go today, Mr. Kawasaki?"

He grabbed a beer from the fridge. "I rode out to the San Luis Reservoir State Park. I took a trail around the lake. It was gorgeous. Granted, I didn't have a run-in with anyone with a handgun or a bikini, for that matter, but it was a relaxing afternoon. I used to fish out there years ago when I first moved out here. I figured once you got on the phone with your girlfriends, you wouldn't even notice I was gone."

I nearly got defensive but had been practicing taking responsibility where responsibility was due. "Yes, we do love to talk. I'm so glad I met Margo and that we put together our group. She is so much fun! I hope I can still be that fun in twenty years."

I figured this was as good a time as any to discuss my weekend plans with him. "Oh yeah, we've made plans for next weekend so you're free. This is your chance to have that poker game and bring in those strippers you've been waiting for me to leave town for."

He pulled out his cell phone and pretended to dial.

I grabbed it and ran to the living room, "Do it and face the consequences, Cowboy."

He chased me around the couch, "Well, you can't withhold sex because, well, because we don't have it."

For some reason, that comment had me seeing red. I threw his phone at him and ran out of the house. He stood there staring at me. I ran out to the road and took a left. The right would just take me to the highway. I needed some time to cool down. I had to figure out what was going on in my head and my heart. I rarely had this kind of reaction to any conversation with Jason. We always just joked around about stuff. I tried to figure out why this was different. Was it his delivery, or was it how I took it?

I kept running then slowed down when I got to Gilroy Hot Springs Road and started walking. I wasn't going to walk all the way up to the springs. It was dark, and I could hear all sorts of wild animals in the woods. Coyote creek ran to the left of the road, and I could listen to it gurgling as I walked. I thought I remembered a bench just before the bridge crossing the creek and leading to the springs. After walking for about ten minutes, I found it and sat down.

I hadn't found a new therapist since moving to Coyote Lake, and I needed one badly. I had gone to the one in Santa Clara a couple of times after work since I'd moved from my apartment, but I hated getting home that late, so I had stopped going. I hadn't been more than three months without a therapist in, well, ever, so I was definitely feeling the loss.

Chaos in the Canyon

I thought about what I would tell her when I showed up at her office, angry and hurt. "Jason and I were just fooling around. I was telling him that I was going away for the weekend with my girlfriends. I joked that he should hold a poker game and have some strippers over. He pulled out his cell phone, pretending he was setting it up, so I grabbed his phone. I jokingly warned him he's better not or face the consequences. Then he said that I couldn't threaten to withhold sex because we didn't have it."

Then she would get a real sincere look on her face and say, "Oh, Miranda. And how did that make you feel?"

And I'd respond, "I was mad! He shouldn't be throwing that in my face. He agreed to my conditions when I moved in here. I'm just feeling vulnerable and want to take things slow. That doesn't mean forever, but for now."

She'd sit there for a minute and then ask, "Well, are there ever times when you wish you and Jason would have sex?"

I'd glare at her. She'd look back at me with a blank expression, the one that they teach in therapy school. Finally, I'd say, "Of course there are. God, sometimes when we are watching a romantic movie, and then he and I get all wrapped up and start kissing and, well, you know."

She'd try to draw me out. Sometimes I wonder if she gets off on this kind of stuff. "I don't actually know, Miranda; tell me how you feel."

I'd close my eyes, trying to relive it. "I feel wonderful and horrible and strong and weak. I feel like I could live forever and like I want to die. I feel like I'm drowning and like I'm lost in the desert, like I'm floating in space and freefalling from an airplane with no parachute. It's the best. It's the worst."

She'd be relentless, "But do you want to have sex with him?"

I'd practically scream, "Of course I do! But I won't do it. Not yet. I don't care how sad he looks at me with those puppy-dog eyes. I don't care that he knows just how to touch me to make me want to. I've moved from the couch to the love seat when he thought he was being clever."

Then just when I thought she'd let up, she'd stick me with the punch line, "So why did you walk out today?"

I would think, knowing if I just blurted out the first thing that came to my mind, she'd keep pressing until I got it right. "I'm afraid."

She'd sit back in her chair, happy I was performing properly for her. A question entered my mind. Why did I need a therapist if I knew exactly what mine would say? I'd have to ponder that some other time when I wasn't in the middle of a session. She'd ask, "Good, Miranda. Now we are getting somewhere. What are you afraid of?"

I'd drum my nails against the arm of the chair, which looked like I wasn't the only one who had done that over the years. "I'm afraid he's going to leave me. Or worse, cheat on me."

She'd ask, "Do you think he loves you?"

I'd laugh. "Of course, he loves me."

"Then why would he leave you or cheat because you wouldn't have sex with him?"

I'd close my eyes, knowing what the answer was, but hoping for something more clever, "Because he's a man, doc. Because he's a man."

I stood, deciding I needed to go home. Talking to Jason was probably a better idea than an imaginary therapist, although I just saved $150. He was sitting on the couch watching golf when I walked in. I could tell he didn't know what to do or say, so I decided to break the ice.

I sat on his lap. "Okay, I might have over-reacted there, just a touch."

Happy and relieved that we weren't fighting anymore, he kissed me hard. I couldn't breathe, and I didn't want to. I wanted to crawl out of my skin and crawl inside of his. All of this sex talk with my make-believe therapist had made me just a bit, how should I say it, needy.

Knowing I was in a weakened state, I went to the kitchen for a glass of wine. I stood behind the kitchen counter, where it was safe. "I'm sorry, Cowboy. Sometimes, I just get crazy. I figured that taking a walk was a better idea than having a knock-down-drag-out screaming match."

He thought about that for a minute. "I think you're right. You know, maybe you're growing up."

I took off my sneaker and threw it at his head.

I sat at the other end of the couch and looked over at Jason. He avoided my gaze, knowing I was going to be asking him something serious. "Jason, if you were starting to feel restless, would you tell me?"

He thought long and hard, knowing this was likely an unanswerable question like, "When did you stop beating your wife?" He decided to answer a question with a question, "Is all this happening because I made that joke about you not being able to threaten to take away sex? Because I was really just kidding."

I looked him directly in the eye, "Yes, and we both know that many a truth is said in jest. It's a socially acceptable way to say something that you really mean in a way that you don't think will make the other person mad. In this case, it backfired." I could feel my anxiety level increasing again and knew that I needed to either back off or get ready for the fight I'd just walked a mile to avoid.

Because he's a perceptive, intelligent man who values his life, he said nothing.

I took a couple of deep breaths and remembered some advice from my therapist in Malibu. "When you feel the most vulnerable, move toward the source of your vulnerability, not away." I slid down the couch and laid down with my head on Jason's lap, lying on my back. "Promise me one thing, Cowboy. If you get sick of me, just tell me, then leave me. Don't find somebody first."

He nodded. "Okay."

I pleaded with him. "I'm serious, Jason. Cheating and lies are the only things my heart couldn't take right now. Anything else I could deal with. I have bad breath. You hate the way I kiss. I'm a horrible driver. My voice grates on you. You hate my friends. My job performance is off. I've lost my sense of humor. You hate my family."

He smiled at me like I was having a breakdown.

I was on the edge of whining and tried to dial it back. "Please promise me. That's all I ask."

He took my hand. "I promise."

He turned his attention back to the TV, and I fell asleep with my head on his lap, dreaming of forever and ever.

Chapter 3

At some point, I must have slogged off to bed because that was where I woke up with the damn rooster at 5:32 on Sunday morning. I felt surprisingly rested and energetic by the time I finished my shower and my third cup of coffee.

Jason had figured out, after years of living here, how to sleep through a rooster crowing. There were some weekend days, if I didn't wake him up, I didn't see him until mid-morning, sometimes even noon. Good for him. That wasn't something I could do.

So, we had developed an informal routine where I would take care of the eggs, feeding the chickens and livestock, and milking the goats on weekends, and he would do it during the week. That seemed fair to me, given the ratio of weekend days to weekdays.

Sunday was also my favorite day to run. Back in Santa Clara, I used to run at least three to four days a week, but my hour commute each way was killing me. When I did run here, until yesterday, I had no idea that I had other options than right, toward the highway. So, after I completed my chores, I headed left toward Gilroy Hot Springs Road. After my internal psychotherapy session last night, I had picked up a trail map from a nearby information board.

It was the Hunting Hollow entrance to The Henry W. Coe State Park. According to the map, the Hunting Hollow entrance provided access to the Jim Donnelly Trail, the Steer Ridge Trail, the Middle Steer Ridge Trail, the Lyman Willson Ridge Trail, and, of course, the Hunting Hollow Trail. The map included contour and elevations, a couple of which climbed from 1,000 feet above sea level to nearly 2,500, but I was up for it.

I had some experience with Coe park over the years. It was one of the best known and best-loved inland parks in Northern

California and spanned over 87,000 acres, including lakes, mountains, and forests with fishing, camping, and hiking facilities. I had done some camping here with some friends when I first moved to LA. It provided me with some much-needed relief from La-La land.

The Jim Donnelly trail looked challenging, so I decided to tackle it, climbing 1,617 feet over a three-mile trek. It was a gorgeous morning, sunny and mid-sixties. Still only 7:30, I doubted I would run into any mountain bikers, but it was always possible. Personality-wise, I had noticed the runners and mountain bikers didn't have much in common, similar to bicyclists and motorcyclists. However, runners and hikers were often very similar.

According to my fitness watch, the trailhead was about a half-mile from the house, so it took me just over four minutes to get there at warm-up speed. I wasn't sure how the footing on the trail would be, so I was ready to dial my speed back if I necessary for safety's sake.

I started up the trail just shy of 7:35, feeling strong and invincible. After the first mile, my breathing was steady but not super hard. I was impressed with my physical shape since I hadn't run on any type of incline since I resumed my running regimen upon my move to Santa Clara.

Not far from a picnic table, around mid-trail, something in the tall grass grabbed my attention. My history told me to keep running and stay on the trail, but something made me stop and investigate further. Around thirty feet from the trail, my worst fears were confirmed; it was a body.

As I got closer, I saw more details. It was a man, a big man, face down with a bullet in the back of his head. I had a terrible feeling, not just the usual anxiety of finding a dead body, but the familiarity of the body, the clothing, the man. There was no doubt

Chaos in the Canyon

in my mind even before I turned him over; it was Burt Roop. And the fact that he was wearing the same thing he had been wearing yesterday told me that he probably hadn't been home since our chance encounter. I dropped to the ground. I had just met him, but he was such a nice man, I felt horrible seeing him lying there. It made me wonder, once again, if I was somehow responsible for these deaths, or they were just a macabre series of coincidences. As I stared at his dead body, I couldn't help but feel responsible. I sat with my arms wrapped around my knees for, probably, twenty minutes, not moving, trying not to think.

After a while, I started to worry. I had been a murder suspect often enough to realize the implications of this situation. I was probably the second to last person to see him alive. Second only to the murderer. However, any law enforcement person worth their salt could easily mistake me for the prime suspect. I had no alibi; not even Jason could vouch for me. I had no idea if Burt had contacted the sheriff or the police when he discovered me at the Hot Springs before realizing that I wasn't the suspect he had been searching for.

I had to think before acting, which I didn't always do. I walked slowly back to the picnic table and sat down, keeping Burt in sight. I hadn't seen anyone else on the trail since I'd started my run, either on foot or bicycle.

Despite putting myself in obvious peril, my first inclination was to dial 911. There were pros and cons, which I ticked off in my head. The pros were: It was the right thing to do. It had the potential of putting me in a good light because I did the right thing. Burt's family would be informed about his whereabouts. And the police could begin to look for his killer. The cons were: I would probably be the primary suspect. I had no alibi. I already had an inexplicable history of drawing dead bodies to me, and this would be another one. This murder could reignite my 'Princess of Death' title on the internet, which I tried so hard to dispel. I could be charged and or wrongly convicted of this murder. And Burt had a jealous wife that I might have to explain why I spent most of yesterday afternoon with him wearing only a bikini.

The list of cons greatly outweighed the pros. Now I had to make a list of the cons of the police discovering that I had come across Burt's body and didn't call 911: I would immediately appear guilty. They were likely to question me anyway since Burt discovered me at the Hot Springs and may have reported it to someone, so I may already be on record as the last person who saw him, so if I reported finding him here, that might be my best course of action. My DNA could be found on the gun Burt rested on my head if they tested the gun for DNA. It was a long shot, but was it one I wanted to chance? My DNA was also probably on his clothes because we hugged before we left one another last evening. His wife wasn't going to like that one, no matter whether I was guilty or innocent of killing him.

As I pondered the pros and cons, I realized I didn't have enough information to know my best alternative. If Burt had kept our encounter to himself, doing nothing might be my best option. However, if he told someone or kept a record of our meeting, stepping forward would be my only smart course of action.

Normally, in these situations, my decisions were governed by the conscience, and this would be no different. I couldn't change my response to the situation simply because I was scared that there was circumstantial evidence that could possibly have made me look bad. I had the truth on my side. I debated calling Jason first, but what for? If he tried to convince me not to call, I would just argue my case. If he tried to convince me to call, I was already going to call anyway.

I called 911. "Gilroy Rescue, this is Samantha Smith. What is your emergency?"

I tried to sound businesslike but not too businesslike, innocent, but sympathetic. "Hello Samantha, I was running on the Jim Donnelly Trail in the Coe Park and found a dead body about halfway up the trail. It's someone I recently met. His name is Burt Roop."

Samantha sounded like she was in her early twenties and that she was writing down everything I said. "And your name is?"

I responded slowly, "Miranda Marquette. Do you want me to spell it?"

She spelled it out. "I think I've got the Miranda. M I R A N D A, right?"

I felt guilty smiling but couldn't help it. "Yes, Marquette. M A R Q U E T T E."

She sounded relieved. "Thank you. I wasn't even close."

She continued as if she were reading a script. "And you said it was Burt Roop? How do you know? Did you check his ID?"

I didn't know how much of my story to share. "No, coincidentally, I met him yesterday. We are or *were,* I guess, neighbors on Roop Road."

She hesitated as if she were reading instructions. "Miranda, have you touched the body?"

I replied, "Yes, I turned him over to ID him, but that was it."

She said, "Okay. Let me give you a few instructions which come to us courtesy of the sheriff's department. Please do not attempt to touch or move the body any further. Please consider it a crime scene, and if it is in any way disturbed, it could significantly vary the outcome of the trial. Please stay at least ten feet away from the body at all times and do not touch or disturb anything around it. Please keep all pets and small children at least twenty-five feet away. If you can do so without putting yourself in danger, please stay where you are until the law enforcement agents arrive at the scene. If, for any reason, you need to leave the scene, please provide us with a cell number, an email address, and a home address where you can be reached as soon as possible after the evidence has been collected from the crime scene. Miranda, do you understand these instructions?"

I nodded out of habit. "Yes."

She inquired, "And where are you now in relation to the body?"

I replied, "I'm about thirty feet from the body, sitting on a picnic table."

She sounded satisfied with the call. "Just stay put, Miranda. Because you're physically in the Coe Park, I'll call the State Park Peace Officers as soon as we hang up, but they may ask for backup from the Gilroy Police Department or the Santa Clara County Sheriff's Department. Either way, it shouldn't take someone long to get to you. They'll probably arrive in a large four-wheeler equipped for multiple officers and personnel, as well as the ability to haul the body out and down the canyon."

I breathed a little easier, having made the call. "Thank you so much, Samantha. You made what could have been a horrific experience more tolerable."

She responded, "You're welcome. I'm pretty new on the job, and I just try not to make matters worse. I know that people are already in a stressful situation before I even pick up the phone, so thank you for acknowledging that. Have a better day."

I was ready to get off the phone and wait for the officers. "Thank you, again." I hung up.

It was now 8:30, so I called Jason, figuring he'd be up. He picked up on the second ring, yawning, "Hello."

"Man, you need to go to bed earlier or get a better mattress."

I could hear a smile in his voice. "I'm still in bed. Why don't you join me?" He purred.

That sounded so much better than where I was now, but I wasn't letting him know that. "Stop that!" Then I hesitated, trying to figure out the best way to break the news to him that I was waiting for the cops. "Um, Honey, don't be mad, okay?"

He suddenly got serious. "Did you smash up my car? I *knew* you were driving the Camaro when I wasn't watching."

He was right. When he took his truck and would be gone for a couple of hours, I would bomb around the back roads in his '69 Camaro. It was amazing. I batted my eyelashes, "Little ole' me?" I then remembered the real reason for my call, "No, it's way worse than that."

"Well, you're still alive, so it can't be that bad."

I took a deep breath. "Well, you remember I told you I met Burt Roop yesterday?"

He jumped down my throat. "Yes. Now you didn't go back to those springs again, did you, Miranda?"

I acted offended. "Give me a break. Of course not." Then I cut him a little slack. "Okay, it's not like I wouldn't ever do it again. But anyway, no, that's not it." I decided I'd better get to the point, or the cops might arrive before I was able to fill him in. "When I went up to the springs yesterday, and later when I took my walk to clear my head, I saw a trailhead just before the bridge that led to the springs. It's the Hunting Hollow entrance to Coe Park. I had picked up a trail map there yesterday and decided to run up the Jim Connelly trail, which was mostly a mountain biking trail but was suitable for running also."

He let me know he was paying attention. "Sounds pretty harmless, so far, but I know you have the capability of going off the rails at any time," he chuckled.

I chuckled sarcastically. "I'd like to argue that point, but you're spot-on. And here's where this story goes awry. My run was going great, it's almost a mile vertical drop, so I was proud of myself. About halfway up, there's a picnic table, and I was debating taking a short rest. When I glanced in that direction, I saw something over in the grass about thirty feet from the trail."

He groaned. "Okay, Princess of Death, here's where the really bad part comes in."

I whined. "Not you too, Brutus! But, yes, I found a body. It gets worse."

He stifled a laugh. "How could it get worse than that?"

I couldn't keep him in suspense any longer. "It was Burt Roop."

There was total silence at the other end of the phone. He must have very quickly comprehended the seriousness of this news. He quietly asked, "Had you heard something on the news that he was missing?"

I thought for a second. "No, I hadn't. Did you?"

He responded, "No, I was just wondering if Sally has reported anything."

I continued, "I wasn't sure what to do at first because I was worried that he had on the same clothes as when he caught me at the springs, and I thought I might have been one of the last people to have seen him alive. But maybe he wore something similar every day, or maybe he went home, washed them, and put the same clothes back on. Only his wife could answer that one. Either way, I decided that I should call 911, and I'm waiting for the police to come up here and do what they do. So, it'll probably be a while. They'll want to investigate the site, question me, and all that. I'm hoping we can do all that out here, and they won't need to take me downtown." I suddenly felt weak in the knees flashing back to when I was thrown in jail due to a 911 call in Venice, Louisiana, a few years back. "Jason, what if they take me in and book me for murder?" I couldn't bear the thought of that.

Jason put on his soothing therapist's voice. "Sweetheart, let's not get ahead of ourselves. So far, you were just running and found a dead body. There's nothing illegal about that. In fact, you were a good citizen by calling 911 and not just leaving him there to be discovered by animals or other hikers."

I smiled. "I knew you'd say that. I concluded when I was making a pros and cons list before I called 911. The truth will set you free, and I have the truth on my side. I didn't kill the guy. That should be enough to keep me out of jail, right?"

He responded maybe a bit too enthusiastically like he was trying to convince both of us, "Absolutely! Hopefully, I'll see you soon. Keep me posted either way."

I smiled to myself, not wanting to point out that he was contradicting himself by saying that he'd see me soon or to keep him posted. "Okay, Honey." I hung up.

By the end of the call, I'd been lying back on the table, basking in the early morning sun. I was relatively sure I wouldn't have much relaxation time today, or at least this morning, once the police showed up. Off in the distance, I heard a siren, disturbing the peace surrounding me. I pictured a police van or truck towing a trailer containing the four-wheeler Samantha had described during our 911 call.

Within five minutes, two four-wheelers, one large one with four people in it, and one more customary one, arrived at the scene, with one passenger and a driver. My initial assessment of the players were four uniformed officers, the Coroner, and an EMT. I stood and brushed the picnic table dirt off my running clothes.

A woman around my age with a clipboard approached me. The other three were men ranging in ages from mid-twenties to around forty. She approached me directly with her hand extended.

"You must be Miranda. I'm Sergeant Tina Bright with the Santa Clara County Sheriff's Department. I'll be heading up the investigation. She introduced the others in order of age. "Bob Carruthers here will provide me back-up. He's a lieutenant with the Gilroy City Police. We have a reciprocal arrangement when it comes to covering crimes committed in the park."

He was obviously fit and had kind eyes. "Nice to meet you, Miranda."

If I'd been single, well, you get the idea.

Tina moved down the line to the next guy who looked ex-military with a shaved head and a square jaw. "This is Randy Bartlett. He's a State Park Peace Officer, which I know doesn't sound like much, but they have all the authority of the State Police when it comes to arresting and apprehending a criminal, including shooting to kill when necessary."

I reached out to shake hands with him. "So the term 'Peace Officer' only goes so far."

Randy agreed. "That's correct, ma'am. We are here to keep the peace, but that doesn't always mean we use peaceful means to do so, even if this is California." I could have sworn he rolled his eyes, but that could have been my imagination.

Tina moved down the line to the youngest and meanest looking of the group. "And this is Jacob Mabry. He's a rookie detective with the Santa Clara Sheriff's Department, and he'll be my chief investigator, digging into the details when I might only have time to brush the surface. You know, ballistics, forensics, stuff like that."

I had a feeling she was telling me more than she would tell a typical citizen who just found a body along a running trail. She confirmed that for me before I had the chance to ask. "For example, he had a chance to research your background to find out that you used to be an undercover detective for the Charlotte

Mecklenburg Police Department in North Carolina. We understand you had a tragic accident, which resulted in your leaving the force and starting your own multi-million-dollar internet-based corporation, which a few years ago was shut down by the government under suspicious circumstances. Since then, you have been working for an international power supplier with relationships with some of the United States' most hated governments, including Russia, Communist China, North Korea, Iraq, and Iran."

I suddenly felt like I was being arrested, indicted, tried, convicted, and sentenced all at once by these officers. I took a couple of long, slow breaths in an attempt to control my anxiety. They all stared at me, so I felt the need to respond. "Your initial description about me being an ex-detective was completely accurate; however, the rest was not. Number one, there was nothing suspicious about my company's demise. Between the time I started my cosmetic surgery company and the time it ended the government had started paying for reconstructive breast surgery after mastectomy. Since I received a part of that reimbursement from my participating doctors, it was considered a commission, not allowed by CMS. So, we agreed to disagree, and my business was dissolved. I was not found guilty of any wrongdoing and never did any jail time. If there are governments who are customers of Ion Systems, I have no idea. I just process orders and deal with customer service issues. The only customers I deal with are commercial businesses in the United States and Canada."

They all remained silent as if expecting me to say more, then Tina dropped the bomb. "Okay, all that even makes sense to me, Miranda, it does. But, what about the fact that you just keep finding dead bodies?"

My ears started ringing, and I closed my eyes, refusing to have an anxiety attack, not here, not now. I took three or four deep breaths. They didn't speak, waiting for me to respond. When I didn't, she said. "I even understand that stuff happens and that the court system works. I have to respect that you were not even arrested for all but one of these murders. On the other hand, I will not be made a fool of. If you have some sick desire to kill people and see that other people get punished for it, that will not happen on my watch. Do I make myself clear?"

I started to protest, but I didn't have the energy, and I could see that this was not the time or the place. "Yes, ma'am," I said and sat down on the picnic table, doing everything in my power to fight the impending anxiety attack.

Chapter 4

I awoke with my head between my knees. I had no idea how long I had been unconscious. There was an EMT sitting next to me as I came to. He asked, "How are you feeling? Would you like to lie down?" He pumped a blood pressure cuff already wrapped around my left arm.

I rubbed my head and said, "Maybe I'll just lie on the table here for a minute or two." My head was pounding and I felt too weak to stand.

He inquired. "Has this ever happened before? Losing consciousness like that?"

I nodded. "It has. I have an anxiety disorder. It's pretty well controlled, but sometimes it just rears its ugly head." I looked around. Everybody else was gone, including Burt. I started to ask, "Where did—?"

He interrupted me. "You missed the excitement, there was a huge wreck out on the 101 and they had to wrap things up quickly. But we've got all the time in the world, so just take your time."

I shut my eyes, wishing I could make my Princess of Death powers go away. I didn't ask for them, and I didn't want them. After probably twenty minutes, I sat up. My EMT friend, Eric, helped me stabilize. He asked, "Do you want to try to stand?"

He helped me to my feet and within a few seconds, I was walking slowly around the grounds.

He smiled. "It looks like you're going to be okay. I have my car at the trailhead. Do you want a ride home?" I declined but he insisted on waiting while I stretched. My muscles develop an odd tightness after losing consciousness, and I wanted to make sure I didn't cramp up on the way down the canyon. Once I felt ready, he escorted me back as far as his car. The rest of the walk back to the house helped me clear my head a little.

Jason lay stretched out in front of the TV playing Nintendo when I walked in. I used to think this was brainless entertainment for him, but I had since learned it was a major stress reliever, and he only played it when many men would have drunk a fifth of whiskey or hired a prostitute. So, I was thankful he had healthier outlets than most men. Mario had just been beaten by some monster to be named later, preventing him from entering the castle when I walked in. He tossed the controller at the TV screen.

He stood and wrapped his arms around me. "How'd it go with the police? At least you're not in jail."

I buried my face in his shoulder, not wanting to talk and bring it all back to my consciousness, but eventually, I knew I'd have to. I took his hand and walked him over to the couch. After we both sat for a second, I changed my mind. "Want a beer? You might need one for this."

He sat with his hands behind his head. "Sure, why not?"

I got up and grabbed both of us a cold one and got comfortable. "Okay, the 911 call went pretty well. The operator was very pleasant and professional. But, when it comes to the police down here, things get very complicated. There are actually three jurisdictions: The Santa Clara Sheriff's Department, the State Park Peace Patrol, and the Gilroy City Police Department. In this case, the Sheriff's Department, in the name of Sergeant Tina Bright, is in charge. She's getting assistance from others, including a rookie detective by the name of Jacob Mabry. He looks like a real piece of work.

"He had dug up more dirt on me in the half-hour it took for them to get there than most cops would have known in a month-long investigation. They knew about my police career. They knew about the rise and fall of my company. They knew about Ion. In fact, they knew more about Ion's overseas customers than I do. And, of course, they also knew about the Princess of Death stuff."

He took a long swig of beer. "That seems strange. I didn't even know Ion had overseas customers."

I took one as well. "I thought it was weird too."

Jason was a great listener. I never felt like he was just waiting for me to finish a sentence, so he could go back to his ball game or reading the sports page. I always had his undivided attention when I talked. "So, they told you all that, and you had no resolution, so you don't know what the next steps are?"

He understood my frustration. "Exactly! Because I passed out, I have no idea if they'll be calling me, if I'm supposed to call them, if I'm a suspect, anything. Although, they certainly seemed to be baiting me. I would imagine they'll call me about Burt to see if I knew him, don't you think?"

He thought about it. "They'd almost have to. He lived a house down and across the street. Even if you hadn't found his body, I would think they'd be around to question us to see if we'd seen anything suspicious." He looked like he was going to kick himself. "I wish I hadn't taken off on my bike yesterday. Then you wouldn't have taken off on yours."

I kissed him. "You can't blame yourself for this. I earned the title 'Princess of Death' long before you entered my life." Then I thought about it. "Well, not that long before you entered my life, but you know what I mean."

He patted my leg, "I know what you mean."

I slapped his hand, "Don't patronize me, Cowboy."

After I had a quick shower and grabbing sandwiches, we switched on the Hallmark Channel and watched sappy and romantic movies until it got dark out.

#

Monday morning came way too early. Last week, I told myself that I would run every day after this weekend, but when the alarm went off at 5 a.m., I just couldn't find it in me to put my feet on the floor.

    Despite our hour commute and the fact that we could have spent another hour together each way, Jason and I rarely drove to work together. It was mostly about the perception of the boss and employee living together that we fought every day. It helped that we were both hard-working and well-liked. But that didn't stop some of the more outspoken employees from doing what people do, gossiping. We got the typical looks and whispers that you might expect under the circumstances. There were times when I was tempted to call some of them out, but I resisted to the death, not wanting to put Jason in an uncomfortable position.

    Rick, one of the new product engineers, was the worst. He was a good friend of Jason's but was relentless with his comments. A part of me knew it was because Rick was jealous of Jason. After all, he knew he couldn't maintain a mature relationship with the opposite sex if his life depended on it, and he secretly wanted it in the worst way. That didn't stop him from badgering Jason about me and his relationship with me, day and night. One of these days, he was going to say the wrong thing at the wrong time, and I would clock him in the mouth.

    When I walked into the Customer Service Suite this morning, Rick was camped out in the small break room, which was normally reserved for my co-worker, Tea, pronounced Tay-a, and me. Evidently, her parents couldn't spell. Tea and I were the only two employees housed in this space, and there was an all-employee break room near the general lobby, which I knew Rick frequented. I often saw him there with his buddies eyeing young ladies from the sales department as they strolled by, loving every moment of their attention.

    My first preference would have been to ignore Rick, but since I had to put my lunch in the fridge in there, that would have been nearly impossible. I bit the bullet. "Rick, what brings you to our humble space?"

Rick looked worried, which was an unusual look for Rick. He was ever the ladies' man and usually looked ready for action. He was mid-forties with salt and pepper hair, nice build, and a face that had a few miles on it, the kind of guy that a certain type of girl could not resist. At one time, I was that girl, but, thankfully, I grew out of that phase at least ten years ago. He motioned for me to sit at one of the small tables.

I joined him, getting a pit in my stomach.

He looked around as if he thought the place might be bugged. He spoke barely above a whisper, "Miranda, you know I *love* you, right?"

I raised my eyebrows. "Well, Rick, I don't—"

He interrupted, "Okay, I don't mean it that way. I know you belong the Jason, and I think that's great. I just wouldn't want anything bad to happen to you."

This was by far the most serious I had ever seen Rick, and I was worried. I looked him straight in the eye, "What is it, Rick?"

He hesitated, then spit it out, "Did you kill that guy in the park?"

I burst out laughing, "Burt Roop? How do you know anything about that?"

He stared at his hands like he was reading his palms, "I'm a Santa Clara County Assistant Deputy Sheriff, and heard the news on the scanner over the weekend. It sounded like they were going to haul you in until you passed out or something."

This was great. Now my co-workers knew about my panic attacks. Could things get any worse? I tried to laugh it off. "Yeah, it wasn't my best day. I guess they'll bring me in for questioning at some point, but I had nothing to do with it, so you can stop worrying."

He looked somewhat relieved but was still wringing his hands. "You've got to watch out for this Jacob Mabry. He's looking to make a name for himself, and he sees you as a once in a lifetime opportunity. He's somewhat of a conspiracy theorist and has traced you to unsolved murders dating back to your relocation from North Carolina to Vegas, including your ex-partner, Melissa."

I stopped dead in my tracks, feeling like a knife was stabbing through my heart. I could barely breathe. Speaking wasn't an option.

Rick stared at me, not knowing what to do or say.

After several minutes, I stood to go to my desk and muttered in clipped words, "Don't you ever mention her name again." I left him sitting in shock, alone in the break room.

I had spent years in therapy but had never been able to deal with her death. I didn't kill her, but I always felt like her death was my responsibility. I had convinced her to quit the force and enticed her to come to Vegas with me. Anger and guilt raged through me as I allowed thoughts and memories to come to the surface that weren't normally allowed. Melissa's death brought a rage in me that even I feared, which was why I pushed it down so far. I hadn't even mentioned her to my last two therapists. Dealing with her death was a lost cause. I would go to my grave with guilt written on my soul.

The irony of the timing of this news was not lost on me. Jason was the first person outside my family I had trusted enough to tell about her. Was it a coincidence all my other relationships had gone down in flames or had just burned out? Probably not.

He was wonderful when I told him. He knew that I hated to cry in front of anyone. But that day, I cried and cried and cried, and he just held me even though I soaked his shirt with tears. He didn't try to make me feel better; he just listened. I don't think I have ever loved him more than that day.

When Tea, all four feet ten of her, raced in, five minutes late, as usual, I stuck my hand up in a wave but didn't comment further. She cocked her head, and her spikey brown hair fell over her huge brown eyes, but she said nothing. Even though she was young, still approaching her mid-twenties, we had developed a mutual respect and a communication style that worked. I knew when not to speak to her and vice versa.

Chapter 5

Around noon, my cell phone rang; the caller ID displayed: Santa Clara Sheriff's Department. Great. "Miranda Marquette."

A perky voice came from the phone. "Miranda, this is Tina Bright from the Santa Clara Sheriff's Department. We met yesterday."

I forced my most enthusiastic response. "Tina, yes, I remember. What can I do for you?"

She obviously wasn't going to address my panic attack, which was fine with me. "With all the excitement yesterday, we didn't get a chance to take your statement, so I was hoping you could come by the station today so we could cross that detail off our list."

She made it sound like picking up toilet paper at the grocery store. I had a feeling it might be a bit more complicated than that, especially now that I had my morning briefing with Rick. But there was no way to avoid it. "Absolutely, Tina. What time works for you?"

She paused, probably checking her calendar. "I have something at two and three. Otherwise, I'm free between now and eight."

I looked at my watch: 12:05. I figured I should just get it over with. Jason would understand if I took a long lunch since I rarely took one at all. "How about now? I can get there in fifteen minutes or so." That would at least give them the impression that I wasn't avoiding it.

She sounded surprised. "That would be wonderful, Miranda. I really appreciate your flexibility."

I smiled, trying to sound as cooperative as possible. "I'll see you soon, Tina." I hung up.

Tea had clearly been listening from her workspace. "Hey, Miranda, is everything okay over there?"

I wasn't sure I wanted to get into detail about my weekend with Tea at this point. "I had kind of an exciting weekend, but I'll have to tell you about it later." I waved.

She stood with her mouth wide open when I walked out. It would take too long to do my story justice, and I'd probably be in a better frame of mind once I had provided my statement to the police.

I was glad I had the car and not the motorcycle today since I had no idea where West Younger Avenue was in San Jose, so I plugged the address in my Google Maps App on my iPhone. Luckily, traffic this time of day was pretty light. Had I opted to go after work, it could have taken me a half hour to get there, but today it only took me ten minutes.

The building was an impressive one for a sheriff's department, but I was getting used to impressive government buildings here in California compared to other parts of the country. When you walked in, hanging on the wall was a large portrait of Laurie Smith, the present sheriff. I wondered if Samantha from the 911 line was her daughter. I realized that Smith was a popular name, but I vowed to look her up online in my quest for the truth.

There was an elevator to the left in the lobby with a sign listing departments and department heads. Tina and company were on the second floor. I pushed the Up button and waited. When the elevator opened, I was greeted by Jacob Mabry. He nearly jumped out of the way when he saw me like I was infected with some intensely communicable disease. Me being who I am, I couldn't resist being as sickly sweet as I could possibly muster. "Jacob, how nice to see you again. I was hoping you'd be part of the team taking my statement."

He muttered something under his breath about going to lunch as he raced toward the exit. I chuckled under my breath as the elevator door closed. *Be careful, little boy. You do not want to be on the receiving end of my wrath.* It probably shouldn't have, but the depth of my residual rage when it came to Melissa's death always surprised me.

I worked hard toward an attitude adjustment by the time the elevator door opened on the second floor. I smiled as I exited just in case someone was standing on the other side. A receptionist sat behind a counter in a small waiting room outside the elevator, which made sense since there was no-one downstairs controlling people's flow to each floor. She was probably mid-thirties with short-cropped brown hair and completely tattooed arms. Her name tag read Tamara Smith. I was beginning to wonder if everyone in the county had the same last name or if the sheriff's whole family worked in the department.

She smiled and welcomed me. "Good afternoon, can I help you?"

I smiled back. "Hi. I'm Miranda Marquette. I have an appointment with Tina Bright."

She buzzed the electronic door lock. "You can go right in. She told me to send you back as soon as you got here." She pointed me to the door to the right. "She's the second office on the left."

I waved. "Thanks, Tamara." Then, as an afterthought, I said, "Hey, are you any relation to Samantha?"

She called after me. "She's my sister."

I fist-pumped no one in particular. "I *knew* it."

Seconds later, I came to Tina's office. She was buried in paper and looked smaller than she had out in the field, leading the troops. She stood as soon as I reached her office door. "Miranda, come right in." She reached out her hand and shook mine. "How *are* you? I'm afraid we had a sudden emergency and we didn't consider your health yesterday. I hope you're okay."

My face reddened. "I'm fine. I'm working through an anxiety disorder but making good progress."

She sounded like she was making a speech, and I wondered if she was concerned about a lawsuit, "Well, let me assure you that we take the mental health of our constituents very seriously, and if there is anything we can do to help, you just let me know."

I pulled a side-chair up toward her desk. "I certainly will. Thanks for letting me know." I wanted to say, "You'll be hearing from my lawyer for leaving *one of your constituents* unconscious on a picnic table at a murder scene with a lone EMT," but I thought I might need to use that as ammunition at some point later on. I wasn't sure what the protocol was for taking a statement here. "So, Sergeant, are we going to do this in your office or an interrogation room?"

She gave me a confused look. "Oh yeah, you're not new to this, are you?"

I wasn't sure if she meant as a cop or a defendant, so I decided to assume she meant as a cop. "Nope, ten years on the force, you pretty much remember the drill."

She leaned back in her chair. "I'm going to record it, so it doesn't matter to me where we do it. It's a lot easier than taking notes or getting someone behind a two-way mirror to interpret what you say. Besides, this is just a statement. As far as I'm concerned, you are a citizen who found a dead body and are doing your civic duty by contacting us. And for that, I want to thank you. Who knows how long that body would have stayed out there before it was discovered, especially as time went on and animals ate the flesh or falling leaves covered the remains?"

I understood exactly what she was trying to do. Someone who had killed Burt would react differently from someone who had found his dead body to the description of how the rigors of time would deteriorate him. It was very clever, and she was very good at it. I admired her conversational style. Some less experienced cops struggled with the conversational approach to interrogation. As an interested third party, I was impressed with her methods. As a potential suspect, I recognized it as the oldest trick in the book and had absolutely no reaction to her statement. The corners of her mouth went down slightly in reaction to my lack thereof. Miranda one—Tina nothing.

She hurriedly flipped on the tape recorder, which looked like a Radio Shack cassette recorder, circa 1980. Some things never changed. Cops using decades-old technology was one of them. I wanted to say, "Hey, you know they have digital recorders now," but why limit their liability of a potentially bad, twisted, or broken tape rendering the whole process useless. I, for sure, was only doing this once, so it was their risk.

She stood the uni-directional microphone on the plastic stand and pointed it in my direction. She sat in her chair and held down the Record and Play buttons because that was what you had to do in those days to record, then said, "This is a test question. Can you please tell me your name?"

I replied, "Miranda Marquette." I thought Minnie Mouse would be funnier, but it seemed like the fun and games were behind us.

She hit the Stop, then the Rewind buttons. She then hit Play. Our questions and answers had been recorded perfectly. She then hit Rewind, and when the tape stopped spinning, again pressed Record and Play simultaneously.

She spoke loudly and clearly, "My name is Sergeant Tina Bright of the Santa Clara County Sheriff's Department. Please state your name."

I spoke toward the tiny microphone. For some reason, I felt like we were in a Saturday Night Live Skit. "My name is Miranda Marie Marquette, 4504 Roop Road, Gilroy, California 95020."

Tina went on. "And on May 15, 2011, around 8 a.m., near the Jim Donnelly Trail in the Coe Park, what happened?

Clearly, she didn't want me to stray too far from the subject at hand. "I was running up the trail and had stopped near the picnic table, which is about halfway up, when I saw something off in the distance, about thirty feet away. I was a cop for ten years and am also just naturally curious, so I went down to determine what it was. It wasn't long before discovered it was a dead body, face down, with a bullet hole in the back of the head." I hesitated briefly, so she took over.

She was a bit of a control freak. "Did you touch the body at all?"

I thought back. "Yes, I turned the body over to identify him."

She frowned. "Okay. So then what happened?"

I continued. "I retreated back to the picnic table and called 911."

She pressed. "You immediately called 911?"

I considered my answer. "Well, I took five minutes to collect my thoughts, so I would provide accurate information regarding my location and what had led up to the call."

She gave me a sidelong glance but let me get away with my answer. "So, Miranda, did you know Burt Roop?" She asked me the question with the attitude that she already knew the answer, and I knew she was ready to pounce on this one.

I inhaled. "Yes, but not well. I met Burt the day before."

She pulled out a pad even though the tape recorder was faithfully operating. "Tell me about that." She sounded more like a therapist than a police sergeant.

I focused on making sure I told the story accurately and succinctly. "I took a motorcycle ride on Saturday and ventured down Gilroy Hot Springs Road, where I'd never been. I moved in with my boyfriend in the fall and hadn't had the chance to venture out much since I got here. At the end of the road were these natural hot springs that had been there forever and some dilapidated buildings. At some point, a pool had been built, which was fed by the springs. There was no-one around and I had a bathing suit in the saddlebag of my bike, so I decided to take a dip."

I knew what happened next was critical to the story. "The pool was heavenly. I laid there with my eyes closed for several minutes but then felt something hard on the back of my head, which wasn't totally unfamiliar. It was the barrel of a pistol. Behind the weapon was Burt Roop. The springs had been in his family for decades, and he was the self-appointed guardian of the property. They had been having some issues with trespassers recently, and he thought I was a repeat offender."

I took a couple of breaths.

She asked, "Would you like some water?"

I smiled. "Please. That would be great. My throat is so dry."

She twirled around in her chair and reached down to a cooler, retrieving a bottle of water which she handed to me. "Here you go. I know I can't talk for more than five minutes without my throat drying up."

I opened it and took a long swig. "Ah, that's much better." I resettled myself. "Burt and I talked for a while, and he figured out that I wasn't the person or people that he was looking for. We chatted for a couple of hours like we were old friends, then I headed home."

She scribbled more notes. "Did Burt follow you out of the area?"

I pictured myself leaving the pool. He remained where he was. "Not that I remember. I figured he would be some checking of things before he left for home. He was very proud to be the guardian angel of that property, and he'd be the first to tell you the same thing."

She stopped writing. "Did you see or hear from him after you left the Gilroy Hot Springs at any time before you found his body off the hiking trail in Coe Park?"

I responded quickly, "No, ma'am."

She leaned back in her chair and pulled out a small beaten-up stenographer's notebook. She read a couple of pages while I watched then set it on her desk and looked me in the eye. "We've got a problem, Miranda. A big problem."

I felt a drop of sweat run down my right underarm.

She had a pained expression on her face. "You see, I actually like you. You seem honest and sincere. You've got a law enforcement background, and I think we could be friends under the right circumstances. Unfortunately," she closed her eyes, then opened them, "these aren't the right circumstances."

I was swirling in a state of confusion.

She picked up the notebook. "We found this notebook in Burt's pocket. What you might not know is we have a program where we deputize citizens who support us on a part-time basis in areas where we don't have many officers. Burt was one of those deputies."

Rick and now Burt. Why have I never heard of this program?

She turned pages in the book. "Let me read you from the May 15th Log. 'Motorcycle on the property. Investigating further. Pretty lady basking semi-nude in the pool. I am convinced that she is the radical group leader who has eluded me for the past six months, using our facilities, trashing the place, using illegal drugs, and organizing anti-American activities. While observing her, I found a Glock 6-inch 10 mm handgun nearby and confiscated such weapon."

I stared at her as if she was speaking Burmese. I tried to hold back, but this was insane. "Okay, so this means Burt was some combination of delusional, blind, and a conspiracy theorist. This is completely consistent with what I just told you. He had me mistaken for someone else, and we got it straightened out. Where he got the semi-nude part, I'll never know, although it is a strapless bikini, so from the back, well—"

She didn't seem to be deterred by my comments. "While we have not recovered the firearm that Burt referred to in his notes, we continue to do ballistics work on the bullet that ended his life. However, we do have some information regarding a weapon that is registered in your name. I believe it is the same model. Is that correct?"

I nodded. "Yes, and it's safely locked in the gun cabinet at home." I crossed my fingers that someone hadn't gotten into the shed where Jason stored the gun cabinet.

Tina looked me in the eye. "There just seem to be a lot of uncomfortable coincidences here, Miranda, wouldn't you say?"

I decided that she had nothing on me and was fishing. "Tina, you're right, coincidences, and uncomfortable. Quite frankly, if Sally, Burt's widow, gets ahold of those notes and believes that I was semi-nude, I'll be running for my life." I forced out a laugh that sounded fake even to me.

Her face was stone cold. "I don't know that I'd be laughing if I were you."

I was getting antsy to get out of there. "Do you have anything else, Sergeant?"

She kept digging. "So your official statement is that you left Burt at the springs on Saturday evening, alive and well, and didn't see him until you found his body on Sunday morning?"

I stood up. "Yes, that's the truth, Tina. Now, if there's nothing else, I'd like to leave." I turned toward the exit.

She said as I reached the doorway, "You don't have any trips planned, do you?"

I forced a smile, "I have a girls' weekend planned for next week in Monterey. I plan on being there." I rushed to the elevator, forcing myself to keep my breathing slow and steady.

Chapter 6

I sat in the Rover for at least fifteen minutes while I tried to get back to where I needed to be to drive—having a panic attack while driving would not work out well for anyone. My conversation with Tina kept running through my mind. Burt's notes. I talked to myself, "Why, in God's name, would he have noted that I was semi-nude? That just downright embarrassing. And the more I hear about Sally, the more frightened I am to meet her. If she thought I had something going with Burt before he died, she'd probably kill me. I'm new here, and the first thing people learn about me is that I'm a semi-nude killer?"

I took a few deep breaths.

And what about this weapon? It did sound just like mine. There were several million Glocks in the world, but the fact that we lived nearby and it had been stored in an unlocked shed for several months didn't give me a warm and fuzzy feeling.

I started to breathe easier, realizing that, as usual, I had the truth on my side. I didn't kill Burt, which meant that someone else had. Even if they had stolen my gun, their DNA would be on the gun, hopefully. And if they could pinpoint the time of death, hopefully, that would eliminate me as a suspect, unless he was killed just after I left the springs.

In the final analysis, I decided to give it all a rest. This had been an unbelievably stressful day, starting with Rick bringing up my ex-partner, Melissa. When I got back to the office, I just wanted to bury myself in order processing; mindless data entry was about all I could handle right now.

I felt like my head was going to explode when Jason called me five minutes after returning to my desk. "How'd it go with the sheriff's department?"

He was so sweet. I didn't want to jump down his throat. "Hey, can we talk about this later. I have a throbbing headache right now."

He didn't interpret my, "Please leave me alone" properly. "Can I get you something? Ibuprofen? An aspirin?"

I had to smile at his effort to make everything all right. "No, I'll be fine. I just need a few hours to decompress."

He got that. "Oh, okay, then. I'll see you at home."

I was happy we had reached a place in our relationship where I didn't have to go into a fifteen-minute diatribe explaining the difference between how men and women process things. "See ya." I hung up.

Even Tea steered away from me all afternoon, which was rare for her. I could even tell that my voice had an edge, and I purposely did nothing to change it.

I walked out the door at exactly 5 p.m. I could count on one hand the number of times I had done that in the two years I had been at Ion. My goal was to get home, open a beer, crank up the Indigo Girls, and get lost in self-pity. But after I exited the 101, I didn't turn into the driveway; I kept going to Gilroy Hot Springs Road. Only my heart knew where I was going. My head would have to catch up.

When I pulled into the parking lot, I had a pang of guilt, remembering that Burt had been alive and well only a few short days ago. Oddly, there was a motorcycle parked not far from where I had been parked on Saturday. When I reached the gate I had entered on Saturday, there was a No Trespassing sign.

I entered cautiously, aware that someone was likely on the property somewhere. When I came around the corner, approaching the pool, I saw a diminutive woman, around thirty years old, with straight black shoulder-length hair, a stunningly beautiful face, with bangs hanging down into her closed eyes. She was sitting cross-legged on the deck, facing the pool. She wore a traditional Native American dress that rode up her thighs, brown leather with beads braided throughout the colorful surface.

Her arms were palms-up on the deck. I studied her face to determine if she knew I was there. She gave me no indication. Her breathing was slow and steady, almost like she was asleep, but my gut said she wasn't.

I inched closer to her. When I got within about ten feet, she said, "Don't worry, I'm awake, and I'm alive." She opened her eyes, staring straight ahead. "I touch the God of the Earth who never mixes with the God of the Water, or the Underworld. I stand between what you would call your God and your Devil. And I am pulled in both directions. I want to stay faithful to the earth, to the good. But the hot spring is the temptation, the evil. I feel the pull, like your gravity. I want to let go. *I want to let go!*" She collapsed on the deck.

I wanted to touch her to see if she was okay, but I felt something bigger than both of us was going on. In front of her laid a piece of cactus about three by five inches. My guess was peyote. I had heard that a tribe of Aulintac Indians lived nearby, and I guessed she was one of them. I wondered if her presence had anything to do with the frustration Burt Roop had felt about trespassers on the property. While this property had been in his family for nearly a hundred and fifty years, if this was sacred ground for these Native Americans, it may have been in their family for centuries.

She hadn't budged since she passed out, and I figured she would be out for a while, so I decided to go home. I had no idea why I had come here in the first place, but I was drawn here like a moth to a flame, and I could only guess this was the reason. I needed to learn more about these people.

As I approached my car, I realized something else I needed to do sooner than later. I needed to visit Sally Roop. The longer I avoided that, the worse it would be. I had no idea whether he had gone home Saturday night, whether he had mentioned me, whether the police had mentioned me to her, or whether she had read his notebook. She was likely to still be in shock from Burt's death, but she sounded like she was a strong and self-reliant woman, so I couldn't picture her sitting in the corner going through photo albums and crying into her tea. In fact, I pictured her with a shot of whiskey and a shotgun.

Since they were only one house down and across the street, I knew which driveway was theirs, so I pulled in on the way home. Jason had gotten used to me working late so he wouldn't worry when I didn't get home at a certain time. As my boss, there wasn't much he could say, not much that would make any sense anyway.

There was a light on in the small farmhouse. I felt confident that I was doing the right thing, so my anxiety level was in check. I walked up to the front door and knocked.

"Just a minute," came a woman's voice from the back of the house.

I stood, making sure I had nothing on my teeth, a nervous habit.

She opened the door and looked at me. "Do I know you? You aren't selling anything, are you?" She was as large as advertised, probably exceeding three hundred pounds, and had a strikingly pretty face.

I smiled. "No. Are you Sally Roop?"

She squinted at me. "Now who might you be?"

I kept smiling, even though my face was starting to hurt. "I don't think so. I'm your neighbor, one house up and across the street. I live with Jason Wall."

She came out onto the front porch. "Oh my, yes, Amanda, right?"

I blushed, although that wasn't the first time in the thirty-five years I'd been called Amanda, "Miranda." I stuck out my hand.

She came over and wrapped her whole body around me. "We don't shake hands out here in the canyon, Miranda. Come on in."

I hesitated. "Are you sure? I know this must be a hard time for you."

She clucked her tongue. "Oh, don't be crazy. I been going nuts around here. Burt was my life. Now, what the hell do I do?" Her eyes misted over. She led me to the kitchen table. "Coffee?"

I had no idea how I would start my story or if she had heard any part of it, but so far, it seemed like she hadn't, or she would have heard of me. "Coffee would be great."

She headed to the stove. "Decaf?"

I nodded. "Even better."

She milled around the kitchen, fetching sugar, cream, and mugs, talking non-stop. I felt like if she stopped talking, she would burst into tears. I hoped this wasn't a huge mistake.

She made small talk, probably wondering why I was there. "So, sweetheart, where are you from? Clearly not a local girl. You have all your teeth." She laughed hilariously.

I wanted to keep it short. "I'm originally from New Orleans. I came here by way of North Carolina, Vegas, LA, Malibu, and Santa Clara. I work for Jason."

She sat on the edge of her seat, hoping to extract more about me. "Sounds like a wild ride. Not sure I ever heard of nobody picking Santa Clara over Malibu."

Chaos in the Canyon

I felt like I was running out of time and nerve, so I just jumped in. "I'll tell you all about it sometime when we have more time, but I'm here to talk about Burt."

Her open expression and body language immediately closed as if I had sunk a dagger into her heart. "Oh?"

I was determined to tell her everything I knew and to let her do with it what she would. I hoped it could help with the case.

"I met Burt the day before he died. I was lounging in the mineral pool and he mistook me for a trespasser he had been tracking down for a while, but we straightened it all out before I left."

I watched for a reaction. Now I had a real judgment call ahead of me. I truly had no idea if the notes that Tina read to me from Burt's notebook referred to me or someone else he followed to the springs that day. The fact that the Native American woman by the pool had also ridden a motorcycle made it even more confusing. Perhaps she was the semi-nude, anti-American he referred to. I decided to try to get more information from Sally before I exposed myself—in a manner of speaking.

I spoke slowly, still unsure of her reaction to my prior information. "Did Burt let you know the details of what he encountered at the springs, such as these people he'd been pursuing?"

She shook her head. "You gotta be jokin'. He didn't tell me nuthin'." She picked up a nearby paper napkin and wiped her eyes. The reference to her late husband apparently brought back a painful memory. "He always did say he was my protector and promised to take care of me. As a Roop, the Springs were his life, and a part of him died when that hotel burned down. He was only eighteen when it happened, but he always thought he coulda stopped it. He knew who did it and blamed himself that they weren't in jail."

I perked up, remembering Burt telling me something about that. "Do you remember his name?"

She nodded. "Oh, yeah. Tommy Pearson. Their family was all money, no brains. His father was government. I think this Tommy kid was even arrested but got off. Burt still knew he did it."

I thought about what she said. *Tommy. That was the rock opera he was humming that day. I knew I recognized it.*

Sally continued her story. "I didn't know Burt back then. We met four years later." She seemed to be considering whether or not she should share this with me. Then she added. "I know Burt thought something big was going on down at the Springs, and he made up his mind to stop it. He would get up in the night and run up there, convinced that he'd interrupt some devilish meeting of anti-Americans ready to take over the country. I was starting to feel like he was losin' his mind."

That information made me feel much better. I was pretty sure Burt wasn't referring to me in his notebook. I wondered, though, if there actually was a sect of Native Americans staging a revolution. In this day and age, that wouldn't surprise me at all. All they needed was a social media account as a means to connect with one another. So, I figured his whole set of notes referred to someone else.

Considering her comments about his conspiracy theories, I decided to keep quiet on the semi-nude question. Maybe it would come back to bite me later, but it seemed like a small detail compared to him being shot in the head, I rationalized leaving it out. "I need to tell you something that happened to me just before I came here. After I left work today and before I went home, I was drawn to the Springs again. When I arrived, there was a motorcycle in the parking lot."

She seemed to have come out of a trance with my words. "Burt talked about a motorcycle lots a times."

No wonder he thought I was someone else.

"What happened today?"

I straightened up, trying to remember the important details. "A Native American woman was sitting on the deck near the pool. She looked like she was in a trance of some sort. She seemed to know that I was there but didn't speak to me directly. She spoke of God and the Devil and the Native American Gods and how they interacted with the earth and the water. I didn't completely understand it. Then she fell over as if passed out. I think she was on Peyote. There was a piece of cactus lying on the deck in front of her."

She looked me straight in the eye. "Did she talk about Burt?"

I tried to think of the words she used. "I don't think so. She was talking about God and the Devil. But, hey, when somebody's on a hallucinogen, it's hard to know what they are really talking about."

She chewed on her lower lip. "Miranda, what time did you see Burt on Saturday?"

I thought back to Saturday, "I don't know the exact time, but it was getting dark when I got home, so maybe 7:30 or 8?" This was where I thought it might get tricky. Burt and I had talked for hours.

She shifted into interrogation mode. Her eyes got squinty. "What time was it when Burt found you in the pool?"

I reddened, knowing that I had left our extended conversation out of the story. "Um, probably around four."

I don't think she liked my answer because she sat up straight, eyes wide open and glared at me. "Four? Until, you think, eight o'clock? And what went on from four to eight? And before you answer, I know the part you told me about findin' you in the pool and puttin' the gun to your head and straightenin' out who you were and who you weren't would take all of about ten minutes. You got at least three and a half hours to account for."

This was exactly the conversation I had been trying to avoid. I had really enjoyed Burt's company, but without Burt to stand up for himself with Sally, I felt helpless to describe our afternoon accurately. I decided to put the best face on it that I could. "I couldn't spend more than twenty minutes in the hot spring without getting light-headed, so as soon as I got out, he suggested that I go change in one of the changing booths. A lot of men would have ogled me in my bikini, but not Burt. He was a real gentleman." *Why did I have to say that? Why? Why? Why?*

She pierced me with her eyes. "He said you looked good in your *bikini*?"

I could feel a bead of sweat running down my face. "No, oh no, nothing like that. He didn't mention my bathing suit. I could just tell it was making him uncomfortable." *Miranda, please just shut up!*

She nodded and went back to her squinty eyes, "So, you think you're so hot that you make men uncomfortable in your presence?" Sally smiled, not an attractive sight, in fact, it was kind of creepy. "You always carry your suit in your saddlebag? Why don't you model it for me?"

This was getting downright uncomfortable. I whispered, "I'd really rather not."

She used the table to help push herself up and leaned over, putting her face close to me. "Oh, you'd *really rather not* now, but you had no problem parading around in it in front of my husband, who is now *dead!* Well, that's just great, *tramp*. Until you can explain what you and my Burt did for the unexplained three and a half hours on the night before he died, I got nothing else to say to you. Now git *out* of my house." She pointed to the door.

I was so flustered; I couldn't even form any words. I tried to reconstruct the conversation Burt and I had that evening, but it escaped me. He was a nice man, a gentleman, and it didn't serve him well for his widow to think anything else, but I needed some time to regroup.

Chapter 7

Thankfully, I only had to drive for about thirty feet before reaching my driveway.

Jason took one look at me and threw his arms around me. "Uh-oh, you've had a rough day. I hope it wasn't work-related."

I rested my weary head on his shoulder. "Work is by far the least of my worries." I headed to the fridge for a cold one.

He grabbed one too. We headed to the couch, hand in hand.

We both sat back, relaxing before I spilled my guts. "Where should I start—Rick, Tina, the Crazy Indian at the Springs, or Sally?"

He looked impressed. "Wow, you *have* been busy." He pretended to count on his fingers. "Let's start at the beginning with Rick."

I kicked myself because I'd been trying to avoid thinking about Melissa again and my deep-seated guilt. Here came years and years of counseling that hadn't even been scheduled yet. And while I had mentioned the topic briefly to Jason, he had no idea how damaged I was. I decided just to touch on the conversation and leave Melissa to my future therapist. I took the next twenty minutes describing my encounters with Rick, Tina, the Native American Woman at the Springs, and Sally Roop. We both sat quietly for a few minutes, then I turned on the TV, and we watched back-to-back episodes of *The Office*, lying together on the couch, until we went to bed.

#

The rest of the week dragged by as I anticipated my girls' weekend. I tried to keep my head down and my fingers busy, entering orders and keeping discussions to a minimum with Rick, Tea or anyone who wanted to know what was going on in my personal life. I figured the less anyone knew, the better.

The sheriff's office had called me with a few more questions about my statement but had left it at that. I held my breath every time my phone rang, thinking it might be someone standing in my way of leaving town. I desperately needed a vacation. My stress level was over the top.

So when I finally burst through the door to head home at five on Friday, it was almost unbelievable. I had ridden my bike in case I had to lane split to get a jump on traffic out of town. If I took the 101, I could stop at home and pack and then decide whether to grab the Rover or stay on two wheels. Of course, I always preferred two wheels, but I might consider driving instead of several grueling hours on the motorcycle.

Jason pulled into the driveway right ahead of me. He picked me up and twirled me around. "Happy Friday!"

I laughed, "You do know I'm going to Monterey this weekend, right?"

He gave me a fake devastated look. "Yes, I know. I thought you might change your mind if I got all excited to see you."

I started toward the house to pack. "Not a chance, Cowboy! I've been looking forward to this for too long. I need some girl time and some *me*-time. This has been a horrible week." I took five minutes to throw some stuff in a suitcase and head toward the door. We kissed as I rushed out. I smiled. "And no strippers this time, and no jail time."

He looked dejected. "You're no fun. I'll have to go fishing."

I blew him a kiss. "See ya."

Since I packed a suitcase, I opted for the Rover. On a good day, the drive was no more than a half-hour, but this was a Friday afternoon, so by the time I pulled up to the Monterey Bay Inn, a medium-sized water-front hotel, it was nearly eight o'clock., and I was exhausted.

I pulled out my cell phone. I had several calls from various members of our yet nameless girl group, and, thankfully, a text from Margo, with a room number: 202.

I grabbed my suitcase and headed up the outside stairs. To the right were rooms 200 to 222. I counted down from 222 to the second to the last room and knocked.

I could already hear excited squeals from inside. I was a little jealous of how much fun they were having without me but happy to be here finally. Margo, in all her splendor, opened the door in her silk robe and pajamas. She grabbed my hand and pulled me inside the room. "It's about time! We were just about to give up on you."

Lyanne was sitting in a chair at a small table, wearing a pair of shorts and a tee-shirt.

She waved with the pinky of her wine-drinking hand. My impression was that she had been imbibing for a while. I wondered if she had been able to get her exclusive interview with Margo before the wine started flowing.

Wanda looked solemn, still in jeans and a tank top, lying on the bed. I wondered if she'd heard through the grapevine what was going on in my life, and it didn't take much time to find out. She said in an annoyed tone, "I never thought I'd have to learn through Tina Bright what's going on in my dearest friend's life." She drummed her fingers on her wine glass.

I suddenly felt guilty having not called Wanda during the week when I was just keeping my head down, trying to make it through to Friday. That was typical of me, pulling away from friends when in crisis, even though I wasn't completely aware of it. I begged for mercy. "Okay, I get it. I should have called you, but it was all I could do to get through the week. I figured I would spill my guts to all of you once I got down here."

Margo pulled up a chair next to Lyanne, and I sat next to Wanda on the bed with my back propped up with a pillow. Margo said, "Okay, girl, you've got the floor, and this had better be good."

I protested, "Wait a minute. I'm the only one without wine."

Lyanne poured, passed the glass to Margo, who passed it to Wanda, then to me. It looked to me like they had this process well-rehearsed. Just how long had they been here, I wondered?

I took a deep breath. "Well, it all started last Saturday. I tuned up Jason's motorcycle, which he hadn't ridden in five years."

Margo laughed. "It figures that it would all start with you doing guy's work. Don't you have a man to do that for you? You should be lounging in a bubble bath, asking him to pour you more wine."

I rolled my eyes. "This is going to take a while, I can tell. Anyway, Jason was so thrilled that I got his bike running that he took off on a ride, leaving me to my own devices."

Wanda put in her two cents. "Any boyfriend of yours should know that's never a good idea. What was he thinking?"

I ignored her. "So, I did a little work on my own bike, and when I was done Jason wasn't back yet, so I decided to take a ride."

Lyanne piped in, "I have a feeling this wasn't just a ride. I'm sure you have a way of making a normal old boring motorcycle ride into something special." She toasted me with her plastic wine glass. I was happy to see that Margo had loosened her up considerably. She was usually the sensible one.

Despite my struggle to get a word in, I said, "Near my house, there are some natural hot springs that have quite a history."

Margo should have been a high school teacher. "The Gilroy Yamato Hot Springs have been famous in Miranda's area for nearly 150 years. During the mid-to late-1800s they were the center of a major resort often visited by the rich and elite from the Los Angeles, San Francisco, and Sacramento areas because it was equally accessible from all three. I spent a couple of days researching the springs when I heard of Miranda's plight, but I don't need to go into all that right now. The most important part of the recent history is that the hotel which had been the center of the resort for more than a hundred years burned down on the Fourth of July in 1980."

I took over the story from there and explained in detail what happened to the point where Burt had the gun to my head.

Then Wanda interrupted. "So you grabbed the gun, and in one smooth motion, turned the tide on Burt Roop and shot him in the back of the head while he attempted to run into the woods."

I laughed when thinking of the irony of it all. "I might as well have. I get the feeling that's what the police think happened. The sheriff's department just hasn't put together evidence that will make it stick yet." That reminded me I hadn't checked the shed to make sure my Glock was still there. Where was my head these days?

Lyanne was on the edge of her seat. "So this guy has a gun to your head. What *really* happened?" She was always the reporter. I was surprised she didn't have a tape recorder and a notebook. I liked Lyanne, but it was a struggle for me to completely trust her as much as I did the other two. Our friendship was a work in progress.

I settled back against the pillow. "We started talking. He initially thought I was the ringleader of a group using his property to stage, he thought, a takeover of the country. I initially thought he was over the top, but the more I researched the Native American group he suspected, he may not be far off."

Margo took over again. "The Aulintac Indians have organized Native Americans from all of the tribes originally in

Chaos in the Canyon

Northern California, Western Nevada, and Northern Arizona. There are at least fifty active tribes, so they have chosen to operate under the Aulintac name for simplicity's sake. They have been amassing wealth, purchasing property, acquiring arsenals of weapons, and training in warfare tactics. While we Democrats, Liberals, Republicans, and Conservatives, fight among ourselves, they have developed a strategic plan to take it all while we are in a weakened state."

We all stared at her like she had lost her mind, and yet she sounded similar to what Burt's widow had told me that he believed.

She stared back. "Go ahead, stick your head in the sand. When you wake up in an internment camp one day, don't blame me."

We could have spent the rest of the weekend discussing that, but I decided to continue my story. "So, anyway, no, I didn't grab Burt's gun. I tried to reason with him. It wasn't long before we were talking, laughing, and joking around. Somewhere in the process, I change into my street clothes because, believe it or not, he seemed uncomfortable chatting with me in a two-piece bathing suit. He was a real gentleman. Let's face it, most men would have had their eyes glued directly at the girls," I said, pointing to my chest. "He had them averted to the point where it was almost *painful* to watch."

Lyanne rolled her eyes and nodded in agreement.

I smiled at the memory. "We talked and talked for hours, which Burt's widow, a jealous woman, reminded me of *very* recently when I went over to have a neighborly chat with her. I honestly don't know where the time went, but Burt and I talked for nearly four hours. Even then, I remember not wanting to go home. Was there something in me that knew this would be the last time we'd ever have a chance to converse? I had no idea, but we definitely got our money's worth. When I left, it was nearly dark, and he stayed behind, I assumed to lock up."

Wanda munched on some brie and wheat thins. "So, how did he die?"

I passed my glass down the line for a refill. "Damned if I know. The next day was Sunday, and I decided to go for a run. We're within walking distance of Coe Park. I had no idea until last weekend what I had at my fingertips. I haven't even explored Coyote Lake yet. It's such a great area." I looked at Wanda, "Sorry, but I don't miss SC at all, and I'm not talking Santa Claus or South Carolina."

She winked. "No offense taken. I might be moving to the beach."

I stood up on the bed. "Oh, do tell! You've been holding out on me!"

She smiled demurely, like the cat who swallowed the canary. "We'll talk later. You finish first."

I sat back down, affectionately messing up the hair she'd just had professionally straightened. "So, the next day I was running up a mountain trail, and I found his body with a bullet hole in the back of the head."

Wanda was piecing things together. "And this is where you met my *friend* Tina?"

I crossed my eyes. "Oh yeah, I figured you two were best buds. I thought you might have invited her down here this weekend." Sarcasm would get me everywhere.

Wanda thought for a minute. "Actually, not best buds so much. She's just so shallow, all perky and fake. Why can't she be more like you three? You tell it like it is. You don't sugar-coat things or make them all nicey-nicey. Ugh, I can't stand that."

I figured I should try to finish. "Wow, that's not the way I read her. Anyway, Tina Bright brings a whole band with her. A

Chaos in the Canyon

state cop, a park peace officer, and a fresh-faced detective from the sheriff's department. And I don't know what it is about that guy, but he's got it out for me. He knew more about my past in the first hour after I called 911 than most people know in a lifetime."

Lyanne suddenly got interested. "What's that guy's name?"

I strained to remember. "Jacob, something. I think it starts with M. Mayberry? No, it's shorter. Mabry. Yeah, that's it."

"Yeah, kind of a scary-looking guy?"

I nodded. "Yeah, that's him."

She stood up to get another glass of wine. "He's a real jerk. He can't even be twenty-five. He hit on me one night after I covered a story. Thought he was really a ladies' man." She shook her head. "I laughed in his face."

"He's out to make a name for himself," I said, "and he thinks I'm his ticket."

Margo had been in the background for most of my story, catching my eye periodically to let me know she was in my corner. "So, Miranda, what do they have on you that's not just circumstantial?"

I thought for a second. "I'm a little worried about the weapon. I have a Glock identical to the one Burt pointed at me, and I have no idea where he got it. We live in the country and don't worry much about that kind of stuff. Our weapons are stored out in the shed. If someone stole it, I'd never even know. If Burt was shot with that Glock and it can be traced back to me, I'm in big trouble. I've got to let Jason know to check that out. I keep thinking about it since meeting Burt, but I haven't taken the time to check."

Wanda puzzled over my statement for a moment. "Glocks are probably the most popular handgun in America. Could be anyone's. Call him now."

I dialed.

He picked up on the first ring. "Wow, you miss me already?"

I laughed. "Yes, I do. But that's not why I'm calling. Could you do me a favor? That Glock that Burt Roop had looked a lot like the one I have, and we have the guns stored out in the shed. Could you make sure the Glock is still there?"

He tried to brush me off. "Of course, it's there. Where would it go?"

I insisted. "Could you just check. I'd feel a lot better."

He sounded like it was a huge deal. "Okay, I'll take the phone with me."

I figured I'd keep him amused while he walked out to the shed. "So, what sorts of fun things have you done since I left?"

He responded in a bored tone, "Oh, you know, goats, chickens, and all that. Okay, I'm in the shed. I'm opening the gun case. And—"

There was silence. "Don't mess with me, Honey."

More silence. Finally, he responded, "The gun case is empty."

Chapter 8

I dropped my phone.

Next to me on the bed, Wanda was the first to react. She whispered, "What's wrong?"

I turned to look at her. "The guns are gone."

She continued whispering as Margo and Lyanne were chatting about something at the table, "*How many did you have?*"

I tried to remember. "Around fifteen or twenty, between my handguns and Jason's hunting rifles. Living in the country, we've both added a couple to our collections."

Margo noticed us whispering. "Okay, you two, this was supposed to be an open girls' weekend. What are you whispering about?"

It wasn't like I wanted to keep it a secret. I just felt so stupid not for locking either the gun cabinet or the shed. "Jason's and my guns are all missing."

Margo put two and two together and got something very bad. "So, your Glock was missing, and the guy that was killed that day after you met him may have had it on his person. That's not good at all. Now you add this Jacob Mabry trying to make a career on your back, and you have a recipe for disaster."

I sat and thought for a minute. "Okay, we need to figure out who Burt's enemies were, fast. The problem is that we don't know what we don't know."

Margo, who was now sitting on the end of the bed, addressed Lyanne, "Lyanne, what do you know about these Indian tribes? Have you done any stories on them? How could they be gaining this much power without anyone knowing about it?"

Lyanne took a sip of wine. "No-one takes the Native Americans seriously. If you want to get people excited, talk about the Muslims, the Middle Eastern Terrorists, the Chinese, the North Koreans, and even the Russians. But the Native Americans? No cares about them anymore. They operate casinos on the barren lands our government allowed them to live on because no-one else would live there. They haven't been a threat since we conquered the west. We were more afraid of the Japanese after World War II than we've ever been afraid of Native Americans."

She set her glass down. "I did an expose on a tribe in the Central Plains doing something very similar to the Aulintacs. They would have gotten away with taking over a huge landmass in South Dakota and Nebraska, but federal troops came in and took them out. It was all very hush-hush because the government never wanted the people to find out about this powerful enemy living among us. But they continue to underestimate the power of other tribal nations who have banded together to take back their land."

I scratched my head. "I had no idea any of this was happening. I always thought the most serious threats to our way of life were from the outside, not from within."

Lyanne nodded. "Oh, there are plenty from the outside also. I'm just saying never to ignore the less obvious answers."

I gave her a quizzical look. "What do you know that you're not telling me?"

She gave me a blank look. "Oh, probably nothing. Probably nothing."

After I refilled my wine glass, I returned to my perch on the bed next to Wanda. "So, if we report the guns stolen now, do you think that helps my case?"

She folded her arms and frowned a moment in thought. "I don't know that it can hurt. The obvious problem is that you will have reported it after Burt was shot. That's assuming the Glock was yours, and it was the murder weapon."

I laughed, "You are fully aware of how my luck runs, right?"

She nodded, not even arguing.

I said to Lyanne, "Do you think the Aulintacs would have stolen our guns? It seems small-time for a huge group of tribes amassing an arsenal."

She nodded. "You're probably right, Miranda, but this could be a splinter group trying to infiltrate. Something seems off. And why kill Burt? Where do the Hot Springs fit in, and who was this drugged-out Indian princess that you saw up there? There's a lot that makes sense and a lot that doesn't."

Margo had been taking notes. "I think you're right, Miranda. We need to figure out who Burt's enemies were. Does he have a social media page? We should troll him. And what about his wife, Sally? You said she was the jealous type. Maybe he had an admirer and she killed him in a jealous rage. Stranger things have happened."

Margo had a laptop, and everyone else jumped on their phones to find out as much as they could about Burt Roop before and after his untimely death.

We all worked in silence for about twenty minutes until Lyanne broke the silence. "What about this Chenoa Gray? She seems to *like* everything he posts. According to her, Chenoa means White Dove in Native-American dialect. What if something was going on between them or Sally suspected there was? Maybe she did him in. And she's your neighbor; she could have easily snuck over and stolen those guns."

Margo pointed to her screen. "Chenoa was also a mover and shaker with the Aulintac Nation. Maybe she was trying to lure him into their clutches so that they could steal the sacred springs away and use the one-time resort as their holy headquarters. Maybe he got in the way of their plan and was eliminated."

I got up to look at her laptop and to get away from chain-smoking Wanda. I love her, but there is a limit to my tolerance. "Is there a picture of Chenoa? I wonder if she's the spiritual leader I came across of the other day at the Springs."

She pointed out several of Chenoa's pictures in full Indian garb, headdress, war paint, and one in the dress she wore when I saw her on the spring-fed pool deck. I was sure it was her. Judging from some of the other more compromising photos, I was also convinced that she was the woman that Burt referred to in his notebook. Margo commented. "Uh-huh. If he were my husband, he'd probably be dead too."

I wanted to comment that all her husbands were dead, but this didn't seem like the time or place.

Wanda had been reclining quietly on the bed but finally spoke up. "I'm just not feeling the jealous wife angle. It's almost too easy. From what you told me about Burt, he would have done anything to protect those Hot Springs, and he adored his wife. He already had some guilt about the 1980 hotel fire, which we have no details about. Was he somehow responsible? Was he playing with fireworks, and one of them went awry? We'll never know. But he had a deep commitment to that place, and I believe it got him killed."

I interrupted. "Wait a minute. There was one thing that Burt said, which was confirmed by Sally. A guy named Tommy Pearson was arrested back in the '80s for setting that fire, but he was set free for lack of evidence. His family was very well connected, which may have had something to do with that. Burt didn't actually tell me his name. Sally did. But Burt said he was after someone and was going to get him."

Wanda said, "So, maybe we are running up the wrong tree with the whole Native American conspiracy theory, and it was something as simple as Burt was after this guy, and he killed Burt."

I nodded. "I guess it's possible, but if he already got off years ago, it's probably a dead issue."

Lyanne, ever the investigative reporter, pulled out a small whiteboard that she's been hiding behind her suitcase and was met with a combination of cheers and jeers from the crowd of three. She bowed then curtsied. I was so glad we had added her to our group. In some ways, we were all so creative; it was like herding cats for us to come to any reasonable conclusions that we could ever hope to agree on.

She started writing. "On the left side of the board, I'm going to write facts. On the right side, conjecture. Maybe once we can distinguish between what we actually know from what we think we know, we'll come closer to solving our case. We did this at a retreat not so long ago, and we actually solved several cases that the Oakland Police Department has considered dead." On the left side, she wrote, "1) Burt Roop is dead. 2) Miranda didn't kill him."

I breathed a sigh of relief, "At least that's not up for debate. Wait!" I raised my nearly emptied wine glass.

"Wait, what?" Margo asked as if suspicious of what I might say next."

I laughed and held my glass out while Lyanne retrieved a bottle, came over and refilled it. When she finished and had replenished everyone's glasses, I said, "Raise your glasses."

They exchanged puzzled glances but did as told.

"Wine as Investigative Tool. All caps. WAIT. Get it?"

Lyanne frowned for a moment while the others also looked puzzled. "What about Ladies in Waiting?"

"Sounds like a bunch of pregnant women," Margo said.

"And just using WAIT makes it sound more cryptic," Wanda added. "Let's go with that. It'll be our secret code. Whenever one of needs the other, we just say, Wait!"

"Maybe our investigations would move along faster without the wine," Lyanne said. "We are an investigation team."

"It's got an extra 'a' in there," I said with a giggle.

"FBI is Federal Bureau of Investigation. It has an extra 'o'." Wanda pointed out.

"True," Lyanne said. "I still think it would read better with something like, WAIT Women's Club. Especially if you want cryptic. We'll know what it's about; others will think we're watching our weight."

Margo tried it out as if she were savoring a new wine. "Wine as an Investigative Tool Women's Club. WAIT Women's Club." We all held our breath as she thought about it, then she nodded. "I really like it! We are WAIT!"

Wanda plunked her glass down on the nightstand. "Well, we've accomplished our goal for the weekend. We can go now."

Lyanne waited for the din to die down. "Wait!"

Everyone stared at her.

"I didn't mean our new name, I meant to wait a minute because I wondered if we have any more facts?"

Margo referred to her laptop where she'd been taking notes. "I'm sure we do. Just not many useful ones." She started reading out the facts. "Burt and Miranda are neighbors. Miranda and Jason's guns are missing. Sally is a jealous wife. Burt was the caretaker of the Hot Springs. Miranda met Burt the day before he died. Three separate police departments are handling the investigation. Sergeant Tina Bright is heading up the investigation. Jacob Mabry is a young detective with an attitude. Burt believed Tommy Pearson burned down the hotel."

Lyanne had been trying to keep up with the list but the more Margo read, the more we realized there were way too many facts to fit on a whiteboard. Lyanne kept writing smaller and smaller until the ones on the bottom were nearly illegible, and there were likely many more to add.

As she struggled to get all the facts down, Margo suggested an alternative. "How about I just email them to everyone?" Lyanne seemed a little put out by relinquishing her role as the group scribe, and Margo immediately picked up on it. "Lyanne, I think you should continue to lead the discussion because you are clearly the most focused of the group."

Lyanne smiled, appreciating the recognition. "Why, thank you, Margo, that's especially complimentary coming from you." I got the idea that was a backhanded compliment, and the two of them were competing for group leader status, but I didn't want to get in the middle of it.

I chuckled, "As long as it gets done, I'm fine."

Wanda didn't comment.

Lyanne stayed at the helm. "Does anyone else have any pertinent facts? Since Margo will be entering the list electronically, we can always add to the list at any time." She looked around for further suggestions.

I suddenly felt that I needed to show that I could keep up with these ladies. "I'm sure that there are other facts, but let's move on to conjecture for now." I wasn't sure which hormone kicked in when women competed, but it was as strong as anything men felt in the heat of battle.

We all yelled out various things. "The Natives are Restless; Miranda's a suspect; Burt was having an affair; Sally killed him; Chenoa killed him; Someone else killed him."

I couldn't resist cutting the tension with some humor. "A bear with really good dexterity and aim killed him."

Wanda rolled her eyes. "Always the comedienne."

I replied, "Gotta love me." She'd been awfully quiet the whole evening. "Are you all right? You don't seem to be really with it tonight."

She looked me in the eye and spoke softly, "We'll talk later. I'm having a bit of a crisis, but I wasn't completely comfortable having group therapy on the topic." She motioned with her eyes toward the other two who were discussing other conjectures.

Margo and Lyanne added to the list. "There are other suspects. There may be witnesses in the park. There could be alternatives that we aren't aware of that the police may be."

I could feel the energy level dropping, so I tried to refocus the group. "Hey, guys, I know that the main reason we're here is to have fun, but I really appreciate you taking the time to help me out with this case. And if God forbid, they decide I'm a serious suspect at some point, we'll already have a head start." I smiled at every one individually. "Now, was there anything in particular you guys wanted to do while we're here?" I laughed, "Margo, since you're paying, I guess you get first dibs."

She chuckled. "Miranda, it's a deal. I'll go first. I wasn't sure that you knew that I was planning on relocating to this area, so I was hoping to look at several houses while I'm here. I understand that it might be fun for some of you or completely boring for others. And that's because we are such a diverse group."

I tried to keep things light and moving forward. "I know that I'd absolutely *love* to shop for real estate with you, Margo. My days of shopping for multi-million-dollar properties are over, but I can still live vicariously through you."

Everyone agreed that it would be fun, but that would be tomorrow. Tonight would involve lots of wine and girl talk.

Because we had two adjoining rooms, we had plenty of space to spread out and four king beds, although it wouldn't have mattered all that much. When we finally passed out some time past 1 a.m., I slept across one of the beds next to Margo. Wanda curled up on the couch, and Lyanne took the other bed. No-one slept in the other room.

Around seven the next morning, everyone started to stir. Both rooms were equipped with full-sized coffeemakers, and thankfully, either the hotel provided coffee, or someone had the foresight to bring some with them. There appeared to be enough to keep us full of caffeine for several weeks. I would have loved to stay that long, but I was sure that wasn't in the cards.

Having two rooms made it easier for us to get ready. By eight, we were all dressed and set to go. Everyone had opted to accompany Margo in her quest to find a new home. Her first appointment was at ten, so we chose to go out to breakfast.

We opted for the Wave Street Café, which was within walking distance of the hotel. The Brioche French Toast with Fresh Strawberries was to die for. Margo opted for the Monkey-Do Cakes, which were pancakes covered with caramelized bananas and pecans. I would have gone into sugar shock had I eaten those, but she already had such a high energy level; if it increased, it wasn't noticeable.

Wanda and Lyanne both had the Sweet Raspberry Pancakes with Coconut and Granola. I was happy to see them eating the same thing. It seemed to help them bond because they hadn't spent as much time together as the rest of us had. While Wanda came across as highly dominant when I first met her, she turned out to be the most introverted and shy one of the group, so this was a breakthrough moment for the two of them.

We spent the rest of the morning and most of the afternoon visiting the most fabulous ocean-front mansions that I had ever stepped foot into. The last house we visited, late afternoon, when we were all exhausted, rubbing our feet, and ready to jump in the hot tub, was on Monterra Oaks Road and it was at listed at close to six million dollars. The general consensus was that this was the house Margo should buy. I wasn't quite sure if it was because this was the best house we saw or if we didn't want to see any more houses, although it was a gorgeous home.

By the time we got back to the hotel, I could barely move from exhaustion. I couldn't speak for the rest of the group, but I was ready for bed. I was relatively sure the other party animals would want to drink wine all night again, so I would have to buck it up and dig down deep for more energy.

I decided to get everyone thinking about Burt Roop again. I figured that tomorrow was a travel day, so this was my last chance. Margo and Lyanne were drinking coffee and amoretto at the small table near the kitchenette, and Wanda was watching golf on TV, lying on the other bed. Everyone groaned.

Lyanne spoke up. "Didn't we flog that dead horse yesterday? Until someone takes some action or we get new information, I don't know what else we can do."

Something had been eating at me since last night. "Well, we did come up with that list of facts and conjectures. But we don't have a plan. I think we need to determine what we do from here. We've got some tremendous resources. Lyanne could be developing some investigative reporting about the Native Americans threatening to take over the country. Margo will practically be in our neighborhood once she moves up here, especially my neighborhood, so as soon as I get more evidence, she can be a point person working with me since I have to work my day job. And Wanda can develop a new and exciting relationship with Tina Bright to help support the investigation." I tried to make it sound positive.

Wanda stuck out her tongue at me and said, "So, what do you get to do, Miranda?"

I laughed and rolled my eyes. "I actually have the toughest job. I have to do everything I can not to get arrested for this. And

I hope that you guys remember this when you're doing your parts. I met Burt the day before he died. I called 911. I hope it's not true, but I'm betting he was killed with my Glock. I have no alibi. Those facts alone could not only get me arrested but get me convicted. I try not to think about it all day, every day, but I have to admit, it creeps into my mind more often than I'd like."

They all hugged me. Besides that conversation, we didn't mention Burt's murder for the remainder of the weekend, which was probably the smartest thing we could do for my sanity.

We split up on Sunday afternoon with a feeling of optimism and hope.

Chapter 9

When I pulled into the driveway on Sunday evening, all I wanted to do was take a hot shower. As I headed toward the back door, a Santa Clara County Sheriffs' cruiser pulled in.

My throat suddenly went dry. I was able to reach the door and walk in before they got out of the car. I quickly said to Jason, who was playing Nintendo, "The cops are here. And I don't think it's for you."

He came over to hug me, but I brushed past him and headed to the kitchen to grab a glass of water.

"Hi to you too," he said as he stood there with his arms still extended.

There was a loud knock on the door. This was not a social call. "Hello?" came the call from a woman through the screen door. I was surprised to see that Tina Bright was making a personal appearance with her sidekick, Jacob Mabry. The screened door was tinted and since I could see them, I had to figure that they could see me, but maybe there was a glare outside, leaving them at a disadvantage.

I crossed myself, even though I wasn't Catholic and headed to the door. The door was only ten feet from me. As I approached, they could see me clearly yet they knocked again. Cops were a strange breed.

I opened the door, ready to face the music. Having spent most of the weekend on the topic of Burt Roop and analyzing evidence, their appearance wasn't that surprising. I figured it was just a matter of time. I was ready to surrender when, much to my surprise, Tina said, "We're looking for Jason Wall. Is he at home?" She had a warrant in her hand. I wasn't sure if it was of the Search or Arrest variety, but I assumed I was about to find out.

The irony was too much to handle after the 'Princess of Death' stuff I had been through over the last few years. Not knowing what else to say, I called to Jason, "Honey, it's for you."

Knowing that I can be somewhat of a joker, and considering my delivery bordered somewhere between complete irony and black humor, he approached the front door with a smirk as I backed away from Tina and Jacob.

Tina stepped up. "Jason Wall, you are under arrest for the murder of Burt Roop. You have the right to remain silent. Anything you say can and will be used against you in a court of law. You have the right to an attorney. Should you not be able to afford one, one will be provided for you at no cost. Do you understand these rights as I have explained them?"

He stared at them with his mouth open as if this were an April Fool's Day prank that was just about to come to an end. But he finally managed to choke out, "Yes, I understand."

Tina cuffed him and led him to the vehicle. I immediately thought of Mark Peterson, my future brother-in-law, old friend, and go-to defense attorney. I yelled to Jason, "I'll call Mark!" hoping he could hear me.

That whole scene was so surreal. Was this the ultimate price Jason paid for living with me, the Princess of Death? He was an innocent man, arrested for a murder that neither of us committed. I had so much information to process and so little time. I needed to talk to Mark, but what would I say? I needed to have the facts straight in my head first. Was it possible that Jason killed Burt Roop? I supposed that anything was possible, but he didn't show up on either the facts or conjecture lists that the WAIT Club put together over the weekend. Was I too close to the situation to see the obvious? Why would Jason kill Burt Roop? As far as I knew, he barely knew the guy, so what could his motive possibly have been? This had to be a mix-up, right?

I dialed Mark's number. I couldn't delay any longer despite not having anything very intelligent to say. He was learning to check his caller ID and answered, "Miranda, good news, I hope."

I confessed, "Mark, do I ever call you with good news?"

"Come to think of it, I've never had a purely social call from you. So, what's up?"

I took a deep breath. "Well, how can I put this?" I figured I'd better just spit it out. "Jason's been arrested for murder."

I heard Mark talking to his assistant in the background. "Sorry, Miranda, but I know what you're going to ask me next, so I'm getting prepared. Hold on just a sec." I heard bits and pieces of his conversation with his assistant, Andrea. He was getting used to flying to California on a moment's notice as I couldn't seem to stay away from murder. Not by my choice. He surprised me when he came back on. "Hey, I've got an idea. I have a new partner who can handle everything here for the time being, and Sabine and I were talking about doing some traveling. How about if she and I come out there, and we can mix some business with pleasure?"

I nearly jumped out of my skin. "You're going to bring my *favorite* sister with you? Oh, Mark, I just *love* you!"

He laughed. "You do know she's your only sister, right?"

I nodded even though he couldn't see me. "Yes, but we're still making up for all those lost years. Besides, once you two get married, I'm going to have you to compete with, so I'd better grab all the time I can get with her now."

He continued. "Hey, let me make our travel plans, but first who is he suspected of killing, is he the only suspect, and would there be any reason for him to have done it?"

I filled him in on the details, making sure he understood I had absolutely no idea why Jason had been accused and arrested.

"Okay," Mark said. "I'll get in touch with the court. Do you think it'll be San Jose?"

I chewed on my thumbnail. "I think so. The arrest was made in Santa Clara County, so I'm almost sure it'll be the same court you were in last time."

He responded, "Okay, I'll let you know when we're arriving. Oh, do you a place for us to stay, or should we stay in a hotel?"

I thought for a second. "Well, once Jason's out of jail, it would be tight. Plus, we're nearly an hour from San Jose, so you'll probably want to be closer to the court. That hotel where you stayed before by the airport might be a good choice again."

He laughed. "You're not trying to hide the other bodies Jason has buried in the basement, right?"

I groaned. "Honestly, if it would keep the press and the internet from focusing on me, I'd probably host an open house featuring those bodies with descriptions on how he killed each one of them." I hesitated. "I guess I shouldn't be joking around at Jason's expense. On the one hand, I'm just so relieved that I wasn't arrested, but worried, on the other, that the internet geeks are going to come after me again. I think with Lyanne in my corner, the press might be a little more forgiving."

Mark was ready to get off the phone. "Okay, Miranda, I'll give you a call or text once I know what's going on. Let Jason know we've got this under control."

I thought for a second. "Hey, do you think I should go up to Santa Clara? I never know what to do when someone gets arrested. Dealing with the police is unpredictable. I might just sit in the lobby for four hours and never get to see him while he's processed."

I decided to stay put. More often than not, seeing a prisoner the day they were apprehended, unless you were an attorney, was next to impossible. I could probably get more done here and keep focused. This curveball was something I needed to pass on to my fellow WAIT Club members to get their take on it since none of us had pegged Jason as a possible suspect in our analysis in Monterey.

Chapter 10

I was pretty sure Margo would have gotten home by now unless she was fighting one of those horrific LA traffic jams. I took the chance that she would be and punched in her speed dial. She answered on the first ring. "Miranda, don't tell me they already arrested you for the murder, and you saved the first phone call for me." She laughed.

I really felt bad for Jason that he had been wrongfully arrested, so laughing seemed wrong, but I couldn't help it. "Well, nope, I was not arrested."

Margo breathed a sigh of relief. "Well, thank goodness!"

I swallowed hard. "There is a caveat. Jason was arrested."

It sounded like she dropped the phone at the other end. "Get out! No way! We didn't even have him on our list at all. So much for the Wine as an Investigative Tool Club, eh? I guess we need to brush up on our detective skills."

"Well, if anyone was going to think of Jason," I said, "it should have been me, and he'd be the last person I'd think of." I thought about it. "I came up with myself as a suspect this weekend and never him. Let's think about his motive. Jealousy? That's a stretch. Politics? Border dispute? Drug war? This is mild-mannered Jason we're talking about. Everyone likes the guy. I have to admit that it drives me crazy sometimes. I really have to work for people to like me, but they are drawn to him like a magnet. Let's take Sally, Burt's wife, for example. I'd say she took an immediate dislike to me, which I'm sure grows every day. Now that Jason's been arrested, I can't even imagine what she thinks."

Margo clicked her tongue, "Oh, Miranda, you can't be so hung up on what others think of you. Imagine poor little ole' orphan me when I became the Princess of Monserrat. If you don't think people talked behind my back every day of my life, think again. I was a gold digger; I was dirt; I should be buried alive in the sand; I should be sent out to sea in an oarless boat, and those are the ones I can repeat. Believe me; you don't want to offend island people."

I smiled. "Leave it to you to give me a fresh perspective. It's hard to remember that you weren't always the socialite that you are now. You are an amazing woman, Margo Prentice." There was something I was going to tell her that was on the tip of my tongue. "Oh, I remember what I was going to tell you. Mark Peterson is coming to defend Jason, and Sabine is coming with him."

She gushed, "Not the international Miss Everything Sabine that I have heard about all these years. God, I hope we get along." She chuckled. "We're both stronger than strong women, so you know it could go either way."

I stuttered. "But I thought you said—"

She interrupted, "I said I didn't worry about what other people thought of me, not that I got along with everyone. That would just be a lie, Miranda. There are tons of people I don't get along with, many of them strong women. Honestly, one of the reasons that the WAIT Women's Club works is because the others know when they should defer to me and when they don't have to."

I had observed that but wasn't sure she was aware of it. "Yeah, I know. I've done it myself." I bit my lip, wondering how she would react.

She chuckled. "Of course you have, Miranda. You value your life."

It was interesting working through the kinds of communications issues that we had as a four-woman group. I wasn't even sure exactly why it worked, but it did. We seemed to rotate roles. No-one was the leader all the time, and no-one sat in the corner all the time either. So far, at least, it was a nice balance.

I realized that, perhaps, Wanda might have heard something about Jason's arrest. She always seemed to know things before I did. "Hey, Margo, I've gotta run, but we need to get together, and you need to meet Sabine. I think you two would really hit it off." I wasn't completely sure, but I wanted to put a positive spin on it. "But, if not, it would be really entertaining watching you two trying to fill the same space."

She pretended to be offended. "You'd be surprised what I am capable of when I'm on my best behavior. I have had to entertain the nastiest and most maudlin queens and princesses in the modern world, and I managed to survive them without starting World War III."

I hoped I hadn't pushed her too far. "I'm sorry. I hope you know I'm kidding most of the time."

She laughed. "Yeah, me too. I'll talk to you soon. I can't wait to meet the great Sabine. She'd better be everything you represent her to be."

I shook my head. "Oh, she is. Believe me. She is."

I tried to picture both of these strong-willed women in the same room but couldn't make the picture work, so I called Wanda. "Wanda Marshall, at your service."

That was a new greeting. "Wow, you must either be in a good mood or standing right in front of your chief."

She covered her phone. I heard her muffled voice tell whoever she was with that she had to take this call. I could hear her walking with her phone and then her office door close. She sounded slightly out of breath. "Miranda, what is going on? They arrested Jason for Burt's murder? Why didn't you call me?"

I was a bit taken aback. "I could have asked you the same thing. In fact, hey wait, oh yeah, I am calling you right now."

She responded, "Yes, but you should have called while they were there, arresting him. Maybe I could have done something."

I wasn't buying it. "Wanda, you're telling me if I called you while Tina Bright and the boy wonder were here arresting Jason, if I'd called you and handed them my phone, you could have said some magic words that would make them change their minds?"

She relented. "Well, okay, maybe not, but I hate hearing stuff like this from my boss, co-workers, or a police scanner. We're friends, Miranda. You're supposed to call me."

I had to shift into therapist mode, or I was going to shift into just pissed mode. "Sweetheart, can you listen to me for just a second? I am calling you right now to let you know that they arrested Jason. I had a few things to do, like calling my attorney first, but you can rest assured that you were very close to the top of the list."

She waited a few seconds before responding. "Sorry, Miranda, it's been a really bad day, and this was the last thing I wanted to hear. My God, he didn't even make our list. He should have at least made the list."

She was right. Jason probably should have made the list of suspects. "So we have some structural work to do on our process, at least we had fun. That's why we do stuff like this, so we have it down before we start trying to sell our investigative services, right?"

She blasted back, "Who said anything about selling investigative services?"

I laughed. "No-one, it's just been a thought that's been kind of running around in my brain since we first questioned Patricia. I know we all have careers, but it's never too early to think about doing something else. Aren't there days when you wish you were your own boss?"

She responded, "Of course, there are. There are days when I'd like to be anything but a cop. And with the way the world is going, I can't imagine that's going to change any time soon."

I said, "Well, let's just keep it in our back pocket for now. We may never do anything with it, but you never know. We all have something of value to add. We'd make a great law firm. Too bad we don't all have law degrees."

Wanda laughed. "Now, that's something I would never do."

I got the conversation back on track. "So, what do you know about Jason's case?"

She sounded like all the relaxation from the weekend had drained from her body. "Well, I came into the office after getting home from our wonderful weekend just to check the docket and see if anything interesting happened while I was away. I like to check the Sheriff's Department activity too because sometimes they horn in on our cases. Or should I say, they make courtesy arrests? Well, I couldn't believe my eyes when I saw what was happening with the Burt Roop case, so I called Tina immediately. But she was, evidently, still en route to the jail and didn't want interference from some competing police agency."

I tried to hide the disappointment in my voice. "Well, when you hear something, let me know. I can't believe they didn't even question him. I keep racking my brain. All I can think is that they made a positive match between the murder weapon and the bullet that killed Burt." My head was throbbing. "All they had to do was ask us, and we could have told them that all of our guns were stolen. This is just a waste of time and taxpayer dollars. I have a mind to run up to Tina's office first thing tomorrow morning and give her a piece of my mind."

She spoke in a soothing voice. "Whoa, there. Let's not jump to conclusions. You may be right, but let me do some digging first, then we'll go from there. The fact that you have me working from the inside is a good thing. I doubt we'll be able to avoid the arraignment, so I would keep moving forward with whatever you're planning, and I'll see what I can find out."

My mind was racing. "Okay, I've got my attorney, Mark Peterson, and my sister, Sabine, on the way out here from New Orleans."

She responded calmly, "Okay, get some sleep, Miranda. You're probably going to need it."

I tried to calm my voice. "Thanks, Wanda. I'll take a hot bath. That usually works to destress me. I know I need to keep my head straight for Jason's sake."

She finished the conversation with, "I'll talk to you as soon as I know anything."

I said, "Bye," and hung up.

It was nearly ten o'clock and probably too late to call Lyanne, but I was curious if she had heard anything. She probably put her kids to bed and was catching up with her husband. I pushed in her contact number on my phone and waited for hers to ring. She answered almost immediately. "Miranda, I knew you wouldn't be able to live without me once you spent a weekend with me."

I chuckled. "If only you knew."

Her voice turned immediately to concern. "Uh-oh. What's up? Is everything okay?"

I got serious. "Well, to be honest, no. Just, when I got home from our girls' weekend, Jason was arrested for Burt Roop's murder."

She gasped. "No way! Are you serious? None of us saw that coming. What do you need from me, Miranda? Just ask."

I wasn't really sure what she could do. "Well, if you're going to do a story on him, could you let me know first?"

She assured me. "Absolutely, you'll be the first to know. I'll try to get the scoop. Obviously, I don't get to do every story, so I'll have to alert my co-workers, but they're usually pretty cool about stuff like this."

I could hear her kids laughing in the background. "Hey, I'll let you get back to your little ones."

She whispered, "I already put them to bed twice tonight. I love them to death, but I'd give anything to have a girls' weekend about twice a month."

I feigned shock. "Lyanne! There's no way you prefer our company to your little darlings." I could hear one screaming and the other one crying. "Okay, maybe I get it."

She sounded harried. "I've been trying to get them into bed for the past hour. I've gotta run, but I'll keep you posted. Talk to you soon." She hung up.

I wasn't really sure what to do when there was a knock on the back door. *Now who can this be?*

I cautiously opened the door enough to peek around the edge to see who might be out there at this time of night, hoping it wasn't the police here to arrest me this time. You could have knocked me over with a feather when I saw Chenoa Gray, the Indian princess, at my door. She wore more typical western clothing than our first encounter: Jeans, plaid long sleeve shirt, cowgirl boots, and a white cowgirl hat. Her hair was jet black and braided down her back, her eyes dark and pleading. Her skin was between olive and peach in color, and she was startlingly beautiful, which was my impression when I first saw her at the hot springs.

My mouth must have dropped open because she looked like she was having second thoughts. She took a step back as is she might flee but then approached the door again and just stood there.

This was feeling weird. As I was about to shut the door on her, she said with what I assumed to be a Native American accent, "Miranda Marquette, Princess of Death? I have so long wanted to meet you." That seemed like an odd thing to say since she was definitely the woman at the Hot Springs the other day.

My head was spinning. Then what she said nearly made my head explode. "Now, we need to work together. As you know, our Jason has been arrested for murder."

I repeated the words in my head. *Our Jason. Our Jason? Our Jason!*

She must have realized that I wasn't connecting the dots. "May I come in?" she asked.

I stepped out of her way and motioned her in, curious and puzzled by her words, *Our Jason.*

She moved like a panther, silently and stealthily. She led me to the couch, which I found odd since this was my house. She motioned for me to sit and sat opposite me.

I was just about to speak when she did. "I presume from your reaction that Jason never mentioned me."

I shook my head.

She nodded with a kind, understanding, and gentle look on her face. "That explains your reaction. Jason and I had a very serious relationship that I ended three years ago. I love him very much, and it breaks my heart every day that we are not together." She paused, letting her words sink in. The fact that she didn't say *loved* him very much was not lost on me.

There was so much I was confused about. I figured I might as well ask one question at a time. "How did you know I lived here, and how do you know about the Princess of Death thing?"

She chose her words carefully. "This probably won't please you. Jason and I still speak, sometimes several times a day."

I could feel my anxiety level rising more quickly than if I had just found a dead body, and honestly, if Jason were here right now, he might just be one. I practiced some of my new anxiety reduction techniques from a book I was reading. Man, I needed a new therapist badly. I smiled with more sarcasm than sincerity. "Oh, you speak several times a day, do you? And just how do you do that?"

The look on her face was anything but smug. She clearly understood that Jason had lied to me by omission every day we had been together. She spoke slowly. "Usually by text, but sometimes by phone. Oh, Miranda, I'm so sorry. He assured me that you knew, so he was lying to me too." She folded her hands in her lap and looked me directly in the eye. I had no reason to doubt this woman and, at this point, every reason to doubt him.

I was seething inside but trying to keep a calm exterior. "So, you know that he's been arrested."

She nodded. "They took his phone, but he called me from the police station."

I wanted to claw this woman's eyes out. He had used his one phone call to call her? I was losing my patience and focus. I closed my eyes for ten seconds, taking deep breaths. I also made a wish, but it wasn't granted. She was still there when I opened them. I took her hand because I intended to lead her out the door. "Chenoa, exactly why are you here?"

I was hoping she'd answer me on her way to the door, but she hadn't picked up on my desire for her to depart. She continued to speak, even though much of it was not registering. I wished I was taping it because I didn't believe my retention would be very high and I might need it in court at some point. "Jason didn't kill Burt Roop," she stated with confidence.

I was reaching the end of my rope. "Listen, White Dove, or whatever your name is—"

She looked at me with a quizzical *How do you know the translation of my name?* look.

I was happy to have gotten her attention and to be in command of our meeting. I said. "I'm sure you are a wonderful person, but this is really not a good time."

She got a very distressed look on her face, seeing that I was trying to give her the bum's rush. She pleaded with me. "I understand that this has been a difficult visit, but there is something very important I need to tell you."

I did everything I could to stay patient. "What is it?"

She grabbed my hands. "Your life is in grave danger, and you need to get out of this house tonight. If anyone witnessed me coming here, I am in danger too, but it was important to protect you. We are sisters of the universe, me of Earth and Water, and you of the Seven Ponds of Death. We will ever be connected as one." She stood and said, "I have to go," and was gone.

Chapter 11

I stayed on the couch for a few minutes trying to absorb everything she had told me. She seemed sincere, but was I really in imminent danger? That wasn't something you necessarily wanted to put to the test.

My mind was racing a million miles an hour. If I truly was in danger, where should I go? Mark and Sabine were due in town tomorrow. How much of this should I share with them? Sabine always felt like she had to swoop in and save the day and that I was incapable of taking care of myself. *That* was not happening.

While I was thinking, I decided I needed to multi-task. I started taking armloads of clothes from my closet to the Rover. I had reclining seats. If I had to sleep in my car a couple of nights while I figured things out, it wouldn't be the first time.

I thought of names, one by one, and eliminated most of them. Margo would have been perfect if she lived closer, but she was still in Long Beach. Even if she had already relocated to Monterey, it would be a stretch to commute to Santa Clara daily.

Lyanne had a husband and two small children. I couldn't imagine adding an outsider that she barely knew to the mix would work. And not that I didn't love kids, but it always sounded like a chaotic pre-school in the background whenever I called her.

While I had met my goal of adding several new friends last year, Wanda was the last one on my list of new friends. Patricia was the only remaining local friend. Since her trial, we had pretty much lost touch when I discovered that she had misrepresented her situation when she moved here from Colorado and consistently lied to me before and after being arrested. We had gotten together one time since she was released, and she hadn't even appeared remorseful, so I had written her off for now. However, desperate times called for desperate measures, and if Wanda couldn't offer me a place to stay, this would certainly be a desperate time.

I had intended to keep in touch with Patricia's mother, Toni. She had moved into my vacated apartment when she relocated from Colorado when her gubernatorial-candidate husband, Charles, wound up in jail for murder. Having had a couple of conversations with her after her husband was arrested, I thought that we could end up being friends under different circumstances. However, blood being thicker than water; it appeared that my unresolved differences with Patricia would prevent me from further advancing any relationship with Toni any time soon.

I figured I could call Patricia or Toni if I got desperate, but I opted for Wanda. I took my last load of clothes, locked the back door, jumped in the car, and hit her number on my phone, starting my drive toward Santa Clara. She was laughing as she answered, which seemed out of character. "Hello," she covered the mouthpiece. "Stop that! I'm on the phone!" I thought I heard a male's voice in the background.

I wished I could be in such a carefree place right now. "Wanda?"

There was a hesitation. "Miranda, is that you? What's up?" Then she giggled again.

I continued. "Did I catch you at a bad time?"

She responded, "Hold on just a sec." I could hear her shoes on the floor as she walked, and then the door slamming. "Sorry."

I was surprised, as I had rarely even seen Wanda smile, much less giggle like a schoolgirl. "Is there something you want to tell me?"

She whispered, "Well, there was something I wanted to tell you over the weekend, but we didn't get any alone time. David and I are together."

I hesitated, trying to add two and two together but got only three. "David, your partner, who's ten years younger, David?"

She went on. "Um, actually fifteen, but who's counting? It was the funniest thing. I honestly couldn't stand him. Then one day, we were arguing in my office over nothing, and I just kissed him."

I tried to picture that but came up blank. "You'd better watch out, girl. I see a sexual harassment case in your future."

I could hear her shift back into Detective Wanda mode. "It's okay. I got him to sign a waiver."

I shook my head. My best prospect to stay with had robbed the cradle. What was the world coming to? I figured I'd fill her in anyway. "Do you have a second? I have to fill you in on something."

She sounded a little impatient, but I figured she could wait a few minutes for her boy toy. After all, she was the one who was annoyed that I hadn't called her immediately after Jason was arrested. I didn't want her angry at me for not filling her in on the latest event. "After we talked, I had a visitor—Chenoa."

She gasped, "The Indian princess?"

I placed my phone on speaker and set it on the center console while watching the road. "Yes, and guess what?" I couldn't possibly tell her everything she told me, so I decided to go with the most urgent. "She said a bunch of stuff, but the most critical right now was that I'm in danger. So, I'm heading up to Santa Clara. I vacated Jason's house. Wow, that reminds me that I'd better call the neighbor next door to take care of the animals while I'm gone. I've never had to think about stuff like this. Jason always takes care of it. Well, maybe he'll be home early in the week anyway."

She responded with interest, "What kind of danger did she say you were in?"

"She didn't say. She was pretty cryptic. There was some other stuff she said that I don't want to talk about on the phone." I hesitated, not knowing what her status was with David and how that might affect my need for short term housing. I decided just to go for it. "So, are you and David living together?"

It sounded like she spit out whatever she was drinking. "God, no!"

She sounded kind of distracted right now; I was beginning to feel unwelcome, but I asked anyway, "Can I stay with you for a couple of days while this all gets straightened out?"

She said immediately, "Of course! Oh, you thought. I'm sorry. I wasn't thinking. I get what that sounded like from the other end now. We were just being immature. My child does come out a little bit when I'm with him. Being the oldest of ten kids, I didn't have much of a childhood. So, he helps me make up for it. It's just fun, Miranda. It's not like we're getting married. Or even anything close. I'm happy and relieved that he has a place to go home to. I'm not ready for anything serious or even full time. But when we do get together, we do have a good time, and what more can you ask for? I'll go back in now and tell him something's come up and I need to end our evening. He'll understand. I'm glad you thought of me."

I didn't have the heart to tell her that my next option involved a Wal-Mart parking lot and a reclining seat. I groaned, "I was in such a hurry to get out after Chenoa left, I forgot just about everything. You should have seen me running from the house to the car with wads of clothes. I have no idea what I even brought. I didn't even pack a suitcase, so I have no toothbrush, toothpaste, shampoo, brush, blow dryer, or tons of other things I can't even think of right now."

She sounded concerned. "You must have been in a panic. I'm sorry I wasn't a little more serious earlier."

I brushed her off. "Wanda, it does my heart good to see you let down a little bit. You're wound just a little too tight for your own good most of the time. I'm just sorry I had to break up the party. I'm glad you can take me in, though; I really need to process the last few hours."

"You've really had quite a time since you got back from Monterey," she said. "What time is it anyway?"

I looked at my watch. "No wonder I'm getting tired. It's after eleven. I'm almost always in bed by now on a work night. Well, at least the boss can't yell at me if I'm late tomorrow." I gave a mirthless chuckle.

She scolded. "There's more of that dark humor you're known for. What do you think Jason would do if he knew you were joking at his expense?"

It just came out. "To be honest, I couldn't care less right now."

She drew in a quick breath. "I guess we do have to talk. I've never heard you talk about Jason like that, and I have a feeling the Indian princess' visit had something to do with that." She giggled. "We're horrible."

I didn't want to talk about that on the phone. "Yes, we are. Hey, I know you want to let David down easy, and I should probably concentrate on my driving, so I'll see you in a half-hour or so."

She laughed. "He'll get over it. He's never had anyone like me and likely never will again, so he's willing to go through a lot for a little. I'll see you soon."

I glanced behind me in the rear-view mirror. My clothes were thrown everywhere. I checked my phone to see if I had the guy next door's cell number, and I did. I knew texting and driving was worse than drunk driving, so I pulled over to get gas and texted him. "Hey, Don, Jason and I had to leave town unexpectedly. Could you take care of the animals for a couple of days?"

Before I could finish pumping gas, he responded, "No Problem" and included a smiley face. He was a divorcee a couple of years older than me, and I got the impression he liked me, so I figured he would take the opportunity to do me a favor. Sometimes you gotta do what you gotta do. I spoke to him a couple of weeks ago and got the impression he didn't have much use for Burt Roop. I'd have to ask him about that. Maybe he was another suspect we hadn't considered.

I was exhausted by the time I reached Wanda's. She had a great apartment in the Tuscany Villas on El Camino Real, not far from the police station and my old apartment. Hers was more than a thousand square feet with two bedrooms, walk-in closets, a balcony, and a nice-sized living room. The kitchen was a little tight, but we'd figure it out. She and I could have probably lived there indefinitely and never gotten in each other's way if we alternated cooking duties or ordered out.

When I knocked on her door, she, uncharacteristically, immediately gave me a warm hug. She was softening up the longer I knew her. "Are you okay, Miranda? I can't imagine what you've been through the last couple of hours."

I held on to her longer than I expected to, and it felt good to lean on her. I whispered, "Thanks for being here for me. You have no idea what this means to me."

She made a hand motion around her apartment. "Honestly, this place is too big for me most of the time. I don't have much company, so the other bedroom just sits there, hoping for a visitor. And now, here you are. It's perfect." She noticed I hadn't brought anything up with me. "I know you said on the phone you might need some stuff, but you really packed light."

I scratched my head. "I couldn't think. I knew I needed clothes to go to work, so I was just running back and forth from the house to the car, emptying my closet as much as I could. I realize now that I might have been in a bit of a panic. I didn't bring anything other than the clothes in my closet. I didn't bring any shoes, no socks, no underwear, no bras, no pajamas, nothing from the bathroom."

She motioned me to sit on the couch. "Hey, we're about the same size. I can take care of you for now, and then we'll see how long you're here. We can either head back down there and get stuff or go shopping. It's no problem. What matters is that you are safe." She settled in next to me. "Now, tell me what's going on. I want the whole story."

I hadn't even had time to process it. I took a couple of deep breaths, hoping that Wanda could make more sense of Chenoa's visit than I could. "Okay. I called you after they arrested Jason, so you know that part. And it's not like that's not bizarre enough in and of itself. Then I called a couple of people, you know, Margo, you and Lyanne, and Mark Peterson, my friend and attorney."

I strained to remember. "I was just resting on the couch when there was a knock on the door. I had no idea who it might be because I don't know any people down there. I was absolutely shocked to see Chenoa, the Princess of the Earth and the Water, in the flesh at my door."

"That must have been disturbing."

"But wait, it gets really bizarre. First, she starts talking to me like she knows me, and I'll never forget this as long as I live, she says, 'Our Jason has been arrested for murder.' 'Our Jason?' What does she mean, 'Our Jason?' He's 'My Jason.'"

Wanda looked at me with a hopeful look on her face, "You know how those Indian Princesses can be, all at one with the Universe, maybe she meant the 'big we.' Like we are all as one."

I responded, "You know, Wanda, I sort of wanted to think that too until she told me this. She's in love with Jason even though she broke it off with him three years ago." I paused for dramatic effect. "Now, listen to this. According to her they still talk on the phone or text several times a day."

She gaped at me. "What? What are you talking about? That can't possibly be? How could that be?"

I wanted to keep talking because I didn't want to cry, not in front of Wanda. "All he ever told me was that he had a bad break up. He never gave me the details of who he was with, where they lived, the circumstances of their breakup, or if she *perhaps lived in his neighborhood.* I never asked anything because I figured he would tell me eventually."

She shook her head. "Oh, Miranda, I'm so sorry."

I didn't want her to be sorry. The last thing I wanted was for her to be sorry. If she was sorry, I was going to cry, and I refused to cry. "Don't you think last week when I ended up at the hot springs, and I described to Jason in detail that I met a Native American woman at the intersection between the Earth and the Water, it might have been a clue *who* I was talking about?"

She sounded noticeably more hopeful. "Maybe he wanted to wait until you got back from our weekend in Monterey to tell you, and then he got arrested before he could."

I nodded. "I actually thought of that too. Then I thought that maybe I was just being a patsy. Jason and I have known one another for years now. There was never an opportunity during all that time that he could have mentioned having continued communication with someone he was very serious with? For all I know, he still loves her, but her tribe prevented them from being together. Wouldn't you think that I deserved to know this?" I could feel my face getting hot and red. My body got the signal. If I wasn't going to allow it to cry, I was going to get angry. "It's not fair, Wanda. I have done everything right. I have called him if I was going to be ten minutes late. I let him know when one of my exes liked one of my posts online. This is huge and not in a good way.

"This may be a dealbreaker." I sighed and leaned back against the sofa, my heart heavy. We had been sitting on the couch, drinking herbal tea when Wanda suddenly smiled, probably hoping it would be contagious. "Would you like anything stronger? I know it's a work night, but you look horrible."

I couldn't help but return the smile, not wanting her to think I was angry with her. "You are a great friend. Sometimes I laugh to myself when I think of our first meeting at the Mission Cemetery. You were one scary cop that night."

She stood up and headed for the kitchen. She brought back a bottle of Crown Royal Vanilla and two shot glasses. "Then, my act worked. My goal is for any possible perp to think that I'm the scariest person they've ever met. I've gotten a ton of confessions that way. They just couldn't handle the pressure."

We clinked glasses. I said, "*Now* you tell me. If I'd known you were so darned nice, we wouldn't have had to waste all that time dancing."

She laughed. "Oh, I let you in way quicker than most. I liked you from day one. That's why I started calling you 'Marquette.' It was my way of being affectionate."

I winked. "I know."

We both took another shot.

Chapter 12

My headache was not as bad as expected when I woke at 6:30 to the phone alarm. It was so nice having my own bathroom and Wanda had it stocked with everything I needed. She was a wonderful hostess. Her apartment had the perfect layout, with the kitchen and living room between the two bedrooms, creating a nice level of seclusion for each bedroom.

I took my time waking up and showering, which was why I had set my alarm for a half-hour earlier than necessary. Before going to bed, we had carried in my clothes from the car and hung them up in the walk-in closet. She was right; by coincidence, we were very close in size, so she left me an unopened package of underwear and a couple of bras with the tags still attached.

Walking out to the kitchen in a silk robe she had left me on the dressing table, I felt so much better than I had when I arrived. I breathed in the aroma of eggs, bacon, pancakes, and coffee. Wanda was my personal chef, flitting around the kitchen serving my every need in her 'I'll Cook, You Eat' apron. I smiled. "Hey, have you ever worked in foodservice? I would love to start a catering business one of these days, and I may need you."

She wiped a bead of sweat from her forehead. "Believe me, don't think there aren't days when I don't think about it. No one knows how it is better than you do. You've been on both sides of the badge. There are days when neither side is that appealing." She sat next to me at the granite countertop. "I love what I do, but it's an uphill battle every day of my life. If I could have a life where the biggest challenge I had was a fallen soufflé or an eggshell in an omelet, that sounds like heaven."

We both stared off into space, dreaming of our best life. Finally, I broke the silence. "Hey, your shower is so awesome. I love showers where the water comes out from all sides. I could have stayed in there all day. It made having a few shots last night a little less painful."

She looked me in the eye. "So, exactly how *are* you today, Miss Queen of Denial? I know that you've got a lot to process."

I nodded. "That's the understatement of the century. I have to admit that I don't know what's up and what's down right now. I'm just putting one foot in front of the other and trying to make it to work on time. Thank you so much for putting me up. I don't want to be a bother, though. If you want me to get a hotel room, I can." I prayed she'd say 'No.'

She grabbed my shoulders. "Slow down. You have been through multiple traumas in a very short time. You were held at gunpoint, then the next day, found the man who had pointed the gun at you, dead. You stumbled upon a Native American woman in a drug-induced trance, to find out a week later that she had been your boyfriend's lover and that they were still in touch and had been for the last three years without your knowledge. And on top of that, he was arrested for the murder of the man you found dead. Does that just about sum it up?"

I rubbed my head, "When you put it that way, no wonder I have a headache."

We hugged. "You are welcome to stay here as long as you like. In fact, I insist on it."

I smiled and said, "If this ends up giving David and you a break, that's probably a blessing in disguise. At the rate you were going, you'd probably both end up getting fired."

She rolled her eyes.

I felt safe in her home. It was so strange, when we met, I never would have believed we had the first thing in common, and now we had an inseparable bond. I felt so blessed. I glanced at my watch. "Oh my God, I'd better find something to wear so I can get to work." I whispered, "Thanks for the undies! You're the best." I headed back to the guest room feeling, at least for the time being, like everything was going to be all right.

#

I appreciated the short commute, having gotten used to driving or riding nearly an hour to work every day. I was somewhat apprehensive about going to work on Monday the morning after Jason's arrest, anticipating lots of emails, phone calls, and visits from various staff wanting to know what was going on.

Tea arrived just after I did and didn't disappoint. She stood at my desk with her hands on her hips, not even bothering to set down her backpack, turn on her computer, or make her coffee. She tried to sound annoyed, but I knew she was worried. "Okay, what's going on? Jason's been arrested? So now you've sucked him into your Princess of Death realm?"

I wasn't ready for the onslaught of Princess of Death garbage, especially from my closest co-worker. I stood up, rather than staying in my seat, staring at my computer screen as I normally would have, going toe to toe with her. "Just what are you *implying*? I had nothing to do with this. If you knew the whole story, you wouldn't even joke about that."

She completely backed down and threw her arms around me. "Oh, Miranda, I'm so sorry. I was trying to keep it light."

I took her hand and led her to the break room. "Let's talk over a cup of coffee. You've known Jason longer than I have. I want to get your take on this."

She hurriedly made a pot of coffee while I scurried around, getting cups, cream, and Splenda ready. After we were done, we sat knee to knee at the small break table. I started slowly. "Okay, how much do you know about who Jason was with before he and I started seeing one another?"

She thought for a minute. "Well, I know from pictures he had in his office, she was Native American and *really beautiful.*"

I glared at her.

She patted my hand. "Okay, maybe that was too much information."

I nodded. "It's okay. I met Chenoa, so I know firsthand."

She sat on the edge of her seat. "Wow, you're a step ahead of me. I never knew her name."

"And for what it's worth, it means 'White Dove.'"

She giggled. "Wow, you've done your homework."

I shook my head. "Not really. Lyanne, my newspaper friend told me. Anyway, do you know why they broke up?"

She thought back. "Well, it definitely wasn't his idea. He just dragged around the office, all depressed for weeks after they broke up. The pictures were gone from his desk, and he didn't want to talk about it." She sat back in her seat for a minute. "Hey, you know who you should talk to? Rick. They're pretty close friends. If anyone knows anything, he does."

I stood up. "You're right. Of course, I should talk to Rick. He's also a volunteer sheriff's deputy."

She looked bewildered. "He is?"

I was already out of the office door, heading to the main building, too late to answer her. I knew that, at this time of day, Rick would be either in the main break room or in the warehouse chatting with the warehouse manager, Dave. I opted for the break room and found him having coffee with one of the Inventory Distribution Coordinators, Sandy. I saw them together quite often and wondered if Rick liked her. It was rumored that her marriage was on the rocks. My advice to him would be to steer a thousand miles clear of that situation. She was just leaving as I walked in.

He motioned for me to sit down. "I thought we might run into one another today. Your situation just keeps going from bad to worse. There is no way Jason did this."

I nodded. "I know. I'm not even worried about that, but Jason's arrest has opened a whole can of worms that I'm hoping you can help me with."

He muttered under his breath, "Chenoa."

I said, probably louder than I should have, "Yes, Chenoa, thanks for waiting until now to bring her up, Rick. You knew he was in touch with her, didn't you?"

He wouldn't look me directly in the eye. "I told him he was playing with fire. He loves you, Miranda. He really does. He doesn't just bring anyone home to Mama."

I shook my head. "He didn't love me enough to be honest with me."

His eyes finally reached mine. "Maybe he didn't think you could handle it."

My whole reason for talking to him flew out the window as I practically spit out the words, "That is the biggest cop-out that you men use. *He* couldn't handle telling me, and you know why? Because *he* didn't want to stop. That's the bottom line. He was afraid that his secret relationship with Chenoa would have to come to an end, or ours would, and he wanted to have his cake and eat it too. Well, you know *what*, maybe he'll end up with nothing." I was seething and took a couple of deep breaths, trying to calm myself down. "Or maybe he just wants her, and he's been working that out behind the scenes. And, you know what else? If that's what he wants, all the better. I'm sure they'd make a lovely couple." I got up and walked out.

I was so agitated, there was no way I could go back to work yet. I waved to Anna, the receptionist, on the way out. She seemed to want to talk, but I couldn't manage a civil conversation right now.

I stormed out of the parking lot and into the mostly residential area surrounding the facility. I hadn't walked around here much, except to walk home occasionally. Within about a block and a half, I found a neighborhood park with an old swing set. I sat down on one of the swings and started swinging. It was a swing made for the older kids, so it was a perfect size. Within a few minutes, I was going as high as gravity allowed. Anyone watching probably thought I was nuts, and I couldn't have argued with them.

My world was coming apart, and I didn't feel like there was anything I could do. The status of my most promising relationship ever was completely up in the air. My boyfriend was in jail. My sister and soon-to-be fiancé were on their way out here from Louisiana. But for the kindness of my newest best friend, I'd be sleeping in my car. I tried to forget everything as I swung up, down-up, down-up, down-up, down-up. I never wanted to stop.

Finally, I let my legs hang still and drifted slowly, slowly, and eventually halted. I decided I wasn't leaving the park until I was able to accomplish an attitude adjustment. Perhaps things weren't as bad as my mind was portraying them. This afternoon, my wonderful sister Sabine was coming into town. Years ago, when I had been shot and left for dead, she had flown to North Carolina and stayed by my bedside for months while I recovered. She was just the kind of support I needed right now.

Mark was also one of my oldest and dearest friends. Perhaps while he was defending Jason, he could extract the truth from him regarding his relationship with Chenoa. Was it possible that I was over-reacting? Had she wanted me to? Was that part of her plan because she wanted him back? Had she seen his arrest and our separation as an opportunity? Did she set him up for the murder?

I had three of the best friends anyone would ever ask for, Margo, Lyanne, and of course, Wanda. If anyone could help me sort this out, they could. So much happened since we were together; perhaps we needed to get together again and re-evaluate all the new evidence. But I doubted we could make that happen any time soon.

Maybe I was being too hard on Jason. There was no way that he killed Burt Roop. He needed my support. I would not open the door for Chenoa or any another woman to step in just because I was angry and jealous. He deserved his day in court, both federal court and Miranda court.

I stood, feeling refreshed and revived. I vowed to find a new therapist by the time this whole situation was over. I owed it to myself and those around me. I was a mess without someone to bounce things off.

One other thing that hit me as I walked back to the office was that I needed to forgive Patricia. We had been best friends before she lied to me and nearly went to prison to protect her father. She had her reasons for doing what she did, and none of those reasons had anything to do with me. Because I was trying to help her, I took all those lies personally and dropped her from my life. That wasn't fair to her or Nate, my nearly three-year-old Godson.

I also wondered if I could befriend Toni, her mother, in the process. Last year when we met, she and I seemed to be on opposite teams, which didn't make for a good start to a friendship. But she had a strong will and a spunky personality that I admired. Perhaps, if I reconciled with Patricia, we could make our friendship work also.

By the time I got back to my desk, it was nearly lunchtime. Tea was diligently working at her desk. I figured she wouldn't ask me where I'd been if she thought I was in a foul mood, so I talked to her first. "Hey, I yelled at Rick and went swinging on a swing set down in the park, so I'm good."

She kept typing on the computer and said, "I know you'll figure it out. If you need anything from me, just ask. I've really tried to know as little as possible about people's social lives around here, so I'm probably just about as useless a person as you're going to find. But, if you need someone to bounce things off, or just to lean on, I'm your girl."

I walked over to her desk and hugged her. "Thanks, Tea. Sometimes I wish I could be as oblivious as you."

She gave me her crooked smile. "Hmm. Not sure that's a compliment, but I'll take it as one."

I kissed the top of her head. "Oh, you have no idea." I walked back to my desk.

Chapter 13

We were both buried in work for the rest of the day, which is sometimes a blessing. True to my word to myself, I took a detour to my old neighborhood on the way back to Wanda's. She had given me a key before I left, letting me know she wouldn't be home before nine, so the timing was perfect. I also reminded myself that Mark and Sabine would be landing at San Jose Airport at 7:25 p.m. I intended to meet them there.

I got a pit in my stomach pulling up to the old apartment house. I had some terrible and some wonderful times there. This house was the bridge from my old life to my new life, and I would never forget it.

As happened so many times when I was living here, Patricia pulled up at the same time. In those days, I would invite her in for a couple of glasses of wine. I wasn't sure what this chance encounter was going to mean. She parked behind me, so there was no way she hadn't seen me. I hesitated, not knowing whether I should get out first or wait for her.

I bit the bullet and got out of the car. She hadn't opened her door yet, so I walked back to her car, unsure why she wasn't getting out. As soon as I reached her driver's door, it burst open, and she came rushing out, took a step toward me, and flung her arms around my neck. I threw my arms around her, and we hugged for what felt like a heavenly eternity. Tears ran down her face into my shoulder. She whispered, "My mom told me that if I just waited, you would come back."

I was overwhelmed by her reaction, but I told myself that I wouldn't cry. She had been so cold when we last spoke, even though I had done everything I could to free her from prison. It seemed like she resented me. I couldn't understand it, so I had to set her free from my life because she was making me miserable. Finally, I said, "Where's that little Godson of mine?"

She took my hand and led me to my old apartment. "Nate stays with my mom now. It's working out perfectly. They adore one another, and I don't have to pay for daycare." She opened the door. Her mom was sitting on the couch watching a kiddie show with a child I barely recognized. "Mom, look who it is. Miranda's here."

Nate scooted himself off the couch and ran to his mom, wrapping himself around her legs. She directed him toward me, "Nate, you remember your Aunt Miranda, right?"

He immediately started playing 'peek-a-boo' with me behind Patricia's legs. Within a few minutes, he was running around and playing with me like it was old times. Whether he remembered me or just decided that I was his new friend, I didn't care. It was a start.

Toni had stayed in the background while Nate and I got reacquainted but approached me while Nate cuddled with Patricia. She finally gave me a warm and welcoming hug. "I'm not sure I ever got a chance to give you a proper thanks for everything you did back then. You saved our lives. I don't know how I can ever thank you, really."

I returned the hug. "This is the kind of thanks that will stay with me forever." I held back more tears, although one was able to escape down my cheek, so I attempted to lighten up the moment. "So, how do you like the apartment?"

She smiled. "It's perfect. Living this close to Patricia and Nate has been a Godsend. You were so gracious to give it up."

I brushed it off. "It was time for me to move on, so you were doing me a favor." Although I wasn't exactly sure how true that was at the moment, I was going with it. Seeing Patricia made me realize how much I needed to talk to an old friend, and she was the oldest friend I had in the area right now. Sure, I'd see Mark and

Sabine later on, but I was here now, and so was she. "Toni, do you mind if I borrow Patricia for a few minutes?"

She smiled. "Absolutely. You two take all the time you need to catch up. I am so happy to see you together again, and I expect to see you around here more often, Miranda, promise?"

I nodded. "I promise."

The weather was beautiful; we opted to walk around my old running route, which intersected several local parks and was an easy three-mile walk. I felt more at ease with Patricia by my side than I had in a while. Unfinished business always wears on me.

She gave me a broad smile, "So what do you need me for?"

I tried to smile back but failed. "I need you to help me check myself. I feel like I'm going crazy. And you know me better than almost anyone." I hesitated, not knowing where to start. "I don't know if you have any idea what's going on."

She gave me a blank look. "If it's something on the news, my mom and I gave up watching the news on TV and the internet after my dad went to jail. It was just too much garbage."

I gave her a high five. "I'm with you there. Okay, then, you're a blank slate. Even better." The whole thing seemed so absurd right now; I could barely figure out a way to frame it that wouldn't sound ridiculous. I decided to start at the beginning. "Okay, get ready for a wild ride. Jason and I live about an hour south near Coyote Lake. Close by are some natural hot springs. Well, the abbreviated version is, I snuck in there, got caught by the owner/caretaker, and the next day he showed up dead."

Her face showed no shock or surprise, she just nodded. "Of course he did."

I hit her on the arm. "Okay, cut me a little slack. Anyway, as it turns out, Jason and I have a shed where we stored some guns that got stolen, unbeknownst to us. Turns out the man was shot with one of those guns. They arrested Jason for the murder, so I'm assuming it was one of his."

She tried to absorb the story. "Well, at least it wasn't one of yours, or you'd be back in jail."

I stopped walking for emphasis. "Do you want to hear the Indian princess part or not?"

She brought a new perspective to what I thought was a serious story. "What Indian princess, Miranda? This is beginning to sound more and more like a Disney movie. This really happened, right?"

"Yes, just listen. I went back to the Hot Springs to find this beautiful Native American princess in a trance. She was mumbling something about the merging of the earth and the water; then she passed out. I think there may have been some peyote involved." I decided to skip the part about the girls' weekend and the Indians taking over the country.

She looked at me like I had either lost my mind or had also partaken in the peyote. "Miranda, you do know how crazy this all sounds, right? You aren't planning on going to the police with this, right?"

I grimaced. "It gets worse."

She poked me in the side. "There's no *way* it could get worse."

We continued walking. "So, right after Jason is taken away by the police, this Indian woman shows up at the house. First, she tells me that she and Jason had been together before he and I were and that they were still in touch on an almost constant basis."

She gaped at me. "No way."

"Then she dropped the bomb, that I was in danger and that I needed to get out of the house as soon as possible. And just before she left, she told me that she was the Princess of the Earth and the

Water and that I was the Princess of Death and that she and I were bonded forever."

We had slowed almost to a crawl as she pondered everything I had told her. Patricia was deep in thought. She surprised me with her response. "I took a course on the history of Native American gods and goddesses, and this has a familiar ring to it. Unlike our society, they believe that the earth and the water are sacred and should be treated as such. If her tribe believes that she is, in fact, a descendant of the Goddess of the Earth and the Goddess of Water, she may be considered a sacred being. It would be strictly forbidden for her to mate with a white man."

My stomach lurched as I pictured Chenoa and Jason together. I thought back to our brief encounter. "She talked of the Seven Ponds of Death. Does that mean anything to you?"

She considered my question. "Yes, it's about the life continuum. They do not believe in the end of life as we do, but seven phases of life. It's all pretty interesting. I can see how, if she is a descendant of the Goddess of the Earth and the Goddess of Water and you are a descendant of the Goddess of the Seven Ponds, how you would be viewed as connected."

I chewed on my thumbnail. "But I'm not Native American."

She agreed, "I know. That's the irony. If you are descended from a goddess, it doesn't matter what race you are."

I thought about it. "Wow, Patricia, I'm glad we got together. I had no idea you were such a font of knowledge on this topic. You are so amazing to me." We hugged, and I said, "So tell me this. Do you think Jason did this?"

We started walking again. "Gosh, Miranda, I just have no idea. I wonder if the tribe framed him to keep him away from, what's her name?"

I don't think I had told her. "Chenoa."

She repeated it. "Chenoa. I wonder if they framed him to keep him away from her."

I protested. "But he's with me."

She nodded. "But they may not know that. You said that Jason and Chenoa have been in almost constant touch. Sure, he's been physically with you, but he's still emotionally with her. You have to face that, Miranda. Otherwise, he wouldn't have hidden it from you." We stopped walking again, and she faced me, grabbing my hands. "You deserve better."

We sat on a nearby bench. I smiled, knowing Patricia was in my corner. It was a role reversal and a powerful one. I put my arm around her. "I really appreciate you. I have missed you so much. The time we were neighbors was one of the best times of my life. I wasn't rich, and I didn't have a man in my life. I was just learning a new job and a new city, but I was happy. And you were a big part of that.

We sat quietly for a few minutes. I finally spoke. "I think I need to get together with Chenoa again. She clearly knows more than she told me during our brief visit. I need to understand her ongoing relationship with Jason and clarify what she believes our connection is in the long term. Maybe I can even find out why she believes that Jason is innocent and if she knows who the murderer is." I thought for a minute. "The only problem is that I don't even know where she lives."

Patricia spoke up. "Let me see what I can find out. What tribe is she in?"

I searched my memory. "Aulintac. Several tribes are coming together right now, but that's her tribe."

She continued. "I had some maps in conjunction with that class that I took, so maybe I can track her down for you. I'll bet she's near Coyote Lake somewhere."

I looked at her with new eyes. "I have always been so self-absorbed; there are so many things I don't know about you. I am so blessed that you are back in my life. I will never take you for granted again."

We both stood up from the bench. Patricia wiped a happy tear from her eye. "This is one of the happiest days of my life without exaggeration. Life is so strange. This was a day like any other, but it has turned into one that I will never ever forget. I love you with all my heart, Miranda."

We walked arm in arm back to her neighborhood—my old neighborhood. Earlier today, I had no idea why I was led back to Patricia, but now I knew. It was not only due to unfinished business, but it was time to move on in many ways, perhaps ways I wasn't even aware of yet.

Chapter 14

My reunion with Patricia went so well, I completely lost track of time and almost forgot that I was meeting Mark and Sabine at the airport. I left Patricia's at 7:30 when Sabine texted me that they had landed. I figured, though, that by the time they got off the plane, used the restroom, and waited for their bags to arrive at the baggage claim carousel, I'd have time to get to the airport.

I was right because I had to sit out front, waiting for them for another ten minutes before they finally emerged through the doors from baggage claim. I hadn't anticipated them having five suitcases, but that was only because I hadn't thought about Sabine being one of the passengers. She had a reputation for packing heavy.

Sabine wore a pink dress, similar to something Jackie Kennedy would have worn in the sixties, but somehow, she could pull it off with style, without a hair out of place after a six-hour flight. I had never seen Mark travel in anything but jeans and, at most, a golf shirt, but today he wore Khakis, a golf shirt, and a cardigan sweater. He looked like he was off to prep school with his mother. They were an unusual pair.

He struggled to pull the baggage cart through the door as Sabine ran to see me. "Miranda, *ma fille,* you look absolutely *exhausted.*"

She always had a way of making me feel like her daughter instead of her sister, even though I was only three years her junior. I smiled anyway. "I'm fine, Sabine. I have been through a little bit of stress with Jason. We'll talk."

She shook her head. "That *Canaill*e, I'll have his head."

I thought, "You don't know the half of it.*"* But then I defended him. "He is *n*ot a scoundrel!" I changed the subject. "Are you guys getting a vehicle now, or should I just take you to the hotel?"

Mark responded, "Let's go to the hotel. We can get a car tomorrow. That worked fine with the shuttle last time. It seems like you always sit around the car rental place for an hour by the time they figure out where your car is."

I nodded. "I agree. I have more trouble with car rental agencies. I thought it was just me."

Their hotel was less than five minutes from the Airport. Sabine and I stayed outside while Mark checked in.

Sabine immediately started grilling me with questions. "Okay, Miranda, what is *really* going on here? I know there's a lot more than what Mark told me. I can't help you unless I know everything."

I didn't really want to tell everything twice. "Let's wait until we get to the room, so I don't have to fill Mark in on everything he missed."

She moved closer. "Okay, how about all the stuff that you can tell only me and would never tell Mark."

She had a point there. If Mark was going to do his best job of defending Jason, it might be better if I didn't get him involved in some of the less flattering parts of the story. I wondered, though, how long it was going to take Mark to check in. I'd probably get partway through a story and then have to finish it later anyway. I decided to chance it.

Obviously, she knew that Jason had been arrested, but I didn't know how much to tell her otherwise. I probably would need to tell her why I wasn't staying at the house sooner than later or she'd think I was hiding something. I'd need to start at the end and go back to the beginning.

She could see the gears turning in my head and couldn't stand it. "Miranda, *mon cher*, you're going to end up telling me anyway; why put yourself through such agony?"

She was right. I would stop if Mark interrupted us. Maybe there was a long line at the front desk. "Okay, after Jason was arrested, I had a visitor."

She exhaled, "Now, we are getting somewhere."

I wasn't exactly sure how I would explain this without ruining Jason's chances with Sabine for good, but maybe it didn't matter at this point. "It was a Native American woman who I had run across the weekend prior, but that's another story. As it turns out, Jason had a serious relationship with her, which he claimed ended at least a year before he started seeing me." I hesitated but figured he dug his grave. "The fact is, he had been in touch with her since then, but I didn't know about it."

She gasped, "Really? How often?"

I could feel my face turning red. I felt like such a fool. "Um, she claims it was pretty much every day."

Had she not been contained in a vehicle she would be pacing around the room like a wildcat. "That *fils de pute—*"

I interrupted, "Let's not jump to conclusions before we hear his side of the story."

She yelled, "What *other* side of that story could there be?"

As usual with Sabine, I felt like a fourteen-year-old who had just been suspended from school.

Sabine tried to contain herself, seeing that I was getting upset. "What else did she say?"

I thought back. "She said that Jason didn't commit the murder."

Sabine bit her tongue but then said, "Was this the plea for a man she still loves or a woman who actually knows who did commit that murder because those are two wildly different things."

This was going about how I expected. "I don't know, Sabine. There seem to be some really crazy things going on with the Native Americans behind the scenes that most of us are not aware of. I'm hoping that somehow that poor man, Burt Roop, didn't get in the middle of something he couldn't handle."

Mark came out with room keys and a smile. "I was able to get one of the bigger suites, so we'll have a place to spread out."

Sabine smiled and said, "You are so good to me."

They were such an unusual pair. I would never have pegged them as a couple, but I guessed that was what made the world go around.

I drove them around to the entrance near their room. I had to work tomorrow and wanted to avoid being grilled all night, so I said, "I'm exhausted. I'll drop you here and you can give me a call in the morning if you need a ride to get a rental car. Otherwise, we can coordinate on the arraignment and all that."

Sabine gave me a 'You're just going to leave me hanging like that?' look but just hugged me goodnight. She whispered, "We'll talk later, young lady."

I laughed, "Okay, *Mom*."

Mark was too busy unloading suitcases to witness the complex communication between two stubborn sisters. It was probably for the best.

Chapter 15

I was glad to be heading back to Wanda's, having avoided a marathon session with Sabine. I loved her dearly, but she could be a lot of work. It was approaching nine when I got back to the apartment, so I just had time to make a pot of decaf and put on my pajamas by the time Wanda walked in.

She looked like the day had chewed her up and spit her out on the sidewalk. I felt better with a possibly cheating boyfriend in jail than she looked.

She tossed her purse on the counter, locked her weapon in the gun safe, and collapsed on the couch. I offered her a decaf. She pointed vaguely in the direction of the whiskey, so I poured a shot in a cup of coffee, hoping my interpretation was right. She responded with a broad smile and a sigh of relief that took a full minute to exhale, "Miranda, have I told you that I love you? If you could be ready with Irish decaf coffee every day when I get home, I'll marry you."

I sat opposite her. "That's not necessary. I'll make your coffee anyway."

She took another sip and asked, "So, what does it mean to you when a cop says, put your hands up and drop the weapon?"

I didn't have to think hard. "You drop the weapon, if you are holding one, and put your hands in the air?"

She gave me a thumbs up. "Right! You don't lower your arms and take off running, right? Which then causes me to have to take off after you, finally tasing you in the parking lot. And for what? Because you shoplifted. Ready for it? A bra."

I was confused. "Who carries a gun with them to go shoplifting?"

She shook her head as if saddened by the whole human race. "Apparently, this guy does."

I giggled. "Guy? Wow, you did have a day." I sipped my decaf sans whiskey. "Well, let me tell you something good about my day. I've been completely avoiding Patricia since we set her free from prison, and I moved out of my apartment, letting her mother move in." She lay back on the couch with her eyes closed. "Uh-huh." Her tone suggested she couldn't be less interested.

I took another sip and continued anyway. "I visited Patricia today, and her mother and my Godson."

She opened one eye. "I'm listening."

I made her wait in suspense, with my goal to take the focus off her terrible day. "And it went great. Toni couldn't have been more welcoming. Nate even played peek-a-boo with me. Patricia and I went for a walk and had a really nice talk. She knows a lot about Northern California Indian Tribes and had some interesting insights regarding Chenoa." I savored the moment. "But, more importantly, I feel like we are back on track with our friendship, which really means a lot to me."

"Good for you, Miranda," she said in a flat voice before taking another swig of coffee. She wasn't as happy for me which I had expected her to be, which hurt my feelings a little.

We sat quietly for a few minutes.

I was confused and didn't want the moment to pass. "Is everything okay? I thought you'd be happy for me."

She fidgeted in her seat. "Oh, it's fine, Miranda. I am happy. I'm just a little worried about you getting involved with her again. I'd hate to see you get hurt again."

I smiled. "Wanda, that is just about the sweetest thing anyone has ever said to me." I went over and gave her a big hug. I also suspected she might be a little jealous of my renewed friendship with Patricia. "My friendship with Patricia or anyone else, for that matter, will never impact what you and I have. We're sisters in blue. None of them, Margo, Lyanne, Patricia, or even my sister, Sabine, will ever have the bond we have."

"What brought that up? I know we are." I continued, feeling like I needed to explain myself. "I left the force because I was no longer in a mental state to stay in. I don't admit that to many people. In fact, other than my therapists, I've never told that to anyone. I was afraid I would let my partner down when it mattered most. So, you're the closest thing I'll ever have to a partner. And don't you ever forget that." I thought I saw a tear in Wanda's eye, but I would never bring it to her attention because she was too proud.

When she held out her mug to me, I refilled with coffee and another dollop of whiskey.

She seemed better with it all and even started asking questions about my conversation with Patricia about Chenoa. I explained, "She thought that the tribe might believe that Chenoa is a descendent of the Goddess of Water and the Goddess of the Earth; that may be why she was forbidden to be with Jason, and subsequently, why they broke up. That's because a true descendent of a goddess could never be with a mortal, especially a white man. But here's something really interesting—if they truly believe that I am somehow the descendant of the Goddess of Death, or in their culture, the Seven Ponds of Death, they also may believe that Chenoa and I really are connected eternally."

She looked confused. "But why doesn't the race difference matter in your case when it does in Jason's?"

I had asked the same thing and have been thinking about it since. "Maybe if I am truly a descendant of a goddess, there is blood between us somewhere down the line, no matter how slight."

We both thought about the implications of this for a while before speaking further. Finally, she brought it back to the reason

I was here. "So, how do you think this ties back to Burt Roop's murder and why you're in danger?"

I shook my head. "I think they are two totally different things. I think I may be in danger simply because I represent an impediment to the Native American's plans because of my alleged heritage. I'm sure that some of them would rather see me dead than have me, somehow, rise to a position of power within the tribe." I rubbed my head, acknowledging the headache I was getting.

"Isn't that a bit of a stretch?" she asked.

"Maybe. But how any of this ties into Burt Roop's murder, I have no idea. I keep thinking that the Indians wanted the Hot Springs, and he owned them, but maybe that's too simple."

Wanda drank more coffee. "There are two people we need to talk to, Jason and Chenoa. I'll bet you'd like to do the questioning."

I nodded. "Maybe for slightly different reasons, but yes, I think we should question them together. No, maybe question them separately, then compare their responses. I don't know. I can't imagine Jason knows anything about Burt Roop's murder, but there's obviously a lot that he knows about other stuff that he hadn't shared. Maybe there's something he picked up in a conversation with Chenoa that he thought was nothing, and it is the key to the whole case. Or maybe she confessed everything to him, him and only him—her sweet boy. Ugh, I could throw up right now."

Wanda looked at me with knowing eyes. I had the feeling she had experienced something similar in her lifetime. Well, of course, she had. She was a woman, after all. She changed the subject for now. "So, how'd it go with Mark and Sabine?"

I rolled my eyes. "I love both of them dearly, but I can handle them better separately than as a couple. Mark and I have a deep friendship dating back to high school, but I get the feeling

Sabine doesn't approve of the level of intimacy that he and I share. Sabine and I have always had almost a parent-child relationship, even though we aren't that far apart in age. That also works better when we are alone. So, trying to manage my relationships with both of them, just from the airport to the hotel, wore me out. I opted to take off and didn't even go up to their suite."

Wanda smiled. "I get it. Whenever I get together with family, it gets weird. We all revert to the roles we had growing up and never progress beyond that. I hate it."

My cell phone rang. It was Mark. "Mark, what's up."

He sounded very lawyer-like. I was sure Sabine was standing right next to him. "Miranda, I wanted to let you know the arraignment is at noon tomorrow. Want to catch an early lunch with Sabine and me?"

I nearly laughed after the conversation I just had with Wanda. "Sure, Mark, that sounds great. Are you going to take care of the rental car in the morning then?"

He responded, "Yes, I just called them. We can meet you at that restaurant near the courthouse in San Jose. The Grill on the Alley on South Market. I had the best steak ever last time I was here."

I laughed. "I'm not sure I'll be ready for a steak that early in the day, but I'll meet you there." I hung up,

Wanda asked, "All set?"

I shook my head. "It'll be fun."

We talked for a while and went to bed. I could get used to this arrangement, so Jason had better watch his step.

Chapter 16

I slept in, knowing my boss was still in jail and that I was attending his arraignment at noon. Wanda checked on me when she left at 9:30 to make sure I was still alive. I stayed in bed until ten, took a long shower, and was ready to go, just before 11:00. I figured I might be a few minutes late, but I knew Mark and Sabine could take care of themselves.

I made it to the restaurant a little after eleven and found Mark and Sabine happily eating Caesar salads and gazing into one another's eyes. The food looked scrumptious, but my stomach was in knots at the thought of the impending meeting with Jason and everything I had learned since his arrest.

A waiter pulled out a chair for me and I took a seat, waving him away for the moment. I asked Mark, "Have you had any contact with Jason, or will your time at the defense table be it?"

He talked while he ate. "I'm going to meet with him for ten minutes before court, so we're on the same page, but it's a no-brainer, really. He's going to plead innocent."

I decided to play devil's advocate since I wasn't particularly happy with Jason at the moment. "Well, unless he actually did it and wants to 'fess up."

Mark looked at me quizzically. "Do you know something I don't know?"

I shook my head. "I don't think so, but you never know if you really know someone."

He gave Sabine a 'Do you know what is wrong with her?' look.

She shrugged.

Mark said, "So, anyway, the food is really good. I wish I could stay for more." He glanced at his watch. "But I've gotta run for my pre-meeting with Jason. You two can head into the court at around noon." He stood up and headed out the door.

Sabine shook her head. "You're a tough one, Miranda."

I smiled. "I'm not doing anything that you wouldn't do under the same circumstances."

She nodded. "You're right." She then looked me straight in the eye. "But if you love him, at least give him a chance to explain. You may reach the same conclusion, but at least you will know you gave him his day in court."

I nodded. "I learned everything I know about relationships from you, so I already know how you feel. I'll give him a chance to explain. But if everything is the way it seems, it's over. I will not stand being lied to."

She patted my arm. "I totally get it. And I'm not defending Jason; I'm just asking you to take it slow and not do anything hasty. You have been under a lot of pressure over the last couple of weeks, so it's not the best time to make a life decision. Remember when I broke up with Mark over what was basically a misunderstanding? We wouldn't be together today if I hadn't just stopped everything and reconsidered my decision, and that would be a shame because I really do love him, and he treats me like gold."

I laughed. "You might want to let him know that once in a while."

She looked at me like I was crazy. "Oh, don't you worry about that. You've only seen us in public." She winked.

She paid the check, and we meandered toward the courthouse. She wouldn't relent. "I know I haven't always been Jason's biggest supporter because I always protect you first, but I just want to make sure you don't do anything reactionary."

I agreed. "I know. Things are crazy right now. I feel like I don't know which end is up. I feel like such a fool that Chenoa had an inside track with Jason that I wasn't even aware of. I'm hurt and, even if he didn't technically cheat, I feel cheated out of the life I thought I had."

Sabine finally gave up and hugged me. "Okay, it sounds like you have your head on straight. I think I'd feel the same way if I were you. It's probably good that you were able to secure a place with Wanda for a while. Maybe not jumping back into playing house with Jason is the best thing you can do for yourself and your own sanity. And it'll give him some time to think."

I smiled. "I completely agree. I think moving back in with Jason when he's released sends the wrong message. Besides, Wanda needs some babysitting of her own right now. She's been seeing her partner, who is fifteen years her junior. Not a good idea on either count. She's almost begging me to stay right now."

Sabine opened the door to the federal building for me. "Everything for a reason, I guess."

Since it was nearly noon, anyone going to arrive for Jason's arraignment was in the courtroom or nearby. While the courtroom wasn't exactly crowded, I was surprised to see three rows toward the back completely filled. I recognized a couple of my co-workers from Ion and nodded as Sabine and I filed in. There were also a couple of members of the press I had become familiar with during my Princess of Death days. It also appeared, judging by their attire, that there were several members of the local Native American community, although Chenoa was not present.

Sabine and I sat toward the front. There was no-one at the prosecution or defense tables. It was 11:55—five minutes to showtime.

I was surprisingly nervous about seeing Jason. It felt like weeks since I had seen him, although it had only been a day and a half. My life and attitudes had changed dramatically since then, and not for good. At least as far as he was concerned. We had had such a carefree relationship and laughed all the time. No-one was laughing now.

Sabine sat quietly, absorbed in her thoughts.

After a few minutes, a couple of suited men entered and sat at the prosecution table. I recognized them as assistant DAs. Apparently, the big gun was not going to appear today. Then, through a door toward the back right of the courtroom, Jason and Mark entered. They were chatting quietly. I could see Jason trying to find me in the crowd, and I purposely avoided his glance. Maybe it was a mistake coming today. I didn't want to send the wrong message either by coming or staying away. It was a tough choice.

I chewed on my thumbnail, and Sabine elbowed me. There was a flurry of activity when the judge entered; the bailiff instructed everyone to stand, we pledged to the flag, and we were seated. The judge, Thomas Wheatfield, was a portly man in his mid-fifties with a deep dimple in his chin. He seemed very pleasant when he greeted the attorneys.

I didn't pay much attention until he addressed Mark. "Mr. Peterson, I'm sure you have plenty of other more interesting things to do with your time here in California, so let's say we dispense with the formality."

He smiled and nodded. I figured they must have introduced one another and exchanged pleasantries outside of the courtroom. It was a nice personal touch. Most judges wouldn't have bothered.

He directed a few comments to the prosecution table. "Mr. Assistant DA, it's my understanding that you have charged Mr. Wall with the First Degree Murder of one Burtrum Roop."

That suddenly made me wonder where Sally was. I looked around and saw her in the second to last row, near the door. She must have come in after we did. I was tempted to wave but thought better of it.

The assistant DA replied, "Yes, Your Honor, we have irrefutable evidence that Jason Wall, the defendant, had the means and the motive to kill Mr. Roop and does not have an alibi. We recommend that he be held without bail until such trial shall take place." I got the feeling that this thirty-something had done his best to memorize his speech but wasn't completely sure what all the words meant. I felt a little bit sorry for him.

The judge jotted down some notes but didn't comment. "Mr. Peterson, do you have a statement that you haven't memorized?"

Mark didn't comment on the obvious snub of the prosecution but smiled. "Yes, your honor. Jason Wall is an upstanding citizen and has been nothing but an asset to Santa Clara County. He's a senior manager at a local manufacturing firm, a seasoned musician, and, in his spare time, runs a small organic farm near Coyote Lake. He and Mr. Roop were neighbors and never had a cross word for one another. In fact, as far as Jason was concerned, they were friends. This case seems to be one of mistaken identity at best, or he is being framed, at worst. Either way, he is clearly innocent. I hope that you can see your way clear to free him on a reasonable level of bail. Thank you, your honor.

The judge briefly read his notes but seemed to know already what he was going to say. "First, I want to thank the prosecution and the defense for their brief and well-thought-out statements. We have gone a bit out of order, but I guess it's only a formality. Mr. Wall, how do you plead to the charges?"

Jason cleared his throat and said, "Not guilty, your honor."

Then the judge said, "I am going to allow bail in the amount of one hundred thousand dollars." He then said, "Court is adjourned," and pounded his gavel.

Mark and Jason shook hands. Jason smiled at me, and I nodded but didn't smile. He gave me an odd look.

Chaos in the Canyon

They then left the courtroom, presumably to arrange bail. Sabine and I stayed in the courtroom and talked about family and what was new in New Orleans. It was a good thing we had come in separate vehicles because I didn't know what was happening after court.

I felt my face turning red when Jason and Mark re-entered the courtroom. Jason walked directly toward me. I couldn't look at him. Mark said to Sabine, "Why don't we leave these two alone for a few minutes?" and led her outside to the lobby.

Once they were gone, Jason tried to put his arms around me, but I backed away. His face was quickly getting red with anger. "You don't actually think I did this, right?"

I could have spit in his face right now. "Is *that* what you think this is about, Jason? *Is that really* what you think this is about?"

His face quickly shifted from angry to confused. "Yes. What else?"

I hesitated, then blurted it out. "*Chenoa.*"

He looked away for a long time with a pained look on his face, like I had taken away his best friend, and maybe I had. "What about her?" He'd turned back to me and did his best to catch my eye as I now looked everywhere but at him. He still didn't have a clue.

I wasn't going to let him off that easy. "Did you think I'd never find out?"

He started pacing around the courtroom. "Find out what, Miranda?"

I glared at him. I honestly didn't want to make it too easy for him. I'd already told him it was Chenoa; what else did he need? Men were so obtuse. Then the more he didn't respond, I started doubting myself. Did she lie to me? Had he not communicated with her? I figured I needed to start asking some direct questions, or we might be spending the day here. I tried to calm myself. "Okay, Chenoa is the woman you were with directly before me, right? The one who broke your heart?"

He hesitated. I guess I shouldn't have asked a two-part question. "Yes, I was with Chenoa for two years before you and I met. But she didn't break my heart. Her people broke us up."

I was crestfallen. This was the worst of all possible worlds. "So, if you had it your way, you'd still be together, which is why you're still communicating with her daily." I didn't even ask it as a question, just a statement. I walked out.

I heard him say, "Miranda," but he didn't come after me.

I ran to my car, fighting back tears. *You will not cry about this, Miranda. It's just a man.*

When I got to my Rover, I climbed in and sat hunched over the steering wheel. I didn't know if I should go to work. Wanda had given me a key. I guess she was expecting me to stay for a while. I hadn't thought, until now, about what Jason was going to do. He was at the courthouse with no transportation, and I had no idea if he had his phone, wallet, ID, or money. I guessed he did since he had them on his person when he was arrested.

I figured that Mark and Sabine went back to the hotel. Jason was a big boy, so he could either call a cab or someone at work to pick him up. So, the last place I was going to go was work. The only place I had left to go was Wanda's unless I went back for him.

I was completely torn. Would going back for him be a sign of weakness or a sign of strength for wanting resolution and not being deterred by his initial response? I needed my therapist badly right now. In lieu of having her and not wanting to go back to Wanda's, eating Chocolate Chip Cookie Dough Ice Cream all day, I opted to return to the Federal Building.

Chaos in the Canyon

Jason was sitting on a bench outside the Federal Building texting or sending an email on his phone. I figured he was texting someone from work for a ride. I pulled up, left my car running, and got out. It was a No Parking zone. Based on my last conversation with him, I didn't think this would take long.

I kept my distance as I approached him, not wanting him to try to touch me. "Okay, so what's going on? You've got one chance, so no crap."

He stood up and put his phone away. He seemed to be seriously considering what he was going to say. I couldn't help but feel that our relationship stood in the balance of the next few words that he uttered. "Miranda, it was nothing."

Oh, this was a bad start, a *very* bad start. He a *no* idea who he was dealing with. I paced in front of him, partially because I was trying to prevent myself from hitting him. I needed to keep moving. "Let me get this straight. You've lied to me by omission from the first day we met. But let's not even go back that far. Let's give you the benefit of the doubt. When we first met, it was none of my business, although it might have been easier to tell me that you were in constant contact with your ex-girlfriend. Or is it ex-fiancé? But, for whatever reason, you chose not to tell me when we were friends. So, where in your little mind did you think it was okay not to tell me when we started seeing one another *exclusively*. Do you know what that means? Let me spell it out for you. That means we aren't seeing or talking to *other* people, that we are *exclusive* to one another."

He gave up trying to follow me as I paced. He mostly studied the pavement before him. "Miranda, it meant nothing. We are just friends."

I stopped and glared at him. "I so *knew* you were going to say that. Then, if that was the case, why didn't you tell me? *She still loves you, Jason.* The elders broke you up. *That* means nothing?" I wanted to tell him to figure out what he wanted, but it seemed to me that he had done that three years ago. I couldn't stay in this conversation any longer. All the answers I was getting were completely predictable. I should have known it was too good to be true. No wonder he didn't mind not getting sex from me. He was probably getting it from her. And if that was the case, I didn't want to know. I headed to the car without turning back. "Have a nice life," I said as much to myself as to him.

I couldn't even tell if he said anything. My mind was screaming too loudly by the time I reached the Rover. I was so angry at myself for having gone back. The definition of insanity was repeatedly doing the same thing and expecting a different outcome, but the outcome was the same as inside the courtroom. I put the Rover in gear, having no idea where I was driving. An hour and a half later, I found myself on Half-moon Bay Beach. I quickly reminded myself this was where I nearly killed myself in a late-night swim a couple of years ago when my life fell apart. I wanted to make sure I hadn't subliminally planned to return to the scene of the crime to complete the job. "Miranda, no guy is worth committing suicide over," I grumbled to myself as I pulled a bikini out of my glove compartment. I had changed a hundred times in my car when I lived in Venice Beach, and I had the process down.

As I headed up the beach, feeling as if the weight lifted from my shoulders confirmed that this was not a self-pity beach trip but a soul-cleansing one. I felt new strength with each confident step forward. My world had been transformed over the past year. I had voiced my desire to add many new friends to my life and found Margo, Wanda, and Lyanne. Now, I had Patricia back in my life with the prospect of befriending her mother, Toni, and seeing my Godson, Nate, regularly.

About a mile up the beach, in one of the most familiar areas, where the crowds always thinned out, I sat down, watching the waves break on the sand over and over again. My head was still spinning with thoughts of Jason. Since I moved to Coyote Lake, I had let my emotions run away with me, and thoughts of marriage and happily ever after had taken me over for the first time in many years. It was an unfamiliar feeling. I had let down my guard and felt carefree. The reality of Jason's betrayal made my heart hurt down to my soul. It felt now like I would never be the same, although I knew from past experience that I would, or at least I'd be close.

I stayed there, enjoying the admiring gazes of guys ten years younger than I was, for a while. I knew bikinis were invented for something. My ego needed a shot. After sitting for an hour or so, five guys set up a volleyball net about twenty feet from me. They invited me to join them. I thought it was odd that they had planned to play volleyball with an odd number of players, but who was I to question them? I hadn't had that much fun in such a long time. I just enjoyed throwing myself in the sand, trying to make the impossible shot, lunging at the net to get a save that they all thought I'd never make. Best of all, my team won every game.

After three games, they invited me to their blankets, towels, and coolers for a couple of cold beers. We talked and relived our games for hours afterward. I hadn't looked at the time for a while and was shocked that it was nearly seven o'clock. I stood up, much to the chagrin of my temporary teammates. "Hey guys, I've gotta run. It was great playing with you. This was just what I needed today."

They all expressed regret and told me to come back any afternoon. I guessed they were college students or independently wealthy. Either way, they provided the kick in the butt that I needed not to stay mired in my Jason-induced funk.

Chapter 17

By the time I reached Wanda's, she was already on her second glass of wine. She hugged me when I arrived. I still had my bathing suit top on and jean shorts over my bottoms. "Hey, you look like you played hooky today, and you smell like it."

I laughed, "Hey, do I smell bad? I can shower."

She brushed my comment off. "No, you smell like salt and sand. I miss the beach so much. Can we go together one of these days? I hate going alone."

Wanda retreated to the kitchen and returned with a glass of red wine for me. I took a long sip, "Umm. You are magical. How did you know just what I needed?"

She put her finger to her lips. "Well, let's see. You were supposed to go to court, and Jason was supposed to be released. Now, it's well after eight o'clock; you've been to the beach, and you're back at my house." She smiled. "Don't get me wrong at all because I absolutely love it. I just want to make sure that you're okay."

I took her hand and led her to the couch. "Okay, let me tell you about my day." I thought first, wanting to get every detail right. "I went to lunch with Sabine and Mark. That was good. Then court went well, just as predicted. They let Jason out on bail. And that's where it went downhill."

She winced. "Oh no."

I continued. "Mark and Sabine took off so Jason and I could have some alone time, and that's when I asked him about Chenoa. He told me that the tribe had broken them up. He never denied or explained why he was in contact with her, whether he still loved her or not, so I left. Then, I thought that maybe I hadn't given him ample time to explain his situation. So I went back, thinking that *she* had misrepresented the situation and that he hadn't been in constant contact with her. But no, he had. He admitted it but said it was *nothing.*"

She had repeated the 'nothing' with me in unison. It was amazing how many women were familiar with this story.

I went on with my saga. "So, I left him there and headed for the beach. I don't know if he went home, to work, or the nearest bar. I don't know, and I don't care. After I sat on Half Moon Bay Beach for a while, a group of guys set up a volleyball net, and they asked me to play. It was a blast. I haven't had that much fun in a while."

She motioned to my bikini top. "I bet they haven't either."

"Yeah, whatever. I had fun; that's all that matters."

We sat knee to knee on the couch. "So, do you think it's over with Jason?"

I hadn't quite thought that clearly yet. "That's where I'm leaning. But you know I'm very forgiving. I never thought I'd forgive Patricia after all the lies she told me. It seems like she's grown up so much. I'm a 'never say never' kind of girl, but right now, I can't look at him and see a future."

Wanda looked me in the eye, "Then make this your home until you know."

I looked away from her intense stare. "I couldn't possibly afford to live here. I can't even imagine what you pay in rent."

She smiled. "We get a pretty good rate because we're cops. Besides, I'm paying a hundred percent of it now, so whatever you can pay would be more than I'm getting now."

I listened intently. "I get that, but I don't want to be a charity case, either. Give me a number, so we can see how close I am."

I could see she was debating whether to give me a real number or to make one up to lure me in. "Okay, I pay $3,200 plus utilities. But it's in my name, and I could throw you out at any time, so that's got to be worth something. How about you pay $1,000, and I'll cover utilities."

I hadn't been sure lately if prayer actually worked, but when she hit the exact number I was hoping for, I almost jumped out of my skin. "Sold!" I hugged her so tight I thought we both would burst. This was one of the best and worst days of my life. I already started to have doubts; it had fallen together so easily. "Are you sure, Wanda? What about David? How's he going to take this?"

She laughed. "Girl, I thank God that you came when you did. Had you waited another week, he probably would have moved in here, and that would not have been a good thing. You probably saved my job, my career, and maybe my life." We high fived.

I agreed. "Don't I know it? I used to live and work with a cop, and it wasn't pretty." She gave me an inquiring look, but I didn't give any more details except, "It nearly killed me."

I couldn't remember how much detail I had given Wanda about my police days and why I quit, but I was sure she'd ask if she wanted to know.

We didn't say anything for a few minutes, each thinking about the gravity of the decision we just made or trying to figure out what to do now. Wanda jumped up from the couch. "Let's go to Wal-Mart, it's about the only store that would be open now." I looked down at my outfit, a bikini top and shorts covering up my bikini bottoms. She looked me up and down, "And that's exactly why we need to go. You need casual clothes, underwear, bras, toiletries, and everything else you didn't bring with you. You're not a houseguest anymore."

I hadn't thought that I might never go back to Jason's or get anything I left there, but that was a real possibility now. I didn't want to overthink that right now, so all I could do was agree. "Okay, let's do it."

Chaos in the Canyon

We took my Rover because it had plenty of room. She had some kind of fuel-efficient little car that fit nothing, but I'm sure it would help the earth survive five minutes longer than my Rover. The enthusiasm with which she approached our shopping I found peculiar, so, finally, I asked, "So why is this so exciting to you?"

She confessed, "Since I moved out of my parent's house, I've never lived with anyone."

I pushed her back like Elaine pushed Jerry on Seinfeld, "Get out! You've never lived with anyone. You are a virgin roomie. Good thing you didn't tell me before I agreed to move in."

She seemed a little embarrassed by the fact. "I guess better late than never."

I said, "You've got to be kidding. You're like the luckiest woman in the world, not having to adjust your lifestyle for someone's crazy friends, annoying habits, dangerous lifestyles. You're in for the time of your life."

She looked terrified. "Which ones do you have?"

I laughed, "I have *all* of them!" I opened my eyes wide and grimaced fiercely at her, showing all my teeth. "You don't mind if I have wild parties with mind-blowing illegal drugs, right? We'll only do it when you're not home."

She looked at me like she thought I might be serious, wondering what she had done.

I patted her on the head. "Sorry, no such luck. I'm as boring as they come. I like to watch Hallmark movies and seventies and eighties TV reruns. I like Christmas movies, the *Wizard of Oz*, and I'll watch *Star Wars* as many times as it comes on, but only the original. I don't care about these new updates."

She noticeably relaxed.

I punched her arm. "You need to learn how to take a joke."

She grimaced, "That isn't my strong suit."

I smiled. "Well, there's always time to learn."

We had a blast shopping for the next couple of hours and could barely carry the bags into the apartment. Moments later, I collapsed in bed, ready for my newest new life.

Chapter 18

I woke on Wednesday, dreading going to work. I knew, or at least figured, that Jason would be there. At some point this morning, I had concluded that this was going to be a tough couple of months. First, Jason and I needed to meander through our boss-employee relationship now that we were broken up. Second, I had promised Mark I would assist with the defense, and I wouldn't let him down.

Wanda left me a note on the counter. *"Hi, Roomie! I had to leave at 6 for a stake-out—hours and hours in a car with David. My day should be as fun as yours. Just remember we always have each other and plenty of glasses of wine. Thanks for taking a chance on me."*

I read it several times, wondering why she was thanking me when she was saving my life. I would have literally been homeless without her kindness. Not permanently, but it was so nice that she had opened up her home to me. I needed to do something special to thank her.

I arrived at work by 7:30, not used to my short commute. My orders didn't get nearly as backed up anymore since I had changed the ordering procedure. I used to be the first step in the process. Now, once the sales and inventory departments coordinated to make sure that the products were either on-site or in the process of being manufactured, final orders came to me. We had cut our turnaround time by fifty percent and cut the paperwork sitting on my desk by seventy-five—without the company having to buy a new system. I felt a little guilty because I wasn't doing anywhere near the amount of work that I used to, but since Jason had hired me to make the place more efficient, I guessed I was just doing my job.

By the time Tea showed up, I had checked email and done reports for a couple of meetings I had scheduled with manufacturing later in the week. If I had my way and the department managers accepted my proposals, my job would be even simpler within a month or two. Tea seemed to be walking slower than usual, and I was worried, knowing that her boyfriend Michael had abused her in the past, however I not recently that I was aware of.

She didn't stop to ask me about court and went straight to the break room, two bad signs. I followed her back, which wasn't always the best idea, but I wasn't going to let her cover-up if he had hit her again and I had unequivocally told her that. She faced away from me when I walked in. I approached her and said quietly, "Tea, are you okay?"

Despite the seventy-degree temperatures, she wore long sleeves and a hoodie, but when she turned to face me, I gasped. Even the make-up couldn't hide her swollen cheeks and black eye. Tears streamed down her face. "Don't say it, Miranda. I already know. I can't go back to him."

I walked over and carefully hugged her, not knowing where else she might hurt. I told her, "You're coming home with me."

She protested, "I really appreciate it, Miranda, but I can't go all the way down to Coyote Lake every day. Besides, that would just be too weird living in the same house as Jason."

I smiled a crooked smile, "Well, this is your lucky day, Missy. Jason and I broke up. I'm staying with a friend in an apartment complex on El Camino Real." I knew I couldn't just assume that Tea could stay with Wanda indefinitely, but I knew, under the circumstances she would be okay with me bringing her to her house for one night.

She gave me a questioning look. "A friend? What friend?"

I wasn't sure if I had ever mentioned Wanda to Tea. They traveled in different circles. "She's a detective with the Santa Clara Police Department. Her name is Wanda Marshall."

She was skeptical. "I don't know, Miranda. I don't think so."

I was reaching the end of my soft sell routine, but I didn't want to push her away. "Let's at least talk to Wanda and see. As a police officer, maybe she's aware of other options. At least come home with me tonight, and we can talk about it. That's not a commitment, just a safe alternative."

She nodded slowly looking like she was weighing her options. "It sounds better than a half-way house for wayward stupid girls who hook up with violent, egotistical maniacs." She managed a half-hearted grin.

I took that as a 'Yes.' "Good girl. You'll be safe there and you can decide what you want to do from there." As I said it, I realized it could be awkward, spending twenty-four hours a day together, but we'd have to cross that bridge when we came to it. "Just promise you'll come home with me tonight, and we'll get it sorted out."

"Okay, Miranda. You're the best." She hugged me gingerly, leading me to suspect her wounds were worse than she was letting on.

I tried to encourage her to go to the emergency room or at least urgent care, but she refused so I sent her off to get some ice from the break room for her swollen eye.

The day progressed much better than I had hoped until around three o'clock when Jason called me on my office phone. I found it odd that he didn't call me on my cell, but maybe he figured I'd have to respond if he called me on official business. He sounded very serious. "Miranda, we need to talk."

I tried to sound as cold as I could. "Fine. When."

He said, "How about now? My office."

I said, "Are you sure we should be having a personal conversation on work time?"

He said, "Yes," and hung up.

This was so weird. We had barely spoken at work since we broke up. My stomach felt like jelly as I approached his office. Anna mouthed, "What's going on?" as I passed the receptionist station, but I waved her off.

He was seated at his small conference table when I walked in, which was totally out of character. He normally chose to stay behind his desk so that he had the upper hand. He motioned for me to sit at the chair opposite him.

I waited for him to speak, but he just stared at me. I felt naked under his glare and pulled my cardigan around me, covering up.

When he didn't say anything, I said flippantly, "So, you wanted to talk?"

He pursed his lips but couldn't seem to make them do anything. Finally, he said, "How are you doing?"

So, this was how we were going to play this? "I'm fine. I found a place to live, and I'm livin' the dream. You?"

He looked like I had stabbed him in the eye. "Come on, Miranda, you can't have moved on *that* quickly."

I spoke louder than I intended. "Oh, you'd be surprised. Lie to me, and I *can* move on *that* quickly."

He protested, "I *didn't* lie to you, Miranda."

I could already feel my pot starting to simmer, and I didn't it want to boil over again. I smoothed my skirt and attempted to keep my attitude in check. "Jason, let's even say that technically you didn't *lie* to me day after day after as you communicated with Chenoa, did you ever *tell* me about it?"

He shook his head. "Well, no."

I almost pounded the table but continued my attempt to restrain myself. "Bingo! You got one right. Good boy. You *never* told me." I figured this was as good a time as any to find out why, since our other conversation had been cut short—twice. "Why did you never tell me, Jason?"

He kneaded his hands together like he was trying to wash away his sins. He said weakly, "I didn't think it mattered."

I jumped on that one. "*You didn't think it mattered?* Oh, I'm sorry. You got that one wrong. Want to try again?" The sarcasm in my voice was reaching a fever pitch, and I wasn't sure how much longer I was going to be able to stay without another dramatic exit. "Since you're struggling, I'm going to give you this one. You didn't tell me because *you didn't want me to know.* Isn't that it?"

Lines appeared on his face that I hadn't seen before. "Well, no, not exactly. I didn't tell you because I thought you'd get mad, and I was right."

I could feel the veins in my forehead straining to be shown. "*Don't even try to make yourself right.* You were wrong, immature, and a bad partner. And as far as I'm concerned, you are a cheater. I call 'em as I see 'em."

It was his turn to try to keep his anger in check. "A *cheater?* I never *touched* her."

I lowered my voice. "I hope that's true, but obviously you touched her heart at some point. And is she still touching yours, Jason? Only you can answer that question." Not being able to bear another lie, I stood and walked out.

As I rounded the corner outside his office, I heard him call my name. But it was much too late.

Chapter 19

At the end of the day, Tea followed me to our new home. She seemed very nervous to meet Wanda as we walked toward the apartment building together from the parking lot. She talked non-stop. "Wow, this community is so beautiful. I could never afford to live here. What's Wanda like? I bet she hates me. Maybe I should just go home."

I stopped just short of entering the building. I had texted Wanda, so she was expecting us, and I wasn't worried at all. "Just relax, Sweetheart. This is the hardest part. I know that you and I are kind of control freaks, so I get it. Just trust me on this one." She hugged me, and we entered the elevator to the second floor.

I used my key to get into the apartment. Wanda was in the kitchen, dressed in work-out shorts and a tee-shirt, looking very un-cop-like, which was a good strategy on her part. Tea still looked very diminutive next to her, and I was sure she felt out of her element. I did my best to draw her in. I put my arm around her. "Tea, this is Wanda."

Tea put out her hand to shake, but Wanda approached her with open arms. I was very proud of her because that was not in her comfort zone. They briefly hugged, and Tea looked a little less anxious.

Wanda grabbed two glasses of wine and handed one to each of us. "I think we all deserve a toast." We held up our glasses. "To living our best life, to making the best friends we can, and learning how to trust in a world that isn't always trustworthy."

We all drank to her toast.

Wanda herded us to the living room. She spoke to Tea. "I hope Miranda told you that you can stay as long as you want. Sleeping arrangements are up to you two. One of these couches converts to a bed, or you two can share the guest room."

Chaos in the Canyon

I spoke up, "I don't know about you, Tea, but I'd rather have you with me than out here on a converted couch. On the other hand, if sleeping in the same bed is freaky to you, I get it. My sister and I did sleepovers for years and slept in the same bed, so it's normal for me, but whatever works for you."

Tea smiled shyly, "I'd rather stay with you, Miranda, if that's okay. I don't snore or anything that I know of."

I giggled, "I've been told that I talk in my sleep occasionally, so maybe you'll learn something even I don't know."

Tea was the first to finish her wine and was uncharacteristically quiet. I could tell she was nervous. She spoke directly to Wanda for the first time. "Wanda, this is so nice of you. I'm sure I'll figure out some housing before too long. I'm sorry about putting you out like this."

Wanda looked Tea in the eye. "Sweetheart, I'm happy to do this for you. I often wish I could take every abused girl off the street, but I know I can't. But to be in a position to help you makes me feel so good. To be honest, I had been lonely living here until Miranda moved in and now you're here too. I love it."

Tea seemed like she was starting to feel more comfortable. "Um, I don't have anything at all with me. Nothing."

Wanda and I laughed. I said, "We bought every kind of toiletry that you will ever need last night, but let's go out and get you some clothes. It'll be the second night in a row."

We headed back to Wal-Mart and spent two hours buying Tea a wardrobe. She kept insisting that she didn't have the money to pay for all of it, but Wanda and I had already agreed to pay before we got to the store. She nearly cried when we told her we would take care of it. "You *guys* do not have to do this. It's *too* much!"

I was so thankful that Tea was away from Mike, and I knew he would never move out of their apartment; that was why she needed to be the one to take action. From what she'd told me when they'd gone to couples counseling, he'd had a rough upbringing, but that was no excuse for how he'd abused her. Sadly, she'd kept going back to him and I hoped this time she was out for good.

The next morning, we decided to ride in together, and I was so thankful we did when I saw Mike's car parked outside the Ion Manufacturing entrance. I told Tea to stay in the car. "And do not get out no matter what happens. Understand?" She nodded.

I got out of the car, ready for anything. Mike sat on the hood of his Mustang. He didn't move as he watched me approach. "What's up, Mike?" I asked, trying to sound casual.

He had a smug look on his face, and I was trying very hard not to knock his lights out. "You have her, I know it. Just bring her back, and there won't be any trouble."

This kid was so green and stupid; I barely knew where to start. I decided to take the direct route. "Are you threatening me, Michael?"

He still hadn't moved from the hood of his car, but I could see his forehead glistening with sweat. He had no idea who he was dealing with. "Actually, I am. You have what's mine, and you need to return it."

I wished he was standing on the ground because I knew I could take this kid in a street fight, or maybe it was better that he wasn't. I couldn't hide my anger, though. "Tea is not an 'it,' and she is not your possession. She will not be returned. We are still debating pressing charges on your latest in a string of assaults, so you'd better wipe that smirk off your face and stand down. You could go away for a long, long time." I approached the vehicle, and he jumped down, probably afraid I would do him harm. Maybe he wasn't so dumb after all.

He stood with his vehicle between us. "You're bluffing. And you're feeding Tea with your garbage. She loves me, and she would never send me to jail. We fought. It's over—time for her to come home."

I could see we weren't making progress, so I decided to change my approach. "Okay, Mike, I get it. Things happen. Let's discuss this like adults." I knew from Tea that he found me attractive, and she hated that, but I figured I might as well use it to my advantage. I smiled at him. He seemed less defensive and moved toward me. I added in the most soothing tone I could muster, "Maybe the three of us could sit down in the break room and have an adult conversation and work this out."

As he was rounding the front of his car, I reached out my hand as if to shake his. I grabbed his wrist, turned it, and pulled him down to the ground face down. I put a knee on his back. He whimpered like a girl, which was my desired goal. Evidently, he hadn't been informed of my police training. I talked in a low, calm voice so that Tea couldn't hear. "If you ever touch Tea again or I hear of you hurting *any* woman, I'll come back and finish you off. Do you understand me?"

He nodded but said nothing.

We could have stayed like this for hours, but I had to get to work, and I was starting to worry about Tea, who was still in the car. She was famous for having second thoughts and forgiving him. During our scuffle, I realized that with a low-cut blouse, I was not dressed for this type of activity, and before I turned him over, his eyes had been anywhere but on my face.

I devised a plan to address this. I got off his back and helped him up as if there were no hard feelings. We strolled toward the driver's side of his car, and I whispered so he'd move toward me. As he approached me, I kneed him in the groin with one fluid motion, opened the car door, and pushed him into the vehicle. "And stop looking down my blouse." I didn't give him time to deny it while he squirmed in pain. "You will leave this parking lot now, or we'll be talking to the police together. And don't come around here again."

He looked at me like he was going to say something but started the car and sped out of the lot.

I was afraid that I'd have to talk Tea off a ledge when she jumped out of the car. But she ran over to me, throwing her arms around me. "Oh, Miranda, you were spectacular! Do you know how many times I wish I could have done that to him? But he's just so big compared to me. How did you do it, though? He's bigger than you are too."

She opened the door to something I'd been thinking about for a while. "Hey, you know what you need? Self-defense classes. I could use a brush-up too, so maybe we should take them together." I probably didn't need them, but I didn't think she would take them alone.

She took about two seconds to think about it. "Yes, I'll do it. I'd love to take classes with you, Miranda."

We spent part of the morning researching women's self-defense courses. This was the most relaxed I had seen Tea in a long time. Hopefully, she would mature into the woman I'd hoped she could be without Mike holding her down. Around noon, Mark called about getting together this evening for a strategy session on Jason's defense. I had to admit my heart wasn't really in it, but a promise was a promise. He, Sabine, and I would meet at six for a working dinner at Olive Garden. I might actually be a more objective assistant since I wasn't necessarily in Jason's corner any longer.

Chapter 20

I found Mark and Sabine at a table in the rear of the restaurant near a large window facing the east mountains. Sabine exclaimed, "I never realized how beautiful Northern California was, Miranda. No wonder you love it here. I'm trying to convince Mark to move. *Magnifique!*"

I wasn't sure how I felt about Sabine and Mark in my life full time but I exclaimed, "That would be great." I thought I saw Mark roll his eyes, but I wasn't going to ask.

Mark then kicked into lawyer mode. "So, Miranda, where should we start with this case? There seems to be a lot going on down there in Coyote Lake."

I nodded. "There really is. From what I've heard, between the upsurge in tribal activity and what appears to be a struggle to control the Hot Springs, I also found out a few weeks ago that Don, Jason's next-door neighbor, wasn't a big fan of Burt Roop. Maybe he's someone we should talk to."

Sabine interrupted, "What do you mean, *Jason's* next-door neighbor? You're still together, right?"

I didn't know how else to answer. "Nope. When you guys left us at the courthouse, we broke up."

Sabine and Mark exchanged glances which I couldn't interpret. Odds were they had a side bet.

"I've thought about it," I said, "and I won't stand for being lied to. I'm done."

Mark used his soothing therapist voice. "Maybe it wouldn't hurt for you two to talk this out and find some common ground."

I was sick of talking about this. "The common ground is between Jason and Chenoa. Maybe they should be talking."

Mark started to speak, but Sabine waved him off. She said, "Okay. I understand."

"Back to the case," I said. "I don't think Jason did it, no matter how angry I am at him right now. I believe our stolen guns were used and traced back to him. That's the only thing that makes any sense. Neither Jason nor I have an alibi for the day of the murder, assuming it was Saturday. We were both on separate motorcycle rides. Well, Burt Roop was my alibi, but he can't verify it." I thought about other possible leads. "We can't rule out Sally, his wife. Everyone who ever describes her uses the term 'jealous wife.' What if she suspected Burt was having an affair? Chenoa is a beautiful woman. What if she suspected something between them? She might have been trying to charm Burt to get Indian control of the Hot Springs. You never know how far people will take things."

Sabine had been studying the notes I provided Mark when they arrived. She said, "You had an interesting comment about Jacob Mabry, the man who arrived with the law enforcement group. You said it was like he almost had *too much* information on you when they came to respond to the 911 call."

I nodded, thinking back to that day. "It was weird. It was like this Jacob Mabry was a Miranda Marquette encyclopedia. He almost knew more about me than I did. How could he have gathered that much information between me making the 911 call and them arriving? It was probably a half-hour, an hour at the most. I thought, maybe, he was the president of the Princess of Death Fan Club or something. The guy's kind of creepy anyway, so I wouldn't put it past him to think me guilty of every murder in California, but now that Jason's been arrested, maybe I was just being paranoid." I thought for a minute. "*Or,* maybe he's secretly *in love* with me and using this case to get Jason out of the picture. And maybe, in fact, *he* killed Burt Roop."

She laughed. "That's about the most outrageous thing I've ever heard, so I'll keep it on my list." She looked through her notes and continued. "There's another angle that we haven't talked about." I was starting to feel like Sabine was a more thorough investigator than I was. "How about the Japanese interest in the Hot Springs? It's still referred to as the Gilroy Yamato Hot Springs, and I couldn't find out based on their website, when the Japanese lost control of the site. Do you think there is bad blood around that?"

I pondered that. "It's very possible. There's a lot of emotion about how we treated the Japanese during and after World War II, including putting them in the internment camps. They were very proud of the Springs, after they'd developed all the lovely gardens in the last century, and we just snatched the property from them. Well, when I say 'we,' I mean the Roop family managed to get it back after the war." I rubbed my head. The more we delved into this case, the less we seemed to know.

Mark who had been quiet, spoke up. "It's a small, close-knit neighborhood, right?"

I nodded, pretty sure where he was going.

"We need to interview everyone that lives there to see if anyone saw anything," he said. "Sometimes people see things and don't think they mean anything or don't want to get involved until they're asked. At least it's a place to start." I could tell he wasn't sure about where to go from here. "Miranda, I know you're not living down there right now. Does that mean you don't want to be the one to do the interviews? You're, at least, a known resident which could help. Sabine and I are complete strangers. Out in the country, I assume they don't take kindly to out of towners knocking on the door."

I nodded. "You're right. I'll do it. These people don't live on a couple of acres because they want people in their business. I'll do it. There aren't many people, I'd say ten houses on that part of Roop Road between the highway and Hot Springs Road. I've only met Don next door and Sally Roop, but that doesn't mean the others haven't seen me around. The others probably know Jason; I can pretend that we're still together, as much as it will pain me." I thought for a second. "I think I can do it this week. How's tomorrow work for you? Then we can get back together on Friday."

Sabine answered for both of them. "That would be great."

Chapter 21

I found Wanda and Tea making chocolate chip cookies when I got home. They were chattering away like two old friends. I just watched and listened, learning more about both of them than I had ever found out on my own. Note to self: *you still need to work on that self-absorbed personality.*

While they baked, Wanda got very excited and directed it at Tea, "Hey, wait a minute. I forgot something very important." She grabbed her purse and dug around in it. She pulled out a key and handed it to Tea. "You can stay as long as you want, young lady."

Tea hugged her. It was such a sweet gesture; I got a lump in my throat. Wanda was one of the most giving people I had ever met. We spent the rest of the evening eating cookies and drinking milk. I was reminded of more innocent days before knowing how my parents' divorce would forever impact my family.

I wasn't sure how to take tomorrow off to interview Jason's neighbors. I figured I could leave Jason a late-night voice mail, so I'd be sure he wouldn't answer it, the way I used to before he and I were together. That would let him know that I was working on his case, softening the blow of another call-out. I dialed his direct work number. "Hey boss, it's Miranda. I'm going to be down in Coyote Lake doing some background work for your case, in conjunction with Mark and Sabine, so I won't be in the office tomorrow. I'm all caught up on orders, so I don't anticipate it causing any work issues. I'll be able to get any orders that come in tomorrow entered on Friday. Thanks much." I thought that was the perfect balance between employee and ex-girlfriend. He should appreciate it.

Tea was an adorable roommate. She knelt by the side of the bed and said her prayers every night. When I only worked with her, I had suspected she was caught between a child and a woman.

I felt like living with Wanda and me, however long, would be good for her. My feeling was that she had not had good female role models, and this was the opportunity to reverse that.

She slept in flannel pajamas in spite of the room being reasonably warm and comfortable. She presented quite a sight with her spikey hair and tattoos while still reminding me of *Little House on the Prairie*. She was far more modest than I would have thought, changing in the bathroom before coming to bed. I think part of that was her age, but most of it was her personality. I respected it and told myself to remember that for the future.

#

Driving down to Coyote Lake, I realized how much I didn't miss the commute. I loved the area, though, and knew I would move out to the canyon someday. I wasn't a city girl and never had been. As I drove, I mapped out a plan to speak to the residents on Roop Road. I had considered calling ahead but thought better of it. I thought it might go better, catching people by surprise and using my charm to question them. I had no idea how it would work, but it was worth a try.

I would start with Don, Jason's next door neighbor, because I knew he was home during the day and would likely welcome me. Because there was no traffic heading toward the canyon in the morning, I was able to get to Coyote Lake from Santa Clara in forty-five minutes.

I pulled into Don's driveway, feeling confident that I had my questions formulated. His house, a 1930s farmhouse, was about thirty feet back from the road. He was somewhat of a loner but was always friendly enough to me.

I breathed a sigh of relief that I hadn't been met with the business end of a shotgun. People around here meant business when it came to property security. I walked carefully to the front

Chaos in the Canyon

door, making sure no boobie traps were laid out for unsuspecting door-to-door salesmen.

When I pressed the doorbell, I could hear old-fashioned chimes ring inside. While I'd talked to Don several times out in the yard, I had never been inside his house and had no idea what to expect. As I waited, I was having second, third, and fourth thoughts. As I was about to turn and go back to the car, the door opened, and there was Don. He was shirtless and wore only boxers. It appeared that I had woken him up.

He attempted to focus on me in the sunlight. "Miranda, what a pleasant surprise. Come in, come in."

I hesitated because of his state of dress or lack thereof. I figured I'd throw out a hint that he had come to the door in his underwear. "Oh, I'm sorry. Did I wake you? I can come back when you're, well, more put together."

He looked down. "Oh, gosh, I'm sorry." He laughed. "Come in. I'll go throw something on."

I had to admit he didn't look bad in boxers. I hadn't paid much attention to Don even though I knew he appreciated me. I had Jason, and I wasn't looking. Now, well, things were different in so many ways. I looked around the parlor as I waited for him to return. It appeared that there hadn't been much remodeling done since this house was built. It had a certain charm, but the wallpaper *had* to go. I admonished myself. Here I was redecorating this guy's house already.

In a few minutes, he returned in jeans and a denim shirt. It wasn't lost on me that he had left the top three buttons undone. It almost made me want to button the second button of mine, but I thought that might be a little obvious if I did it right now.

He sat in a chair next to mine, just a little too close for comfort. "So, Miranda, what brings you to my humble abode? And please forgive the mess. I don't get much company."

I figured I'd jump right in. "Well, I'm sure you've heard that Burt Roop was found dead in Coe Park."

He nodded.

I continued. "And I'm sure you've heard that Jason was arrested for the murder." I wasn't sure how much I had told him when I asked him to take care of the animals; I had so much going on.

He said, "Yes, it's such a shame."

I couldn't help but note a hint of sarcasm. I knew there was no love lost between Burt and Don. "Anyway, I'm working for the defense, so I'm just in the process of gathering evidence that may be important to the case."

He had a confused look on his face. "I thought you and Jason broke up."

I laughed. "My, my, word does travel fast in these parts."

He said, "You know what they say, the words they echo down the canyon."

I smiled. "Hmm, I didn't know they said that." I tried to ease away from him and tugged the hem of my skirt over my knees. "I guess you could say we're taking a break. I'm not totally sure what our status is exactly, to be honest."

He took my hand, which was downright uncomfortable. "Are you living in the house? Are you calling each other during the day? Are you planning vacations together?"

I coughed and used that as an excuse to pull my hand back to get a tissue from my purse. "Well, no."

He laughed. "Then you're broken up. Welcome to my world." He raised his hand to high-five me, and I couldn't very well reject his without it being very awkward, so I raised mine.

I decided I needed to refocus our meeting because this was turning more and more into a first date. "Okay, Don, so can I ask you some questions about the days leading up to the Sunday Burt's body was found?"

He put his hands in his lap, which was fine with me. "You can ask me anything, Miranda, but I'm pretty sure I'm not going to be able to help you."

I smiled, hoping that would make him want to cooperate. "So think about the Saturday before last, the day before Burt Roop was shot. Describe what you did and where you were that day."

He tilted back in the chair, making me nervous that he was going to fall back on his head, but I guessed he knew his furniture better than I did. "I spent the morning doing typical house and farm stuff. I fed the chickens, collected the eggs, milked the goats. You know, pretty much the way it is over at your, oops, I mean over at Jason's place." He smirked, probably thinking he was clever. "That afternoon, I went into town, you know, Gilroy, and picked up some feed and groceries."

I took notes. "When did you get home?"

He thought for a minute. "Oh, I'd say about five. I remember I was hungry because I ate right after I got home. After that, I watched TV and went to bed. It's kind of embarrassing, but that's my life."

I shook my head. "I'm not here to judge, just get facts. Besides, you're a nice-looking guy. I'm sure you could have an active social life if you put yourself out there."

He shrugged and looked down at his hands for a moment before looking at me again. "Yes, I suppose. It's tough to recover when you find out your wife's been having an affair for five out of the ten years of your marriage. I still haven't quite recovered." He seemed a little choked up. "I'm not sure I ever will."

I wanted to hug him and tell him it would be all right, but that was exactly why I hadn't gone into social work; I would want to hug everyone, which could give some people the wrong idea.

"Did you see anyone strange walking around on Roop Road, Hot Springs Road, or coming off the highway?"

He shook his head. "Not that I recall. The only unusual things I saw or heard that day were your motorcycles coming and going. It had been a while since Jason had been on one of those."

I stood, not wanting to overstay my welcome or to imply that I was here for any reason but to gather evidence. I stuck out my hand, and he shook it. "Well, Don, I really appreciate your time. I'm sorry for waking you up. I guess I should have called first."

He laughed. "Miranda, a pretty lady like you can drop by anytime."

I let myself out and nearly ran to my car. That seemed like it was a waste of time. Although I did verify that Don would be a likely candidate if I ever were desperate for a date. It seemed like he had some issues, though. I'd have to send him to a counselor to work those out first.

I got in the car, hoping the rest of the day didn't go like this. I dreaded seeing Sally Roop again, which was exactly why I was visiting her next. I had gathered a lot of information since she and I had first met, and I wondered how much of it she was aware of.

After our last meeting, I didn't even know if she'd allow me on the property, but I wouldn't know unless I tried.

Chapter 22

I had my motorcycle the last time I visited Sally, so maybe she wouldn't set the guard dogs free when I pulled in the driveway, at least until she recognized me. I felt like my feet were a hundred pounds each as I slogged to the front door. My stomach was doing cartwheels as I rang the bell.

"Comin'," she yelled from somewhere deep in the house. She opened the door and blinked as the sunlight hit her eyes. She wore a bright floral muumuu. I wanted to turn and run, not knowing what she was going to do next. You could have knocked me over with a feather when she said, "Oh, thank God it's you, Miranda. You saved me a trip."

I guess she could tell by the look on my face that I was completely dumbfounded.

She motioned for me to come inside, then she gave me a huge hug, nearly suffocating me. "First, let me apologize for how I acted, last time we met. I have a something of a jealous bone. So when I pictured you with those," she pointed at my chest, "in a bikini, sitting around with my Burt, I near had a conniption—my problem, not yours."

She released me and I smiled in relief both for surviving the hug and her apology. "Apology accepted."

She patted the seat of the couch, indicating I should sit next to her. "That ain't the worst of it, though. I lied to you. The Indian woman you described is Chenoa. I know that by the way you described her and by Burt's notebook. He always made shortened notes so that if some crazy kidnaps him, they won't be able to figger 'em out. I couldn't tell you at the time. I guess you now know who Chenoa is and what she means in the tribal unrest."

I gaped at her, wondering where she got her information.

She patted me on the leg. "I know you'd love to know how I know that you know all this, but I can't tell you. Just be happy as hell knowing that it's all true."

My head was spinning. I was relieved that Sally didn't hate me, but I had a growing sense of unease about the State of the Nation as I thought I knew it. "Chenoa came to me last Sunday and told me to move out of Jason's house because I was in danger. Do you think she was telling the truth?"

Sally chuckled, "We used to have a saying back in the day: Redskins, love 'em or hate 'em, they don't lie."

I looked her in the eye. "I wish I'd asked her more questions, especially about her and Jason."

She bit her lip. "Sorry about that too. Guess you didn't know."

I shook my head. "No, I didn't. And, actually finding out about the fact that Jason had been with her would have been tough to take, but I think we could have gotten through it. Finding out that he's been communicating with her every day since he and I have been together was too much for me to handle."

Sally folded her hands in her lap. "I understand how you feel. Just be careful you don't make any decisions based on pain you're suffering right now. Here's something I learned early on in my long, long marriage. Men are weak. They like to call women the weaker sex. Hogwash! That was something men came up with to hide how weak they are. Find me a man who can resist a kind word from a pretty woman, and I'll show you a dead man."

I stared at her trying to comprehend. "But, Burt—"

She interrupted, "I ain't saying Burt wasn't a good man. Burt was a great man, but he wasn't perfect neither. And he loved me with all his heart and soul. But he couldn't ignore a kind word from a pretty woman. Am I saying Burt had affairs where he was out in other women's beds having all sorts of sex? Of course not. He was just sometimes pulled off track, and I had to pull him back. Do I regret marryin' him? No. He loved me, and I loved him. He wasn't perfect. No man is, Miranda. No man is. Don't be convicting Jason and lose something and someone you love over a text or email. He loves you, not Chenoa."

I thought about my conversation with Jason. "I guess if he loves me more than her, that will become self-evident. He thought of no one but her for two years before he was able to let go and begin to date again. I will never say never, but right now, I need some space."

She patted my leg again. "That's all anyone can ask for."

My questioning almost seemed anticlimactic after this conversation, but it made me wonder what else she knew. "Sally, do you know who killed Burt?"

She thought for a minute. "Miranda, I wish I did, darlin'. I've thought of nothing else since you found him. I had a couple suspects, but they didn't pan out. And I know there's a struggle going on behind the scenes for the Hot Springs, but killing's not the Indian's style, especially with a gun. They would have sent a message in a traditional way, with a knife or an arrow. They are a very proud people. A coward murdered Burt."

One question had been bothering me since Sally threw me out the last time I visited her. "Did Burt come home the night before he was killed?"

She wiped a tear from her eye. "No."

With everything she had said to defend his honor and all the progress she and I had made during this visit, I almost didn't ask, but I thought it was important. "I'm sorry to have to ask this but—"

She asked it for me, thank God, "Do I think he spent the night with another woman?" She wiped a tear from her eye. "If he did, God damn him, he's gonna have a fight on his hands when I git up to heaven."

I decided not to pursue that line of questioning any further, but then this one slipped out. "If so, who?"

She drummed her fingernails on the coffee table as if sending morse code to Burt in heaven. She said, barely above a whisper, "Chenoa was supposed to meet him at the Hot Springs after he met you that afternoon. She was meant to bring him some stolen guns. That's why he stayed there."

I looked at her with disbelief. "What stolen guns? What are you talking about? How do you know she didn't kill him? What if there was some sort of misunderstanding, and she ended up shooting him with one of the guns?"

She thought of something but changed her mind. "You met Chenoa. Can you picture that?"

I still wasn't sure but agreed. "No, not really."

Then she explained about the guns. "The sheriffs have amnesty once a year, where guns can be turned in, no questions asked. Because the Indians trusted Burt, he was chosen as the go-between for the hand-off."

That was the first I'd heard of that program. "Oh, I had no idea they did that here."

She nodded. "I got a feelin' Burt was meeting with someone after turning in the guns, but he didn't tell me."

I stared into her eyes. "Did you kill him, Sally?" Suddenly, I felt like a cop, and not a very good one. But her reaction would tell the whole tale.

She kept her cool. "Oh, Lord, Miranda, I almost wish I did, then at least we'd know."

Chaos in the Canyon

My experience told me that was not the answer of a guilty woman unless she was a very skilled liar who had been practicing for that moment since the day he died. She didn't strike me as the pathological liar type. I decided to use her as a resource to set up my interviews for the rest of my day. "Is there anyone else on Roop Road that would be worth talking to about this? You know, people who pay attention to people coming and going, strangers walking down the road, stuff like that."

She smiled. "Yes, there's only two I'd bother with, and they both live toward the Spring from here. Angie Booker and Jerry Carter. She's a retired schoolteacher and don't miss a trick. He was government, CIA, I think. Well 'nuf said about that. He's like a jackpot witness. Not sure why I didn't think of him earlier."

I stood up, ready to take on the two best options. "Have you spoken to them yet?"

She mock scolded me. "Miranda, would I waste your time? I already tol' you I crossed the others off the list. I'm your best friend, you just didn't know it until now. But 'cause you and I are buddies, it'll all be good. So, tell me if either of them pans out. I might become a PI to help pay the bills. I want to know if I'm any good."

I nearly laughed out loud at the idea of Sally trying to sneak around unnoticed, but the fact was, I hadn't thought about how she would make ends meet with Burt gone. "I definitely will." I hugged her. "I'm so glad I came by. I have to tell you; I was a little bit frightened after last time."

She smiled. "Good, it worked." She winked.

I headed for the door. "You're a trip, Sally Roop. See ya."

She waved from the dining room. "See ya. Soon, I hope."

Chapter 23

I hopped in the car, knowing that some people put their names on their mailboxes out here, hoping these two did. That wasn't as common a practice as it used to be in this world of anonymity. I was in luck with the first one. About three-quarters of a mile down the road a mailbox on the left said Booker. I pulled in the driveway.

In her early seventies, a diminutive black woman with graying black hair nearly ran out the front door as I pulled in. She carried her phone in one hand and a Yorkie in the other. "Miranda? Are you Miranda? Sally just called me and told me to expect a visitor. I love having visitors, so I wanted to come out and welcome you," she called to me as I parked the car.

Her house was a darling cape cod style house with yellow siding and black shutters, an oddity for California. I waved as I got out of the car. "I love your house!"

She grinned broadly, obviously pleased with my comment. "When I moved out here from the east, I couldn't find anything I liked, so I had it built. I wanted a basement, but they refused, so I built it twice as large as I originally planned and added an attic. I still can't look at it without thinking of those summers I spent in Maine with my grandmother. Please come in and have some iced tea." I followed her into a bit of New England in California. The walls were adorned with pictures of the ocean, lighthouses, lobster pots, and peaceful harbors. If she loved Maine so much, it made me wonder why she was here. "Before you ask, it's the weather. If Maine had California's weather, I'd be there in a second. I just can't handle the snow and below zero temperatures anymore."

"It's lovely," I said as she took me from room to room. It had a warmth that you rarely find in a home out here. It's hard to explain. I'd never been to New England but visiting her made me want to go there.

We sat in the living room, sipping iced tea. After a few moments, she asked, "So what was it that you wanted, dear?"

I smiled. "I was having such a wonderful time; I almost forgot why I was here."

She laughed. "Then I've achieved my hospitality goal."

I shifted gears. "I'm sure you heard that Burt Roop died, especially if Sally has you on speed dial. I wanted to see if you knew anything, had any feelings, saw anything unusual, heard anything, stuff like that."

She looked me in the eye. "You don't pull any punches, and I like that, not like that cop who came snooping around here, asking all sorts of twisted double-crossing questions. I finally had to ask him to leave."

I had a hunch. "That wasn't Jacob Mabry, was it?"

She looked at me with amazement. "How did you know?"

"It sounds like his style. He's not my favorite of the group they have assigned to this case." I sipped my iced tea. "I don't want to take much of your time. I'm sure you've given it a lot of thought. Is there anything you remember about the day before Burt was found dead that seemed odd or unusual?"

She shook her head. "No, nothing. The thing that has bothered me most about this whole thing was that cop. He kept trying to lead me down a certain trail, and I have to be honest, Miranda, it was to you."

I gasped. "Me? He was trying to aim you toward me as the killer? Was this before or after Jason was arrested?"

She was adamant. "Oh, this was after, Miranda. This was yesterday."

I was stunned. "Did he give you any indication of why he would be focusing on me when Jason was the one who had been arrested?"

She looked confused. "No. I thought maybe he thought you were an accomplice. I thought maybe he had it out for you. I really didn't know what to think. You seem like a perfectly lovely young lady, and if Sally Roop says you are okay, you're more than okay in my book."

I pushed for more, "So he didn't ask about possible other suspects, like strangers wandering around the area, people like that?"

She was clear. "Oh, no, not at all. All the questions he asked me were about you."

I was just about finished with my tea. "I hate to cut my visit short, but everything you've told me has been so helpful. Now, I need to get going. Thank you so much. Let's get together when we have more time."

I nearly ran to the car. That information was really disturbing. I had a bad feeling about this Mabry guy before, but this made it worse. I wondered if they had spoken to the ex-CIA guy Sally had referred me to. I hoped she had done a pre-introduction for me also. That was really helpful.

I continued down Roop Road to the one remaining house on the right before the intersection with Hot Springs road—the Carter house. It was a typical sixties ranch house. I could picture the inside without even going inside. It sat down in a gully with a creek running nearby, most likely fed by Coyote creek, which was on the other side of Hot Springs road.

I turned onto the driveway to see a mishmash of antennas and satellite dishes in the field behind the house. It figured. He was ex-CIA, after all. I was probably under surveillance the instant I pulled onto the property. This should be an interesting visit. I was surprised that Sally hadn't mentioned connecting with him before this.

Chaos in the Canyon

As I approached the front door, a good-looking medium build man in his late fifties or early sixties opened the front door. He had the leading man good looks of a Sean Connery in his 007 years. He gave me a broad smile. "Miranda, I assume."
I smiled back. "I love it when my reputation precedes me."
He waved me through the door and into a room next to the kitchen that normally would be considered a family room, but it was stacked with computer terminals, printers, and all sorts of hardware I couldn't identify. He surveyed it with pride. "Welcome to my central information processing area. I have surveillance all around the world. It's ironic how much is going on right in our own back yard."
I look at it all with wide-eyed amazement. "What is all this stuff?"
He minimized the immensity of what he was able to do here. "Oh, I have a few satellite hook-ups that tie to several of the underground networks here and abroad. I pretty much can follow anything and anyone in the world given time and coordinates."
I would have loved to spend the day here seeing what he saw, but I couldn't spare the time. I dove right in. "Have you been following the Burt Roop case at all?"
He adjusted one of his video feeds. "I have video feeds all around Coe Park and the Hot Springs, generally tracking any movement. These honestly were put into play because of some vandalism taking place a couple of years ago; I just never dismantled them. The video quality isn't very good because I haven't cleaned off the lenses for a while."
I explained what I was looking for and he immediately set up his equipment to find the time and place so we could check it. The cameras were set with motion detectors so we watched a lot of wildlife wandering around in the hillside and then—there it was—someone dragging a body up the side of a mountain and

leaving it in a field. It was hard to tell in the dark, but that appeared to be where I found Burt. He stopped the video, increased the light, and ran it in slow motion. But the slower he ran it, the grainier the picture got, and the harder it was to recognize anything.

He was frustrated. "The more times I run it, the less I can tell from it. All I know, at this point, is that he wasn't killed where you found him. It was probably a man based on size and strength. That's all I can tell. Well, we know that he was dragged up the mountain, not down. But that's it."

I asked, "So you don't have another camera to pick up where this one left off?"

He shook his head. "The only other cameras we have are at the Hot Springs." He played around with some switches and then said with a broad grin on his face, "Well, in fact, we have some very clear video of you and Burt Roop the day before, and him and Chenoa later on."

I was excited by that news. "You have him and Chenoa? Do they look like they were arguing or have an altercation of any sort?"

"No, they talked for a couple of minutes, and both left. There's nothing after that. Here, see for yourself." I watched the brief video and had to agree, they hadn't been arguing.

After a flicker of hope, I was deflated. "So what's your gut feeling, Jerry? Was this a conspiracy-based thing, a robbery, a crime of passion, something random or something else?" I thought for a second. "Hey, wait a minute. Let's look at that again. Did they leave *together,* or did they just leave at the same time?"

He switched to a different camera. After flicking a few switches, it showed the two of them getting in his vehicle and driving away. I said, "Oh my God! He didn't go home that night; this means *something.* I don't know what, but it means something.

You're from around here. What do you think it means? Aren't they supposed to be on opposite sides?"

He thought for a minute. "Yes, technically, but Burt was everybody's friend. You saw how quickly he turned around after putting a gun to your head. You two talked for hours. I could see him befriending Chenoa, but I couldn't see anything untoward happening between them. That wasn't his style or hers."

I pushed him. "So where did they go, and how did he end up dead?"

I could see by the veins bulging in his head that he thought he should be able to answer these questions but was unable to. "I just don't know."

I asked the obvious question, "Don't you have any way of tracking where they went from the Hot Springs?"

He gave me a look. "Well, Miranda, I have some of the most sophisticated equipment available in the world today, but the real answer is 'No.' The problem is that they were local, and they were driving. Had they been flying or nearly anywhere else in the world, I could have tracked them."

I asked, "So, what time of day was he carried up the trail and dumped off?"

He checked the video. "About 4 a.m., and he left the Hot Springs around 8 p.m. on Saturday. So that's a lot of time to get in trouble."

I stood to go. "Well, I guess you gave me a more compressed time frame, but I don't know where to go from here."

He winked. "Well if all else fails, you can accuse that police guy who was here. I don't know that he did it, but he was obnoxious enough, I'd like to see him locked up."

I stopped in my tracks. "Do you mean Jacob Mabry? Why does his name keep coming up?"

He looked me in the eye. "You know he was talking trash about you, right?"

I couldn't believe he was doing that here too. "I didn't know that until earlier today. I'm going to give his boss a piece of my mind, though. What is it with that guy?"

He shook his head. "I don't know, but it seemed like if he had his way, you'd be in San Quentin by now."

I nodded. "I'm getting the message loud and clear. Well, you don't think I did it, right?"

He laughed, "No, you're a lot smaller than the guy that carried him up that mountain."

"The police need to see this," I said.

"I'll make copies and send them over to the sheriff's office. They need to see this," he said. "It makes it clear you had nothing to do with the murder."

I waved on my way to the car. I decided to pay a visit to Tina Bright of the Santa Clara County Sheriff's Department.

Chapter 24

Within an hour, I was pulling up to the sheriff's department building in downtown, a typical California Mission-style office building—all stucco walls and red tiled roof. I didn't have an appointment, so I hoped that Tina would see me. The receptionist at the front desk talked briefly on the phone to Tina who was apparently amenable to a meeting as the young woman pointed me to the elevators and said, "Go right up."

Within five minutes, and a short elevator ride, I was seated in her ten-by-ten office crowded with file cabinets surrounding an ancient, oversized metal desk, leaving just enough space for her chair and one straight-backed visitor's chair. Everything was buried in papers and files. "So, what can I do for you?" she asked.

I didn't want to come on too strong about Jacob Mabry, so I figured I would start with some general questions. "So, how's the investigation going? As you may know, I'm working for the defense, so I thought this might be a good chance to compare notes. I've been interviewing some of Jason's neighbors down in Coyote Lake and hearing some interesting things."

She reviewed some notes on her desk. "Oh?"

She clearly wasn't going to share anything with me. "I don't know how close you are to the investigation, but I just met with two neighbors, Jerry Carter and Angie Booker, who indicated they had recently met with your staff."

She nodded, very noncommittal. "Yes, my staff has been doing some routine questioning as you can imagine having been a cop yourself. As far as I've heard, they haven't uncovered anything too interesting in the case."

"Well, you ought to be getting something interesting pretty soon from Carter. He has video of Burt Roop's body being dumped on that hillside."

Her eyes lit up at that information. "Really? Why didn't he let us know right away?"

"He forgot he even had cameras on in that area until I asked him about it. You couldn't believe the equipment he has in that house."

"I'll keep an eye out for it. Is that what you wanted to tell me? If so, I really appreciate it."

I mentally hemmed and hawed, unsure how to approach her about the behavior of one of her deputies. She watched me as if waiting for me to either get up and leave or to say something else. I decided to cut to the chase and looked her straight in the eye. "I'm having an issue with some of the questioning coming from one of your employees, namely Jacob Mabry."

She raised her eyebrows and said, "Oh?" again, which made me feel like she was playing me.

I tried not to sound frustrated or angry, "Are you saying that you aren't aware of what the focus of his questioning has been?"

She seemed genuinely interested. "I actually give my employees quite a bit of latitude in their jobs, so I can't say that I've reviewed his questions or even discussed what his plan of attack was."

I couldn't control myself any longer; I blurted out, "It's me, Tina. His focus is me."

She immediately defended him. "Well, you are the defendant's girlfriend, so I can see how you might come up in the questioning. It's inevitable."

I could feel my face turning red. "No, *Tina,* I get that. But his focus was solely on me like *I* was the defendant. I heard this independently from two people. When I heard it the first time, I thought, perhaps it was an overreaction, but the second time, it was from an ex-CIA agent. I couldn't imagine him over-stating the case. They said Mabry was asking about my character, my relationship with Burt Roop, if they were aware that I had an encounter with him the day before he died; stuff like that. He didn't ask one question about Jason. Doesn't that seem odd to you since he's the one you arrested?"

She agreed. "That does seem odd. Well, it's our lucky day. Jacob is in the office today, so let's call him in here and see what he has to say about all this."

She dialed him direct on speaker, and he said he'd be right in. Within seconds, Mabry was in her office. He looked surprised to see me. He stuck out his hand, "Miranda, how nice to see you again. To what do we owe the pleasure of your company?"

That seemed like an odd statement from someone who had made no secret, from day one, that he didn't particularly care for me.

Tina explained, "Miranda had some questions about a couple of Coyote Lake residents who claimed that you seemed to be treating her as more of a suspect than Jason Wall."

He tilted his head. "How so?"

I wasn't buying the act but tried to keep my composure. "The two people I spoke to said that you didn't ask any questions at all about Jason, his whereabouts, or his relationship with Burt Roop. All your questions pertained to me."

He maintained his composure completely, "That sounds like an exaggeration. Of course, your name would come up since you were living with Jason at the time, although I understand that you have now moved out."

Tina looked at him, and then at me, to make sure he had his facts straight.

I nodded. "Yes, that is true, but I am still working on his defense. We're just taking a break. It's a stressful time for all of us." That was kind of true. I really didn't know what our future was at this point. Sally had made some compelling arguments for giving him another chance, and she had a lot more life experience than I did. But he was getting off-topic. "I'm not talking about pulling me into the discussion about Jason. I'm talking about asking questions solely about me. This came from two separate sources. Why would they say that, Jacob?"

He mumbled something under his breath that I couldn't hear or interpret.

While I had him here, I figured I should address another issue that had been bothering me since we first met after the 911 call. "Which reminds me, I have another question since you're here. When I made the 911 call after I discovered Burt Roop's body, you seemed to have a *lot* of information on me. It seemed unlikely that you had accumulated that much information in the short time between the time I called and when you arrived."

He looked like the cat who swallowed the canary. As if as much for his boss as me, he hesitated like he didn't want to give away his professional secrets. He folded his arms and leaned against the wall as if he were buying a little time before he explained. "There are some locals that we keep files on, even though they don't have a criminal record or haven't committed a crime that we are aware of. Their notoriety alone makes them a person of interest. We accumulate information on those persons so that if and when they become suspects, we don't have to start our investigation from scratch." He looked directly at me like he was waiting to deliver the punch line. "With everything that had happened since you'd arrived here, and before that, you quickly became one of those people. You're quite a legend, actually."

I looked at Tina to see if she seemed surprised by his response. I figured that if she did address it with him, it would be after I left the office. "So, I guess I'm your back-up suspect?"

Jacob laughed, "Oh no. Those were just routine questions as the girlfriend of a murder suspect, nothing more and nothing less."

Tina seemed ready to move on. "Okay, then, I'm happy we were able to straighten that out."

I wasn't sure that anything had been straightened out, but I was in enemy territory, so my expectations were low. I decided this was the best I was going to get. "Okay, thanks. I appreciate you taking the time to see me without an appointment." We shook hands, and I left her office.

She had asked Jacob to stay behind when I left, so I wondered what was *really* going on. I, unfortunately, couldn't count on these people for the straight story. I would check their story with Wanda to see if they handled things the same way in their office or if this was either something unique to the sheriff's office or to Jacob Mabry.

It was such a nice day, and I wasn't going to work, so I drove to the park to get my facts together. I had lists of suspects in my head, but no idea of who did it, not a clue. I was pretty sure Jason had nothing to do with it, but now that I was not with him, it seemed harder to eliminate him completely. I sat on a picnic table, staring off into the blue sky, hoping for a sign from somewhere that would point me in the right direction.

I listed the suspects in my head, Jason, Sally Roop, Chenoa, other Native Americans in her community, someone else Burt ran into after he and Chenoa left the Hot Springs. The key was finding out where Burt Roop was between Saturday evening and early Sunday morning. That would be the key to determining his killer.

I wondered what Wanda's hours were today. I texted her. *'Hey, are you working now?'*

She responded, *'Yes, but leaving soon. Where are you?'*

I was happy, '*I'll be home in a few minutes. I need your help with sleuthing.*'

She responded immediately, '*It's what I live for.* ☺'

Chapter 25

I was waiting for Wanda when she got home. She looked like she had worked all night because she had. She had large, dark circles under her eyes. But she was a good sport and tried to stay awake for me. I was brewing coffee in the kitchen, anticipating that she'd probably be exhausted.

She sat at the kitchen table. I asked, "Do you have a whiteboard around here anywhere? I need to organize my thoughts."

She went to the hall closet and, like any good detective, had one stashed in the back. She set it up in viewing distance of the dining room table. She grabbed a marker, "Okay, so what do we have? Did you find out anything new in Coyote Lake?"

I bit my lip. "Kind of, but I don't know what any of it means." She wrote it down as I said it.

"1. Burt Roop left the Hot Springs with Chenoa around sunset.

"2. Burt was dragged up the mountain to where I found him around 4 a.m. the next day.

"3. Jacob Mabry has been asking questions about me in the neighborhood as if I'm the suspect and not Jason.

"4. Mabry said he was just asking routine questions because I was Jason's girlfriend, but I'm not buying it.

"5. When I asked Mabry how he had so much information about me when they arrived after the 911 call, he said they already had a file on me because of my local notoriety.

"What do you think about that?"

She looked at me intensely. "Five is completely bogus. No police department in the world has time to keep files on people who might break the law someday. So, let's step back for a second. Your ex-neighbors didn't have anything else, even that former CIA agent?"

I responded, "Carter came up with the first two based on his surveillance of the area. He's sending copies to the sheriff's office. But he's set up more for global stuff than what's going on in his back yard. It makes me want to do some more questioning down there to see if anyone saw Burt Roop on Saturday night. Although, I'm not even sure where I'd start or who I'd ask. Now that I have Sally Roop on my team, maybe she could tell me if he's ever just gone out after going to the Hot Springs, like to get a beer or something. I guess I could call her on the phone, but in-person interviews work so much better."

Wanda looked at her watch. "You know, it's only forty-five minutes down there. If you believe she's the key, maybe you should head back down there. I have a feeling you're onto something, but I have no idea what."

I looked at her and smiled. "You're not just saying that because you want to go to bed, right?"

She tapped the whiteboard with the end of the marker. "Well, to be honest—"

I laughed, "I get it. In my frustration, I may have left there prematurely."

She looked me in the eye. "No, I don't think so. You needed to meet with Tina Bright and Jacob Mabry today also. That's a piece of this puzzle, I think, but I have no idea how or why."

I stood up and put my coffee mug in the sink. "You're right, of course. I'm going to head back down to see Sally. I don't get the impression that she goes much of anywhere during the day, so I think it's a low risk, showing up without calling. I like to surprise people and find them in their own space. I think they are more authentic."

She waved as she headed to the bedroom. "I think you're making progress. Keep on plugging. You probably can't afford another day out of the office, so make the most of it."

I nodded. "You're right. I definitely can't. I'm not even sure how much slack Jason is willing to cut me right now," I went out to my car. Wanda was right, I was making progress and would at least have something to talk to Sabine and Mark about tonight. Another forty-five minutes later, I pulled into Sally's driveway. She was outside, hanging her laundry on the clothesline. She gave me a broad smile when she saw me.

She finished her last towel and approached me with open arms. "Miranda, didn't think I'd see you again this soon. Good news?"

We hugged in the driveway. I could get used to being appreciated this much. "Well, not exactly. I still need you to fill in some holes."

She led me inside. "Coffee?"

I grinned. "I'd love some! This driving is killing me. I've already been back to Santa Clara today once."

She sounded impressed. "And you drove back down here just to visit? Gotta be important."

We sat on the couch. "I think it is. I've narrowed down Burt's death between 9 p.m. on Saturday and 4 a.m. on Sunday. And I don't know if it means anything, but he was seen leaving the Hot Springs with Chenoa. Did he talk about having a meeting with her or with the tribe?"

She chewed on her lip like I do when I'm thinking. "Like I told you, Miranda, he kept me out of his business. He thought the less I knew, the better in case he ended up in hot water. I heard him a couple of nights before he was killed talking to someone about those stolen guns. They wanted to buy some, but he said that they were all going to the sheriff. That was all I heard."

I stood and started pacing. "Sally, you do know that he was killed with one of Jason's guns that was stolen from our shed? That's why he was arrested."

She watched me pace. "Well, I guess so. I did hear that, but I don't believe it for a minute that Jason would have done that. What reason would he even have? But I still haven't got a clue how we're going to track down the killer." She paused as if she was considering whether she should tell me what she was thinking. "Miranda, I don't know if this is important, but I've been getting threatening phone calls."

I perked up at this news. "First off, it's not your job to find the killer; it's up to the police and well, me, because as you know I'm working for the defense. As for threatening phone calls, of course, that's important. Are they coming in on your house phone or your cell phone?"

She thought for a second. "My mobile, but there's no caller ID. Says 'Number Blocked.'"

I tried to be patient, but I couldn't help but wonder why she hadn't told me this earlier. "So what is the caller saying, and how are they threatening you? Do you recognize the voice? Is it male or female?"

She shook her head. "'Got four or five since Burt died. First, I just thought they were crank calls and ignored 'em. You know how crazy people are these days. But they kept gettin' more specific about who I was and where I lived. I don't feel safe now."

I watched her eyes to make sure she was telling the truth. I asked again, "How are they threatening you?"

She closed her eyes, thinking back. "It was a man, soft voice, but pretty creepy. I didn't recognize the voice. He just says, word for word, 'Leave it alone, or you'll end up the same way Burt did.'"

I scratched my head. "So, they didn't tell you what to leave alone. That's pretty frustrating. I understand, though, why you wouldn't feel safe. Is there somewhere else you can stay?"

She grimaced. "I hate to bother anyone. I could ask Angie, I guess. She always says she got plenty of room and loves company."

I smiled. "That's a great idea. Let's call her together before I leave."

She seemed relieved. "Okay, sounds good. Now, before we forget, weren't you gonna ask something about the guns?"

I nodded. "I was thinking that if the guns were changing hands the night Burt was killed, maybe either the people who originally stole them from us or those who bought them killed him. Did you tell the police about this?"

She nodded. "I think so— that Mabry guy."

I shivered. "And how did he react?"

She thought back. "He didn't. I remembered thinking that he must already know about that 'cause he seemed bored like I was wasting his time."

I remembered what the other two had told me about Jacob Mabry. "When he questioned you, what did he ask?"

She looked at the ceiling, trying to remember. "I was out of it. I had just found out my Burt was gone. Lemme think now. He asked me if I knew you or Jason. Then, he asked if Burt knew either of you two. He asked if I had seen you heading toward the Hot Springs. He asked something about the queen of something; I had no idea what he was talking about."

"The Princess of Death?"

She snapped her fingers. "Yeah, that was it. Darned if I'd ever heard of that."

I said quietly, "That's me."

She gasped. "No, how can that be you?"

I didn't want to get into it but had no choice now. "I've been nearby where several people have died over the past several years, and now Burt." I cringed, waiting for her reaction.

She smiled and put her hand on my shoulder. "You didn't kill him, did you?"

I smiled back. "Of course not."

"Then we have nothing to worry about."

I thought to myself, "Thank God!" I still needed more information on the guns because he was killed with one of them. "So, tell me again why Burt would be in the middle of a stolen gun issue? What did it have to do with him?"

She thought for a minute, "The Indians didn't trust the sheriff not to arrest them on the spot if they brought the guns themselves, so they figured Burt could do it."

I had a crazy idea. "Was Jacob Mabry involved in that program?"

She shook her head. "Not a clue. Never heard of the guy 'til he came here questioning."

I smiled and took her hand. "It's fine. Something happened, and it has to do with this exchange of firearms, I'm almost sure of it. Something that got Burt killed. And that is such a waste since the only reason he was in the middle of it was that he was a nice guy, trying to do what was right." I thought for a minute. There was something I had to do. "Do you know where I can find Chenoa?"

She shook her head. "No one knows where the tribe lives. They move 'round all the time. All I can say is go to the Hot Springs around sunset. Sometimes she's there. Stay here until then? We can cook dinner and just have some woman to woman talk."

Her kindness touched me. "I'd love that."

Chapter 26

We had a wonderful meal of spaghetti, homemade sauce, garlic bread, and lots of love. Whether or not I ever moved back into this neighborhood, I planned on visiting Sally regularly. Her aspirations to become a private detective made me wonder if I should introduce her to the WAIT Club, but I'd save that thought for another day. To start with, it would probably sound really insulting if I said it before explaining what the club was about.

Before I left, we called Angie together on her cell phone about Sally staying with her until the dust settled around this case. Angie was thrilled about being able to help and the idea of having some company. It was a perfect solution. I just hoped whoever was threatening Sally didn't find out about it.

I was a bundle of nerves as I approached the Hot Springs and nearly turned back several times before crossing the bridge over the Coyote Creek near the Coe Park Trailhead. I had enough personal issues with Chenoa that I would have been willing to avoid ever seeing her again, but I had to put my feelings aside for now.

As I approached the small parking lot, I saw the same beat-up motorbike I saw when I first encountered Chenoa. I pushed down my anger as much as possible. This woman had singlehandedly changed my life in a moment, without remorse or accepting responsibility. The human side of me wanted to make her pay for that, but I tried to tell myself I needed to be professional at the moment.

I trudged up toward the pool, where I had found her last time, and sure enough, there she was, this time dressed in jean shorts and a tank top, not the most intelligent riding attire in my opinion, but I already didn't like her, so she was just accumulating more reasons on my list. She appeared to be meditating with her legs crossed and her hands, palms up, resting on her knees.

Without opening her eyes, she said, "Miranda, you made it back to me."

Here she was, already speaking in riddles. "Chenoa, can we stop this before it starts?"

She didn't move an inch. "Stop what, My Princess?"

I walked over to her and sat facing her. "That, 'My Princess.' What's that even supposed to mean?"

She was coming out of her meditation-induced mood and scrunched up her face. "You and I are sisters of blood."

I wasn't letting her go. "And what does that mean?"

She finally opened her eyes. "Do you really think it is a coincidence that you and I both ended up with Jason, of all the men and women in the universe?"

I thought about it. "Yes, why not?" Now that I had her grounded, I asked her the question that had been on my mind since I left Jason. "Tell me this, Chenoa. Now that I have cleared the way for you, are you going to go back to Jason?"

I was finally able to get some attitude from Miss Calm Indian of the Year. "Oh, don't worry, Miranda. It was never *you* who was keeping us apart."

This conversation had become tiresome. "While this is fascinating, I need to find out what happened after you and Burt Roop left here the night before he was found dead."

She stared at me. "We recovered stolen firearms from renegades and told Man with Kind Eyes that we wanted to return them."

I tried to fill in the gaps. "So Burt is Man with Kind Eyes."

She nodded.

I was finally getting a straight answer. "So once you gave him the firearms, what happened then?"

"He left me with my people and took the firearms with him. He said that he would take them to the White Man for disposal so no-one would be harmed with them."

I acknowledged. "So he was going to turn them into the sheriff's office to get them off the street. About how many guns were there?"

She thought back, "Around a hundred guns of all kinds—automatics, handguns, hunting rifles. We could save many lives. We were not banding together as many were accusing us of. This was how we would demonstrate that."

So, this was a political gesture on their part. I wasn't sure I believed it, but I would accept it for now. "Who do you think killed Burt?"

She blinked, then closed her eyes and said, "Man obsessed with Princess of Death hides the truth."

I shook my head in bewilderment. This woman really was spaced out. "Come on, Chenoa, stop being so cryptic. Can you explain more clearly?"

She was silent. I was apparently dismissed.

I turned to walk away, not giving her the satisfaction of looking back.

Chapter 27

I sped back to Santa Clara, knowing I was late for my meeting with Mark and Sabine. They were just finishing a late dinner in their suite when I arrived.

Sabine got up to load the dishwasher. "Look what the cat dragged in. *Vous avez l'air horrible!*"

I laughed, "I've had quite a day, and I still don't know which end is up. I've been to Coyote Lake twice, visited with the Santa Clara Sheriff's Department, and even had a moment to compare notes with Wanda."

Mark was on the edge of his seat. "What have you got for us?"

I pulled out my notes. "I'll give you the Reader's Digest version. I talked to Sally Roop twice and a few people on Roop Road, mostly based on her recommendation. She seemed to have a good handle on who knows what down there. I spoke to Don, our next-door neighbor. He had nothing because he was in town most of the day. Then I spoke to Angie Booker and Jerry Carter, a couple of neighbors down from Sally, toward the springs. Both of them said that Jacob Mabry was trying to get more dirt on me than Jason for the murder. Jerry was also able to narrow down Burt's murder between sundown on Saturday to 4 a.m. on Sunday, and a male with the strength to carry him halfway up the mountain where I found him is likely the killer. Carter made copies of the videos and should be sending me a copy for you."

Mark was quickly scribbling notes. "Excellent. Anything else?"

I responded, "Oh yeah, that was just from my trip down there this morning. Based on the comments about Jacob Mabry, I felt like I had to drop in on Tina Bright, his boss. She was pretty defensive of him. She called him into his office where he explained that his questions about me were just routine and get this—he had put together a file on me based on my status as the Princess of Death last year even though I never even committed a crime, *just in case* I ever did."

Sabine seemed to question the value of the information about Jacob Mabry. "I hate to say it, Miranda, but I think you're barking up the wrong tree with this guy and chasing your own tail. If you want my opinion, he's got a crush on you, and he's afraid to tell you. He's trying to get your attention like the kid who pulls your hair on the playground. He's that kid. I think he's getting in your head."

Mark and Sabine had clearly already discussed this. "I have to agree, Miranda. If you can't work with him because you have a personal issue with him, we can try to get him taken off the case. Otherwise, grin and bear it."

I felt a bit unheard, but it wouldn't be the first or last time. "Okay, guys, just looking at every angle. I went back down to Coyote Lake to see Sally again, and she said something shocking that she hadn't shared before for whatever reason. She's been getting threatening calls, several of them since Burt was killed. It sounds to me like they're from the killer. She felt so threatened since the last one that she doesn't feel comfortable staying at her house and is staying with her neighbor, Angie, the one I spoke with earlier."

Mark nodded for me to continue.

"So after I talked to Sally, I went to talk to Chenoa, because I found out from Jerry Carter that she and Burt left the Hot Springs together around sunset. She may have been the last person to be seen with him alive, except for the killer, of course. She claimed that the tribe was giving Burt guns that some renegades had stolen, and the tribe was turning them in as a show of good faith and solidarity with the White Man. She claims that they are not banding together with other tribes to create unrest, and this was proof of that."

Mark said, "This is good stuff, Miranda. If we can figure out what happened during or after that firearm transfer, we'll have our man. I think it was during or immediately after because there was no reason for Burt not to go home right after that, and he never showed up at home that night."

I rubbed my eyes. "Hey, I hate to be a terrible guest, but do you guys mind if I head home? I'm exhausted, and if I don't get back to work tomorrow, Jason will have my head on a platter."

Sabine hugged me, "Of course, *ma belle*."

Mark spoke up. "I forgot to tell you, the preliminary hearing is next Wednesday."

I whined. "Next Wednesday? How can it possibly be that soon? Isn't that illegal?"

Mark laughed, "Actually, no. It has to take place within ten court dates of the arraignment in California."

I responded, "Oh, oops. So, do you think there's any way of getting him off at the hearing? But, then again, I suppose they must have ballistic records."

Mark chewed on his pencil. "That's what I'm guessing, but we won't know until then exactly what they have, so we'll have to keep working whatever angles we have. Anything you can do to fill in the blanks between sunset and 4 a.m. will be the key."

Exhaustion overwhelmed me as I dragged my feet to the door. "I'll see you guys."

#

When I got home, Wanda was either asleep or at work. I needed to ask her for a schedule. Tea was in bed, so I sneaked in quietly and fell asleep as soon as I hit the pillow.

I was so happy it was Friday when I saw the sun leaking through the curtains. Tea, who could literally sleep through an earthquake, hadn't stirred yet. Sometimes I wanted to put a mirror under her nose to make sure she was breathing.

I stared at her, willing her to wake up, and suddenly she started to stir as if she couldn't bear the feeling of me staring at her. I hadn't touched base with her since Wednesday and our encounter with Mike, and I wanted to make sure she was staying strong. I *accidentally* brushed her cheek with the back of my hand. She tried to swat it away like a mosquito then her eyes fluttered open.

She smiled with a sleepy look on her face. Her voice sounded froggy. "When did you get home?"

I laughed. "I've been here most of the night, but you're such a heavy sleeper, you never knew it."

She glanced at the clock. "I guess I have to get up."

I agreed. "Yup, the bus for work leaves in an hour." I wanted to ask about Mike but chose the indirect route. "How was work yesterday?"

She thought for a minute. "It was uneventful. Pretty quiet, actually." She started to get out of bed. "Oh, wait a minute, Rick was looking for you. He said it was important."

I laughed. "Yeah, he probably wants to ask me out now that I'm not with Jason." I looked at her cross-eyed. "That's not happening."

She didn't laugh. "I'm serious, Miranda. I've never seen him like this."

I would have to check on him today, but I had a question for her. "Has Mike bothered you since Wednesday?"

She looked away, which I knew was a bad sign. "He's been texting me, and he says he's really sorry. I don't know, Miranda, maybe I rushed into this."

I took her cheeks in my hands and directed her to look at me. "Do not, I repeat, do not backtrack. You are doing so well.

This is the hardest part." She nodded, but a stray tear drifted down her cheek. I brushed it away. "Okay, what's wrong?"

She looked me in the eye, which I felt was a good sign. "I'm lonely. No offense to you, but I miss sleeping in the same bed with him, just the familiarity of my life with him. Sure, I don't miss the fights and the bruises, but we had good times too."

This was typical of the many young girls I tried to rescue from abusive relationships and marriages when I was on the force. The story was always the same, and most of them grew up with abusive fathers, so it was all they knew from childhood. I begged her, "Just promise me you'll talk to someone if you're considering going back, a counselor or professional that specializes in this, okay?"

She hesitated, and I knew she probably wouldn't, but she said, "Okay, I will."

We rushed around in typical fashion for the next forty minutes and showed up just in time for work. At least Mike was smart enough not to show himself in the parking lot again. I doubted if he would be around me much in the near future if he knew what was good for him. This morning, Rick didn't have the patience to wait for me in the break room; he was seated in my chair with a very serious look on his face.

Tea slipped into the break room to make coffee. I asked as I motioned for him to get out of my chair, "Rick, to what do I owe the pleasure of your company today?"

He whispered, "Why didn't you call me? I told Tea it was urgent."

I brushed him off. "I didn't even see Tea until this morning. What's so urgent?"

He spoke slowly. "You know Jason didn't do this, right?"

I responded, "I suppose," even though I was sure he didn't.

He ignored my comment. "Okay, I'm not supposed to tell you this, and I'd deny it to the death, but Mabry is gunning for you."

I feigned shock. "Really? Why me?"

He insisted. "I'm serious. He wants to take you down, especially after you went into the station the other day and called him out." He looked around to make sure no one was listening except Tea, who looked scared to death, sitting in her office chair with her knees tucked up under her chest. "He has a private social media page now called 'Lock Her Up' where he describes your exploits since high school, including all your alleged victims."

I offered him my computer. "Show me."

Within a few seconds, my life, well not *really* my life, but the deranged presentation of my life as the Princess of Death was tied together neatly in one package on one site. I knew this website would be a destructive force the first time I saw it in action. There were all sorts of pictures, articles, blogs from other Princess of Death followers, and just about anything you could think of if you wanted to implicate me in a murder case. The most disturbing part was the information on the Burt Roop case, which seemed to put the nail in my coffin, so to speak. It was conjectured that his death was my signature that I had relocated to Coyote Lake. I was shocked to note that the page had 2,356 members and more than ten thousand 'likes.'"

I had been living with the POD title for several years, so while this was another step up from what had been done in the past, I couldn't say I was shocked. I wondered, though, what had Rick so excited. "I know this seems shocking when you see it all in one place, but there's nothing new here. You're just learning what it's like to be me."

He asked, "So why do you think Jason was arrested for this murder?"

I responded. "Well, we had some guns stolen, and we've been told that one of them was used to kill Burt. We'll probably have that confirmed next Wednesday at the preliminary hearing."

He scratched his head. "That makes even less sense. Why would Mabry be trying to pin this on you when they have this evidence against Jason?"

I shrugged. "I've given this a lot of thought because Jacob has been focusing on me when questioning witnesses. Maybe he believes that I used Jason's gun to kill Burt. I get that. We were living together, and I would have had access to it. *And* I'm the Princess of Death and have far more history with murder than Jason does."

He seemed to have calmed down, his coloring was better, and he had his silly half-grin on his face. "I'm just worried about you, Miranda."

I touched his hand. "Thanks, Rick. You really are a good friend as much as I like to bust on you. But let me tell you where I am at with the investigation since you're a deputy. You might be able to help me with the last piece of the puzzle."

He nodded eagerly. "Anything for you. And, of course, Jason."

I went on. "I've narrowed down the timing of when Burt was killed and the circumstances. Burt was in the process of turning in stolen guns to the sheriff's department, which included the ones stolen from Jason and me. Somewhere between then and 4 a.m., the next day, he was killed, and his body was dumped off a hiking trail in Coe Park."

He looked impressed. "I haven't heard any of this from my brothers and sisters at the department, so good job, no matter how you came up with that information. Just be careful. I worry about you. I worry about Jason, too, but when I see a social media page like that, it's pretty disturbing."

I chuckled. "Welcome to my life."

He waved as he headed out the door.

By the time he left Tea worked quietly at her desk. Eventually, she came over to my workspace. "They're not going to arrest you, are they?"

I shook my head. "I don't think so. I'm used to all that noise whenever anyone near me dies. I'd almost be disappointed if it didn't happen." That might have been an overstatement, but I didn't want Tea to worry. She had enough on her plate.

I wondered if it made any sense to share everything I had with Tina Bright. I realized they were on the other team but didn't we all have the same goal in the end? I would discuss that with Mark before taking any action.

Tea's phone rang just before the end of the day, and all indications were, based on her secretive behavior, that it was Mike. She took the call in the break room, spoke very softly, and then returned to her desk, not looking at me or speaking to me.

A couple of minutes later, I asked, "So what did Mike want?"

She glanced at me. "Nothing." Then she looked away.

I strolled over to her workstation. She refused to look at me. She typed on her keyboard, pretending I wasn't there.

I decided to try a different approach. "Is he trying to get you to come home?"

She typed.

I placed a hand on her cheek and turned her to face me. "Is he being really sweet to you?"

She stopped typing and burst into tears. "Oh, Miranda, I don't know what to do. I miss him so much, and he's acting like he did when we first got together. He's in counseling, and he's learning a lot about himself and finding out why he does the things he does."

I doubted it but let her continue.

She sniffled. "He says that he needs me home as a part of his therapy."

I stopped her there. "Okay. If he were truly in therapy, which I doubt, his therapist wouldn't want you two within miles of one another. He is lying to get you to come home. I guarantee it. If you don't believe me, ask him for his therapist's number and talk directly to them. They would not want you two together at this point in his therapy."

Her face started to soften. She glanced at her watch. I looked at mine; it was 4:45. She turned to me. "Can we go home now? He's going to be here in ten minutes."

I hugged her. "Good girl." We shut down our computers and headed for the door. Mike wasn't anywhere in sight. I wasn't concerned about him because I knew he wouldn't mess with me. It was Tea I was concerned about.

Chapter 28

I had another appointment with Mark and Sabine after work. I was relieved that Wanda was home when we arrived. I didn't want to leave Tea there alone.

When she went into the bedroom to change, I had a brief conversation with Wanda. "Can you keep a close eye on Tea this evening? She's a flight risk. Mike has stepped up his pressure on her. He pretends that he's in therapy, but from some of the things he's saying, I seriously question that. I think he's using that as a ploy to get her to come home."

She patted my shoulder. "We can make cookies again and then watch a movie. I'll take care of her. She likes spending time with me, I think. We don't get much time together. She seems to view me as a parental figure. I'll try to work some valuable information about abuse into the mix."

I hugged her. "Thanks so much. You're a lifesaver."

I headed out the door, not really sure about what to talk to Mark and Sabine about. Not much had happened since we met yesterday.

We had decided to meet at a seafood restaurant to shake things up where they were known for their fresh lobster and homemade breads.

It was crowded, and I was happy they already had a table. At least twenty people waited outside and in the lobby.

We all hugged at the four-person table they had been seated at. They were sitting across from one another, so I sat to the side and folded back the napkin to expose the fresh warm rolls. "Great! They're my favorite." I plucked one up and took a bite.

Mark nodded. "Happy to oblige." He helped himself to one also. "Let's cover what's going on at the preliminary hearing on Wednesday. It'll be here before we know it. Let's assume that they are going to use the fact that a gun registered to Jason was used in the murder."

I agreed. "I'm guessing that's all they have. You should be able to eliminate that as strong evidence easily. Our guns were stolen from the shed. Unfortunately, we didn't notice they were gone or report the theft until after Burt's death."

He shook his head. "Yeah, that doesn't help. I'll just have to be super convincing, as usual." He reviewed his notes. "It's very important to present that Burt had the guns in his possession and that Chenoa had given them to him. That makes the crime far less random. The murder had to be committed by someone who knew he had the guns or someone who discovered that he had the guns."

I was frustrated. "How can we ever find out about the missing time frame?" I wracked my brain. "Wait a minute. He was supposed to be meeting with the sheriff's department, right? Wouldn't there be a recording on a DashCam on the police car where they exchanged the guns?"

Mark brightened. "Great idea. There should be, depending on if they were facing the right way. It's a possibility, though. It's something we can request."

I was excited. "That might also tell us if Chenoa was still with him when the guns were exchanged and if they picked up anyone else along the way. I wonder if one of the renegades who the elders forced to turn the guns over kept one for their own use and perhaps killed Burt with it later on." I thought about the possibilities. "Do you think we can get the recording before the preliminary hearing?"

Mark shook his head. "I can try, but this is pretty late to be asking. I won't be able to request it until Monday morning now. But nothing to lose. It's probably going to trial. To be honest, that's probably the best thing that can happen for you, Princess of Death.

It'll buy us some time if we have to develop a defense for you when Jason goes free."

I punched his arm. "Thanks for the vote of confidence."

Sabine had been uncharacteristically quiet this whole time. "I'm sure you've been on this new social media page 'Lock Her Up.' It seems to me like 2,356 suspects haven't been considered. Maybe the only thing Burt did wrong was to live in the wrong place."

I looked at her like she was out of her mind.

She continued. "Don't be so quick to dismiss me, *mon amour*. You have to know that some of these people on those social media platforms are just, how do you say *fou* in English, *crazy* enough to kill someone, in this case, Burt Roop, to keep the Princess of Death legend alive. If you relocated and *no one* died, it would be over."

I was stunned by her statement, and yet, I couldn't deny that it was possible. I had to verbalize it to make sure I was getting it right. "And if Jacob Mabry was indiscreet enough to post a social media page like that one, with how many people did he share that he was collecting up firearms for the sheriff's department to be disposed of? He seems like the kind of guy who needs constant kudos from those around him. That's typical behavior of people with very low self-esteem." Another thing suddenly struck me. "Oh, my God. Just like Tara and Annika's deaths, I was indirectly responsible for Burt's death also."

Sabine spoke in soft, soothing tones. "I didn't mean that, *cherie*. You are not responsible for what crazy people do. Even indirectly, any more than you were responsible for the deaths of your teammates. I know you will always feel responsible, but you weren't."

I started to argue, but deep inside, I knew she was right. I was suddenly tired, full of lobster, and ready to get out of there.

"Okay, guys, I think we have done everything we can do for tonight. So, Mark, you're going to request the DashCam from Jacob Mabry's cruiser on Monday morning?"

He nodded.

I did my best to muster a smile as I stood to leave. "I'll see you guys on Wednesday or sooner."

Sabine said, "I hope sooner, *ma belle*." I think she knew it probably wouldn't be unless I came up with something that would change how we would approach the preliminary hearing.

#

The aroma of chocolate chip cookies again wafted through the elevator as I took it up to the apartment. I was happy to be home. It was funny seeing my two roomies dressed in corny aprons when I walked in. Until I met Wanda, I didn't think anyone actually bought those aprons. Hers said, 'Kiss the Cook', and Tea's said, 'I Cook for Wine.' They were just finishing their third batch of cookies, so it looked like the evening had been a success.

I mustered up more enthusiasm than I thought I'd be able to. "It smells great all the way down to the parking lot."

They both looked proud as they sipped on red wine.

Wanda spoke up. "It was a labor of love. Now we all have to gain at least five pounds eating them."

I laughed, "Yeah, I'll probably gain ten." I groaned. "Well, we can take a bunch to work on Monday. Did you guys have fun?"

Tea chimed in, "Yeah, we both decided we've sworn off men for the foreseeable future."

I mouthed, "Thank you," to Wanda, while Tea was looking the other way. Then I said, "I'm going to join your sorority. I've had it with men too."

The three of us high-fived.

Since they were still baking, I took the opportunity to go to bed. I had been tired all week, and this was a great time to catch up on my sleep with nothing to wake up early for tomorrow, which was finally Saturday.

Chapter 29

I awoke as the sun peaked through the curtains. It was barely eight o'clock Saturday morning. I could probably sleep for another couple of hours, but I felt alive and refreshed. I hadn't woken up at all during the night and had no dreams, that I remembered anyway.

It seemed like all I could think about these days was the case. I suppose it was really Jason's, but it didn't feel that way. It felt like it was my case, either now or would be later once Mark won Jason's case. I was tempted to go back to the sheriff's department, but I thought they might start to consider me a stalker.

I realized that the part of my personality that tended to be obsessive was taking over. I had set up an appointment with a new therapist, Rachel, but we weren't connecting until next week. If we were meeting today, she would probably suggest that I focus on something else—call a friend, take a bike ride, go for a run, or just do something different.

I grabbed my phone and dialed Margo. She answered after one ring. "Miranda, it's about time you called me. I thought you'd dropped off the face of the earth."

I smiled. It was so good to hear her voice and her scolding me for this, that, or the other thing. "You can always call me, too, you know." I wished I could see her. Hearing her voice made me ache to see her. "Are you in Long Beach?"

Margo laughed, "You're not going to believe it. I'm back in Monterey, looking at houses. A couple of new ones hit the market, and I couldn't resist." She fumbled with some kind of paper. "Why don't you join me for lunch at the Sandbar and Grill. I've got a reservation for lunch. I'm meeting a realtor there at two, so I'll have a couple of hours to talk."

I couldn't believe it. "Oh, my, that's music to my ears. I need a break. I'll be there."

At some point, I would have to address the fact that I had left my motorcycle at Jason's, but I had a car, so that would do for now. And while it was closer to Monterey from Coyote Lake, it wasn't a bad drive from Santa Clara on a Saturday morning.

I was pulling into the restaurant parking lot by noon. I had taken the Cupertino route to avoid going past Gilroy and Jason's house.

Margo was already seated at a table overlooking the marina when I arrived. We hugged. She looked me up and down. "What have you been doing with yourself? You look like you haven't slept in weeks."

I agreed. "I am a little stressed."

She *tsked* me. "You should have brought the other two so we could take some of that stress from you."

I smiled. "I thought about it, but Wanda's working, and I figured Lyanne would have something going, either with the TV station or with the family."

She grabbed my hands. "Truth be known, I'm happy just to see you anyway. You'll always be my special friend."

I was touched. "You'll always be my special friend too, Margo. I'm so glad you're moving. We're going to be neighbors, practically."

She suddenly turned serious. "So, what has you so stressed out, my Miranda? And what can I do to help?"

I tried to smile but failed. "I've been working on this case day and night, and I feel like I'm so close. You know they arrested Jason for the murder, and I know he didn't do it. And, oh, by the way, we broke up, and I moved out."

She practically jumped out of her chair. "What? When did this happen?"

I started thinking back. It had only been a few weeks since Burt's death, and since we had all met down here to work on the case. "Well, right after you and I spoke, just after they arrested Jason, the Indian woman who we had determined was Chenoa, came to my door. She dropped a bomb. She had been with Jason and would have married him, but the tribe's elders broke them up. But she also admitted that she and Jason had been in nearly daily contact since their breakup and that she still loved him."

Her mouth dropped. "Small world, right?"

I nodded. "So, I asked him about it, and he didn't deny having feelings for her and admitted that he had hidden their continued communications, so I broke it off."

She was sorting it out in her mind. "But he wasn't seeing her any longer, right?"

I agreed, "No."

She put her hand on my arm. "I get it, Miranda. He hurt you, and he *was* wrong; just don't throw the baby out with the bathwater."

I was getting frustrated with women who didn't seem to understand. "He *lied* to me about *another woman* for at least two years. What else is he lying to me about? Or what else is he going to lie to me about in the future? I can't trust him, at least not right now."

She nodded, seeing that we were getting nowhere on the topic of relationships. "So, how's the sleuthing going? I'm assuming that's why you're here."

"Yes, it's crazy. Just when I think I'm getting close, I get thrown a curveball. I thought a pair of fresh eyes and ears might help, plus, I've missed you."

She pulled her ears out like Dumbo. "I'm all ears."

I laughed. "Okay, here's what I have. Burt Roop was murdered between sunset on Saturday and 4 a.m. on Sunday."

"Hold it a minute." She held up a hand like a stop sign. "Let me find my notebook and a pen." She scrabbled around in her oversized purse for a moment and then pulled them out, holding them up like prizes. "Carry on."

I waited a second for her to find a blank page and hold her pen poised over it. "Right. He left the Hot Springs with Chenoa around sunset with the intent of collecting some stolen firearms that he was going to provide to the sheriff's department. Somehow, he ended up getting shot with one of them, one registered in Jason's name. In the meantime, the Princess of Death movement online has heated up again under that name of 'Lock Her Up.' Look it up. It's precious."

She took notes and looked up for me to continue.

I tried to remember everything I could. "There's this cop in the sheriff's office that confuses and worries me. He's involved in this 'Lock Her Up' site and spent a lot of time interviewing witnesses about Jason, but mostly asking questions about me. He's also the one who seemed to know a lot about me when I called 911 when I found the body, more than he could find out in the time it took him to respond to the call."

She smiled. "Maybe he's sweet on you, Miranda."

I gagged. "You're not the first person to have suggested that. That's gross." I remembered Sabine's comment. "Do you think it's possible that somebody murdered Burt Roop because I moved to Coyote Lake?"

She took my hand. "Let's take a step back for a minute. Maybe we're making this more complicated than it needs to be. Let's face it, more often than not, murder is about relationships. I know it's possible someone would kill Burt Roop just to keep the string of Miranda-related Princess of Death killings alive, but how likely is that, really?"

I felt foolish. "Not very?"

She talked to me like I was four. "Who was Burt Roop having relationship issues with? Do you know? Maybe you need to talk to Sally again."

I protested, "She was so solid the last time we talked. I was convinced she had nothing to do with it."

She pressed me. "But the first time, she almost chased you off the property, and that was when she didn't have time to rehearse."

I shook my head. "I don't know, Margo."

She let up a little. "Well, maybe it had nothing to do with Sally, but just don't count her out. But what about other people he had relationships with? Granted, I have no idea how to find those people, but he knows more people than you've talked to, I'm sure."

I thought back. "I keep thinking back, too, to something Burt said to me just before we parted. He knew who started the fire at the Hot Springs back in 1980, and he was going to get them. Then, when I talked to Sally about that, she remembered a kid who had been arrested and released for lack of evidence: Tommy Pearson. I guess we've got to consider him a suspect."

Margo nodded. "I agree."

I looked at the menu while we talked. "My problem is that the preliminary hearing is next week, and I'd really like to have enough evidence not to have to take this to trial."

She stared me down. "Whoa, little girl. Is that you or Mark that wants that outcome?"

I thought for a minute. "Well, it's not to my advantage for him to be acquitted since I'm probably the next candidate."

She nodded. "Exactly, and don't forget that."

We ordered salmon salads to complement our bottle of Pinot Noir.

I absorbed what she said after we spent some time catching up about other things in our lives. "So when all is said and done, you think it's Sally or someone else that he had a close personal relationship with."

She nodded as our food arrived. "I would suggest heading home through Coyote Lake and seeing what's up with Sally. She mentioned to you that she wanted to pursue a career in private investigation, right?"

I responded, "Yes, she did."

She set her pen and notebook aside and dug into her salad. "So see if she's worth her salt. Maybe she's not involved in the murder at all, but if she's not, she's the closest person to it and the most likely to solve it if she takes the time to do so."

I looked at Margo with awe. "Just how do you know so much? I lie awake at night and can't think of half the stuff you come up with during lunch."

She laughed, "Hey, I didn't come from nothing to become the Princess of Monserrat because I'm dumb."

I nearly choked on my salmon. "You're hilarious." We spent the better part of an hour on girl talk. She and I always had a great time together, and I couldn't wait until she moved permanently. We hugged and said our 'Good-byes,' and I was back on the road.

It only took me forty minutes to get to Angie's house, where Sally was a houseguest. Angie welcomed me with open arms. "Miranda, you have made my life so much more exciting these past few days. To what do I owe the pleasure?"

I smiled. "Nice to see you too, Angie. Is Sally around?"

Angie led me to the dining room, where she and Sally were working on a jigsaw puzzle.

Sally seemed surprised for a second to be seeing me so soon but recovered quickly. "Miranda, good to see you. Hope you have good news." She started to get up but I waved her back into her seat. Just watching her exhausted me.

I sat with them at the dining room table. I didn't waste any time explaining why I was there. "I'm running into a lot of dead ends in the investigation. Can you think of anyone else that Burt was having issues with? Someone he'd had a relationship with for a long time, maybe?" I was thinking about Tommy Pearson, but I wanted her to bring up the name.

Angie excused herself to go wash dishes and give us some privacy.

Sally took a sip of what appeared to be cold coffee. "No one comes to mind. I'm sure those Indians are involved. I don't trust that Chenoa."

This wasn't going to be as easy as I'd hoped. "I don't know, Sally. Burt was bending over backward to help those people. The fact that he volunteered to be the go-between in the firearm exchange doesn't show any bad blood."

Sally bit her lip. "How 'bout the sheriff? Maybe they got a bad egg and he took guns for himself."

I thought for a minute. "We are requesting the DashCam from the police car just in case, but it's unlikely." I looked her in the eye. "Sally, can you think of anyone that we haven't talked about who might have wanted to harm Burt? Someone with a long-standing grudge, someone he got into a bar fight with, someone he beat in a football game in high school?"

Sally gave me a blank stare. "Got me, Miranda. He'd tell me what he wanted me to know. But if he thought something could harm me, he would keep it from me like a fort. If you're talking about Tommy Pearson, if he got the chance Burt would've down and made him pay for burning down the hotel. He woulda done it in a heartbeat. But after all this time, that don't seem likely."

Relieved that she brought the name up herself and dismissed the possibility, I clicked a pen sitting on the table in front of me. "You're probably right."

Sally leaned on her elbow. "He hadn't brought up Tommy to me in years. But Burt was funny that way."

I spoke just above a whisper. "But anything like that is just what I'm talking about. Did Burt keep notes about any of this stuff, who he suspected of various activities around the Hot Springs, who he had talked to?"

She smiled. "Burt was always taking notes. Figuring them out is a whole different animal. But I'd go through everything I have if you thought we could find his killer."

I felt like we might be on to something and, despite Margo's suspicions, I still believed that Sally was innocent. I needed to believe that for my plan to use her assistance to work, so I hoped my sixth sense was right.

I got up to leave. "It would be helpful if you could look through Burt's notes. I'll call you later in the week to see if you unearth anything. We still have a preliminary hearing to get through on Wednesday, but worst-case scenario, they decide that Jason goes to trial. That doesn't mean that we won't win it."

She hugged me on the way out the door. "Wish me luck looking for new suspects. I hope this isn't a wild goose chase."

I reassured her. "I'm pretty sure it's not."

Chapter 30

Wanda and Tea were making brownies and chocolate chip cookie squares when I arrived around seven on Saturday evening. Wanda must have taken me literally to keep Tea busy every second I was gone, and I appreciated that she had followed through. I had half-expected Tea to be back with Mike by the time I returned.

I rushed into the kitchen to join in the fun. "I hope I can have some even though I didn't help."

Tea winked at Wanda. "Um, I don't know. We might not have enough," eying the stacks of baked goods that it would have taken an army to eat.

I pouted. "Just one?"

Wanda rolled her eyes. "Miranda, please. Begging doesn't become you or any smart and strong woman."

I could see that she had been working with Tea on strong woman values, and I needed to step up to the table. "You're right, Wanda. I demand a brownie *and* a chocolate chip square."

Wanda high-fived me. "Exactly. We women deserve far more than we ever ask for or expect, and that is going to change today." Wanda thought for a second and asked me, "So what's new in the case? Anything hopeful that will get the judge to drop the charges at the preliminary hearing?"

I wasn't sure how much to share since Sally seemed to be grasping at straws other than the death threats from some anonymous party. "I had another conversation with Sally, and I'm working on some angles. I don't think we'll have anything solid enough to convince a judge to drop the charges besides the fact that Jason's gun was stolen, and he didn't even have access to it at the time of the killing. That would be enough for some judges, but unfortunately, it's hearsay because we hadn't actually reported them stolen."

She checked the cookies in the oven. "So you haven't figured out who did it yet?"

I shook my head. "In a word, no. But did I tell you Sally's been receiving death threats? She was feeling so unsafe; she moved into her neighbor Angie's house temporarily."

She scratched her head. "How long has that been going on?"

I thought for a second. "Pretty much since Burt's death."

She shook her head. "And she didn't think to mention it until today?"

"No, she told me a couple of days ago and that's when I suggested she stay with Angie for a while. There's been a lot going on and I forgot to tell you. I just wish I could figure this out once and for all."

She smiled. "Well, it's not for lack of trying. I'd think you still had feelings for Jason, the way you're putting yourself out there to defend him."

I chuckled. "To be honest, I feel more like I'm defending myself. It's absurd that Jason was even charged. But the 'Lock her up' movement online stands ready to make sure I'm next in line when he gets acquitted. It's so nice to know that the Princess of Death is alive and well and living in Santa Clara."

We spent the rest of the evening baking and eating decadent treats. I was starting to realize how enjoyable life could be without a man. I just felt like I could be myself and didn't have to live up to anyone else's idea of who I *should* be. My attitude on that subject had changed considerably in the last few weeks.

#

We finally fell into bed after midnight and slept well past mid-morning. It was noon before the three of us were assembled around the kitchen table. I sat quietly with a cup of steaming coffee in front of me. I kept thinking about the details of the Burt Roop case, wondering what I was missing. Someone somewhere knew the truth. I just needed to find them. The killer alone might be the sole person with this knowledge.

Tea sat at my right. She kept glancing at me, not saying anything. Finally, she spoke. "Miranda, I know this case is driving you crazy. I'm younger than just about everyone you know. I wonder if I could give you a different perspective."

Wanda nodded. "Hey, not a bad idea. A fresh perspective is always a good idea. You keep running pretty much the same stuff past the same people and getting similar answers. And maybe there's some new stuff I haven't heard either since our girls' weekend in Monterey."

I figured it was worth a try, although I was getting tired of giving out the details. I asked Tea, "Have you heard anything about the case at all? Or do you want me to start from the beginning?"

She laughed. "It's hard to spend any time around you without picking up dribs and drabs, but why don't you start from the beginning so that I can get the whole picture."

I settled in my chair. "Okay. Down in Coyote Lake, where Jason and I were living, a guy named Burt Roop, a neighbor of ours, was killed, his body left near a hiking trail in the nearby Coe Park. Burt's family operated the Gilroy Hot Springs, a few miles from our house, off and on since the 1800s. At one time in the last part of the 1800s and early 1900s, they were at the center of a resort for the rich and famous from both San Francisco and Los Angeles. The facilities had fallen into disrepair since the resort hotel burned down on the Fourth of July of 1980, and it has not been open to the public since then.

"There are several local American Indian tribes who have been attempting to take control of the Hot Springs for several decades. Burt has been fending off these subversive attacks on the springs by various means and, so far, has been successful. Several weeks ago, Indian renegades stole several weapons from various households in the Coyote Lake area, including mine and Jason's. Through Chenoa, a local American Indian Princess, it was communicated to Burt that the tribe was in possession of these weapons. In exchange for access to the Hot Springs, they were willing to turn them in to the sheriff's department through Burt.

"Burt arranged to meet with Chenoa, who coincidentally happened to be Jason's ex-girlfriend with whom he had been communicating by text and email, without my knowledge for the past two years. She was going to deliver the firearms to Burt, and he would deliver them to the sheriff's department. This was to happen on Saturday evening. He was seen was with Chenoa around sunset. The next time he was seen was around four a.m., dead. Shot in the back of the head. Jason was arrested because a bullet from one of his stolen guns was used to kill Burt."

I paused. "That's pretty much it. Any questions before you offer a solution, Sherlock?"

"So, something happened either during or after the gun exchange. Do I have that much right?"

I smiled. "Yes, very good. Thanks for paying attention to a story I am getting tired of telling. Let me tell you some of the suspects we've had so far and pretty much eliminated. Burt is married to a very nice, if not a touch jealous, woman named Sally. Because of her jealous tendencies, we initially suspected her. Having met with her several times since Burt's death, she seems well-grounded and seems to have loved him very much. My gut says that her devotion to Burt trumps her periodic bouts with jealousy."

I thought about other suspects. "We also thought it might have been Chenoa or some of the other Native Americans in the area. But that didn't seem to make sense because Burt was actually providing them with something they wanted through this firearm exchange."

I laughed. "Oh, I forgot my favorite part. There are also about two thousand people on an internet page called 'Lock Her Up' who believe that I'm responsible for his death. I thought they might have killed Burt to keep my Princess of Death persona alive, but that seems a little farfetched even to me."

Tea asked, "Had Burt lived in that area his whole life?"

I responded. "Yes, he's been there since birth."

She nodded. "Then that gave him a long time to collect enemies. Remember that guy you rejected in junior high who never go over it?"

I grinned at the memory. "I forgot I told you that story. Yes, but he had good reason to hate me because I called him 'Larry Lepper' and it stuck with him for life."

She acknowledged the fact. "Well, maybe there's someone in Burt's past who has a similar story."

I agreed. "Yes, but if that's the case, how would we ever know, other than through random luck?"

"My point is you can never know someone's complete past. I think you should be working equally as hard to discredit the prosecution's case instead of just trying to solve the case yourself."

I agreed. "You make a good point. But in the process of trying to find a motive for the real killer, it becomes more and more obvious that Jason didn't have one." I thought for a minute. "So, based on what I told you so far, do you think any of our initial suspects did it?"

She shook her head. "Not that I can see unless there's a lot of other supporting information that you didn't share." She laughed, "You can never completely eliminate the jealous wife as a suspect. If you were to find out that Burt had been cheating and that she found him in bed with another woman, a bullet in the back of the head would be fully expected and deserved."

Wanda listened with interest. "This case is exhausting. Have you talked to Sally Roop since we last spoke?" I wondered. "Yes, we talked yesterday."

She held her coffee mug in the air and pointed at me with her other hand, jabbing at me as she spoke. "She knew Burt better than anyone. She knew his friends and his enemies. I wonder if there are things she knows that she doesn't even realize."

I gently swatted at her pointing finger and pushed it down to the table. "I'm one step ahead of you. She and I talked, and she acknowledged that he kept volumes of notes about people, places, and things that she would review. He had a long past in Coyote Lake and had been assigned to protect the Hot Springs since 1980 when the resort hotel burned down. Oh yeah, I almost forgot the newest suspect. It seemed that a kid named Tommy Pearson was arrested for burning down the hotel back in 1980 but was released for lack of evidence. His family was well-connected, and Burt was convinced that he did it, despite his acquittal, and vowed to make the change stick. I don't even know if there is a statute of limitations on arson. Do you, Wanda?"

She had her laptop in front of her and typed in a few words. "According to this, there is no statute of limitations for felony arson. The hotel fire qualified as a felony arson due to the size and value of the structure. So, if Burt had some sort of indisputable proof and was threatening to prosecute this Tommy Pearson, he might have put himself in harm's way."

Tea nodded. "Well, I don't have anything more based on what you guys told me. Sorry."

I said, "Thanks for assisting, Tea. Another set of eyes and ears are always helps." I focused on Wanda. "Do you have any other ideas?"

She leaned back in her chair and looked at the ceiling. "You know, there is one more person you should touch base with, Lyanne. She's got a good head on her shoulders and was the only one of us who knew anything about the Native Americans' underground activities in this area. I wonder if she's got any history on the Hot Springs that she hasn't shared."

I agreed. "Let's call her right now."

I dialed her number. She answered on the first ring and I put her on speaker. "Miranda, is everything okay?"

I laughed. "Yes, but thanks for thinking I would only reach out to you if I were dying."

She chuckled. "I didn't exactly mean it that way. Anyway, what can I do for you?

I spent the next ten minutes explaining everything that had come up and concepts and suspects who had been rejected since the four of us met in Monterey.

She sounded impressed. "Wow, you guys haven't stopped moving since we were together. I feel kind of guilty."

I laughed. "We do understand that you have to maintain your standing as one of the top news reporters on the West coast day in and day out."

She sounded like she was smiling. "Thank you, Miranda. It's nice to be on the same team."

I didn't want to push but valued her input. "So, Lyanne, can you think of any other angles we should be pursuing? You've been reporting around here for a while. Is there anything you've ever reported about the Gilroy Hot Springs that comes to mind in the context of this case?"

She hesitated. "I'm going to have to check out my records. It sounds familiar, but it's not ringing a bell right now. I put some feelers out after I got back from the weekend. I'll give them a call to see if they came up with anything."

I was glad we called. "Thanks so much, Lyanne. We hope to see you again soon." Wanda yelled. "Bye, Lyanne." She laughed. "Bye, Wanda." She hung up.

Tea asked in amazement, "Wow, that was really Lyanne Melendez from TV?"

I smiled. "Yes, Tea, you'd be surprised who we know."

Chapter 31

Monday and Tuesday flew by, and suddenly Sabine and I were in the gallery of the court of Judge Thomas Wheatfield again. Much of the scene was déjà vu from the arraignment, although the gallery was nearly full now compared to half full then.

I recognized some of the neighbors I had interviewed and, of course, Sally Roop, who was flanked by them. She waved at me from her seat, which was about three-quarters of the way back. It seemed odd to be working for the defense in the murder of her husband when I felt like we were becoming good friends.

It was five minutes before the hearing officially started, and the prosecution was still getting organized, with several ADA's assisting the DA with the case. It wasn't surprising that the DA was in first chair today since this was a murder trial.

A few minutes later, Mark and Jason filed in. They both looked relaxed and confident, which was a look I hadn't mastered when I went to court as a defendant. I sincerely hoped I didn't have to sit in that chair again any time soon.

I stared at Jason's back, wondering how I had fallen out of love with him that quickly and if I would ever love him again. Love was a delicate and precious feeling.

As I pondered that thought, the judge came in through the back door. The bailiff announced him. "All rise. The Honorable Judge Thomas Wheatfield is now presiding over this court." His honor climbed up to his chair behind the raised bench, eyed the packed courtroom, and sat down.

"You may be seated."

All eyes were on the judge as he addressed us. "Ladies and gentlemen, today, we will be determining if the case of the United States versus Jason Wall will go to trial. It will be the prosecutor's responsibility to make the case that they have sufficient evidence to support the charge. This can be done in several ways: physical evidence such as DNA, factual evidence such as firearm registration and forensics, eyewitness evidence, and circumstantial evidence.

"It will be the defense team's job to convince the court that there is insufficient evidence to take the case any further. This may be because of insufficient physical or factual evidence, or the eyewitness or circumstantial evidence lacks credibility."

He directed his attention to the prosecution. "Mr. Prosecutor, your opening statement, please."

The DA stood and directed his comments to the judge. "Your honor, this is an open and shut case. We have a murder weapon registered to the defendant. We have the defendant's DNA on the murder weapon. And we have the defendant's DNA on the spent shell that was used to strike down the victim in cold blood. We have a video of an assailant approximately the size and weight of the defendant carrying the victim up a trail in Coe Park, and coincidentally, the defendant's girlfriend found the victim there just a few hours later."

The judge responded, "Thank you for the brief statement." Then he directed his attention to Mark. "Mr. Peterson, your statement?"

Mark stood up and wasted no time. "Your honor, this is the most ridiculous murder case I have ever heard of. There has been no motive identified by the prosecution. It is well known that several of the defendant's firearms had recently been stolen, and of course, his DNA was on his own weapon and ammunition. And, as far as his girlfriend finding the body, she just happened to be running in Coe Park that day."

The judge pointed to the prosecution. "Do you have any response to these serious allegations?"

The prosecutor stood up. "Your honor. According to our records, the firearm in question was never reported stolen until last week. That hardly constitutes a valid report of a stolen weapon, more like a desperate attempt to distance oneself from a murder weapon. I must give the defendant kudos for creativity, though."

The judge nodded in acknowledgment of the prosecutor's statements without asking for anything further from Mark, which was not a good sign. He then said, "Your first witness, Mr. Prosecutor."

The prosecutor remained standing. "I call Sally Roop."

That didn't seem like a good sign. She never told me that she was a witness for the prosecution. I watched her approach the witness stand carrying a briefcase and get sworn in. She squeezed uncomfortably into the witness chair. Beads of perspiration rolled down from her forehead and dripped onto her blouse, then disappeared into a swirl of eighties psychedelic colors.

Sabine whispered to me. "What is she doing up there?"

I whispered back, "Darned if I know. I sort of thought she was on our team."

The DA approached the witness stand. "Mrs. Roop, I am very sorry for your loss."

She half-smiled. "Thank you. You can call me Sally."

He continued. "Okay, Sally, then. When did you learn about the unfortunate and untimely demise of your loving husband, Burt?"

She thought back. "It was on Sunday morning, the seventeenth. I'd been worried sick all night because he didn't come home. I knew something was wrong, and the call I got from the sheriff told it all." Tears joined the drops of perspiration rolling down onto her blouse.

The DA moved a box of tissues toward her then he spoke in a very calm and soothing voice like Mark liked to use. "Did you have any idea who did this?"

She spoke up. "No, sir. Everyone loved Burt." Then she corrected herself. "Well, everyone but the Indians in the canyon." I wondered what the angle was here. I was still taken by surprise by the fact that she'd never told me she was testifying.

"So was there anyone in particular in the tribes who didn't get along with Burt?"

She practically jumped out of her seat. "Oh, yeah. Chenoa Gray." She made air quotes as she added, "Princess of Earth and Water."

The DA seemed confused. "And, of course, not everyone in the world can get along all the time, but why is Burt's relationship with Ms. Gray relevant to this case?"

She sneered at him. "Because him and Chenoa were *lovers*. He would do anything for her."

That comment tripled the size of the pit in my stomach. She never, ever mentioned that little fact to me.

Mark and Jason were whispering at the defense table. This was a curveball even I didn't see coming, but I hoped we had talked all this out enough that Mark could go after her.

The DA continued. "So your testimony is that the defendant and Chenoa Gray had an active relationship. How can you be so sure?"

Sally removed a few papers from the briefcase she'd carried in. "I went through Burt's notes and found this dated March 25, 2011. "Found IP and EX BF in CR at HS. I told them both to go. He always wrote in code, but I know what that means. Found Indian Princess with her ex-boyfriend in a changing room at the Gilroy Hot Springs. You get the rest."

I gasped. While this was open to interpretation. I was pretty sure she was right in hers. I couldn't help but believe that Sally had unearthed these notes because of my prodding for her to review them. Life could be very ironic. I glared at the back of Jason's head, looking for a clue as to whether or not this was true. The back and forth between him and Mark told the story.

Sabine took my hand. She whispered, "I love you."

I replied, "I love you too." I watched, even though I was in shock.

The DA continued his questioning. "So, Sally, what do you believe happened the night Burt was killed?"

She started the story I supposed she believed to be true. "Burt and Chenoa left the Hot Springs together at around sunset on the sixteenth so she could get the stolen guns that he was gonna take to the sheriff. But it didn't happen. Someone stopped them. Chenoa and Jason planned it all. During a fight over the guns, Chenoa ran away with the weapons, and Jason shot and killed Burt. Later, he hauled the body halfway up the trail in Coe Park, and he went home."

This was all so unbelievable. I was so confused because it was my understanding that the guns had been turned in to the sheriff's department, which made this story completely bogus. And since the gun that killed Burt was registered in Jason's name, they could have included that part in the story and still had him with his own gun. Someone wasn't a very good liar. I hoped Mark picked up on it.

The judge asked Mark if he had a cross-examination of the witness.

Mark stood up. "I do, your honor." He approached the witness bench. "Sally, it's so nice to meet you after everything Miranda has told me about you."

She blushed. "Nice to meet you too."

Mark started slowly as usual. "Let's go back to your interpretation of Burt's code. Was there a key in the document or any way to assist in the interpretation?"

She shook her head, "No, but I've known Burt a long time, almost forever, so I just know."

He nodded. "So there is no other possible interpretation? Like Found Inpatient with Excellent Black Fly in Crater at High School. Let's face it. There are millions of possibilities. So, I don't expect the court to buy the one that implicates my client just because that works for you."

Her mouth dropped open. She gasped and craned her neck to look at the judge who ignored her. Her beady little eyes squinted at Mark as she waited for the next bombshell to drop.

"But let's continue with your firearm theory," he said, "most of which I believe you stole from my assistant, Miranda. However, the part where they are ambushed by Jason and Burt is killed makes no sense. Let me tell you why. The guns were actually turned in to the sheriff's department. It's documented in their records and was recorded on a DashCAM on the police cruiser. So while you have demonstrated a vivid imagination, I do not see any facts to back up your story. Thank you." He sat down.

Sally's mouth clamped in anger as her face turned dangerously red.

The gallery exploded in chatter until the judge glared at them and banged his gavel several times. They immediately quieted. He continued with the hearing. "Mr. DA, do you have any more witnesses?"

The clerk told Sally she was excused and she lumbered from the witness box across the room, glaring at Mark the whole time until she passed through the gate that separated the gallery.

The DA stood again. "Yes, your honor. I call Mr. Jacob Mabry of the Santa Clara Sheriff's Department and lead investigator on the case."

I whispered to Sabine, "This cannot be good."

Mabry took his time getting to the stand, enjoying the spotlight, leading me further to believe there was something wrong with this guy. He swaggered slowly so that we could observe his spit shined shoes and the creases ironed into his uniform pantlegs. He must have spent an hour in the mirror before court this morning. I wanted to gag.

The DA began his questioning after Mabry was sworn in. "The defense has brought into question whether the defendant had a motive in this case. It's my understanding that you have taken on motive as your primary focus."

Jacob seemed to have been waiting for this moment on the stand and was poised and ready. "Thank you, Mr. Prosecutor, and Your Honor for the opportunity to serve."

They both acknowledged him with a nod.

He continued with intense concentration. "The concept of motive was what bothered me most about this case. I asked myself, why would an intelligent and successful young man like Jason Wall kill a neighbor he barely knew in passing? And as far as anyone could tell, including Sally, they had never had a cross word. They weren't best buddies, but we all have a neighbor like them. We wave when we're mowing the lawn; he might come over with jumper cables when the car battery dies, stuff like that."

He hesitated. You could hear a pin drop in the courtroom, and he glanced directly at me. I felt like I was going to throw up. "Then the little coincidences started creeping in," he said. "Was it a coincidence that his girlfriend, Miranda Marquette, had just moved in a few months earlier? Was it a coincidence that she had just met Burt Roop less than twenty-four hours before his death? Was it a coincidence that she miraculously *found* his body?"

I looked over at Sabine, whose anger was written all over her red face. I'd never seen her like that. She whispered to me, "We will take this guy down."

I took her hand and whispered back, "Welcome to my life. I'm just glad you're here."

Once the murmur in the gallery died down, he said, "I know that Miranda is not on trial here, and I have no doubt she won't be charged or convicted in this crime. What I do know, though, is that she influenced Jason Wall to kill Burt Roop in cold blood. As an officer of the court, I don't believe in coincidence. You shouldn't either."

He was done. It amazed me what passed these days for fact when he had presented nothing more than opinion and hearsay. I was interested to see how the judge would react. He said nothing other than to pass the witness on to Mark.

Mark approached the stand. I was happy that we had spent so much time reviewing this information. He was as much of an expert as I was. Sometimes, it felt like we went over things too much, but now I knew why. He began quietly as he always does. "Good morning, Jacob."

He responded politely, "Good morning, Mr. Peterson."

He smiled. "Call me Mark."

He repeated, "Mark then" Mark stood close to the witness stand. "You are a man of the law, correct?"

Jacob responded. "Yes, definitely."

Mark kept his interrogation conversational. "So, as a lawman, you deal in facts, correct?"

He nodded. "It's all about facts."

Mark's posture and tone shifted. His back straightened and he took a step back from the witness stand. "Okay. I know you weren't privy to any conversations between Jason Wall and Miranda Marquette." He turned to scan the courtroom before continuing. "I'm trying to figure out just where the facts are here. You refer to Miranda and Burt meeting the day before he died. You're right. In fact, they did meet that day *and* developed a quick friendship, to the point that they talked for nearly four hours. And I can't tell you why whoever killed Burt dumped the body in Coe Park, but she was merely running up a trail that's utilized by thousands of runners and mountain bikers annually. So, let's stick to the facts." He whirled around and faced Mabry. "Okay, Jacob?"

I wondered if Mark was going to hit Jacob with his obsession with me and his tie to the 'Lock her up' page or if he was going to save that for the trial if he needed it.

It didn't take long to find out. "On a similar topic, let's talk about your involvement with this page, Lock Her Up." He had a projector hooked up to a laptop. I didn't see that coming, but I was jumping for joy. He had the screen placed perfectly so that Jacob, the judge, the DA, and the gallery could see it clearly. Mark scrolled through the website until he reached the particulars of the site including the creator's identity which was Santa Clara County Sheriff's Deputy Jacob Mabry. "Could you describe just what this is all about?"

Jacob's bravado immediately became embarrassment as he was exposed to the court, his co-workers, the press, and the gallery. I think the fact that I was sitting there glaring at him even had an impact because, bottom line, he was a coward hiding behind a keyboard. He spoke flatly and quietly as he described his handiwork. "Some of us have been following Ms. Marquette for several years because death seems to follow her around. While she had never been convicted in a court of law, she was arrested for one of the murders, and there has been speculation that she was involved in some or all of the others."

Mark had him just where he wanted him. "May I be the first to say what other people must be thinking. You are a disgrace to the court and to the legal system—shame on you for abusing your law enforcement position to promote this internet garbage. I plan on using this as a prime example when I go to the legislature to beg them to put laws in place to address this travesty of justice that is allowed to exist simply because someone as twisted and depraved as yourself gets off on lies and deception." He approached Jacob, and I thought he was going to spit on him for a second, but he turned and went back to the defense table and sat down. I wanted to run up and kiss him.

The judge addressed the prosecutor. "Do you have any further witnesses at this time, Mr. DA?"

He responded. "No, your honor."

He addressed Mark. "Mr. Peterson, do you have anything further?"

Mark stood up. "Your honor, based on what we have seen here today, I respectfully request that all charges against my client be dismissed."

The judge hesitated, then responded, "Mr. Peterson, I understand and, to a large degree, concur with your request. However, I cannot ignore the ballistic, DNA, and forensic evidence in this case. It will go to trial. Court is dismissed."

Chapter 32

I was disappointed with the outcome of the hearing but not surprised. Hard evidence was the direction most courts went these days, even though the killing defied logic. I believed the judge was responding to public pressure as much as anything.

Sabine, Mark, and I went out for coffee afterward. It was kind of ironic that I was working as hard as I was to get Jason acquitted when I could barely stand to be in his presence. I hugged Mark. "Thank you so much for taking on that Mabry thug. I think he should be fired."

Mark laughed. "If looks could kill, he'd be dead. And I'm talking about the prosecution, some of his co-workers, and his boss, Tina Bright. She looked not only embarrassed but angry. I wouldn't want to be in his shoes when he tries to return to work."

I patted him on the back. "That was brilliant to have the technology at your fingertips in case you needed it. Sorry, it wasn't able to get you out of a trial, but that's always a long shot."

He nodded. "I figured with the registered weapon and the DNA, and the fact that they likely have no other suspects, they weren't dropping the charges. The press would have the judge's head."

Sabine sipped her coffee quietly. "I was disappointed with your friend Sally. But tell me, do you think her interpretation of Burt's code was correct?"

I wished I could lie, but I couldn't. "Yes, I do. And the bad thing is that it might not even be Jason. Chenoa may have ten exes for all I know. That is something I'm going to have to ask Jason about at some point." They both looked at me with expectation. "Okay, let's clear the air. I know I'm angry with him right now and that I've moved out. I don't know if that means just now or forever. He's a sweet man and made me very happy when we were together. But I can't stand to be lied to. I have a lot of sorting out to do, so I'm glad to do it away from him. It's a lot easier than trying to live with him every day."

We all drank our coffee in silence for a few minutes.

I thought about what Sabine said. "I was disappointed with Sally, too, though I understand where she was coming from. She needs closure, and so if she had to throw Jason under the bus to make that happen, at least she didn't throw me under too. I still think there's a chance she can lead me to the real killer. She's got Burt's notes, and I'll bet she hasn't even scratched the surface in reviewing them."

Sabine agreed. "I don't know who else there is to help solve this thing. There's a good chance that Burt knew he was in some kind of danger and didn't want Sally to know. That seems to be the kind of relationship they had. It was sweet in a way but makes it hard to solve a murder."

I turned to Mark. "How long do you think we have until the trial?"

He pulled out his phone to look at his calendar. "If I were a betting man, I'd say around four weeks. I doubt it will be any sooner, and it could be later, but that's my guess. I know they don't want this to drag out any longer than it has to. I guess that once the press gets hold of the details from today's hearing, the court will want to get this case closed even sooner." Mark's phone buzzed, and he laughed. "Well, look at that. Trial date is set for exactly four weeks from now."

Knowing there was no time like the present, I decided to drive to Angie's to clear the air with Sally. She was my only hope. I could have gone to work, but I doubted I would have gotten much done. I didn't even know how Jason was handling the time I was taking off recently so I could work on his behalf. Hopefully, he wasn't docking my pay because I couldn't possibly afford it now that I had to pay rent.

On the drive down to Coyote Lake, I thought of various speeches I would make when I got together with Sally. No one could have been more shocked when she opened Angie's front door and smothered me in a hug. She whispered. "Please forgive me, Miranda. Please forgive me."

Eventually, needing to breathe, I pushed myself away and held her at arm's length. "Okay, now. What, exactly, am I forgiving you for?"

She blushed, "I should have told you I was going to court. I should have given you a heads up. That's what friends do. I should have told you what I found in Burt's notes. Mark did a good job, but we both know what his notes meant."

I agreed. "You're probably right, and I'm going to address that with Jason when the time is right. But I forgive you. I can't say I wouldn't have done the same thing in your shoes. I get it; we're not technically on the same team. I'm with the defense, and you're trying to get a conviction. That relationship has some built-in conflict. So, let's continue doing the best we can and hope that we can find some mutual ground."

She stood back and looked at me. "Now come on in. You're a strange woman, Miranda."

I laughed. "I've been called worse." I wasn't quite sure how to ask her my most important question. "Okay, I need to ask you something."

She nodded. "Okay."

I drew a deep breath and plowed ahead. "I want to work with you going through Burt's notes. That way, we can cover more ground more quickly. And maybe I'll see something that you don't notice since I'm coming from a different place."

She looked at the ceiling, which I've noticed over the years isn't a good thing when you are hoping for a positive response. "I don't know. Some of those notes might turn out to be personal and they're all I have left of Burt."

I wasn't sure how to convince her. I even understood her hesitation to a certain degree. "I get it, Sally. But I'm not going anywhere with it. I'll work on it right here in Coyote Lake with you. Then if I have questions, you can answer them in real-time. Besides," I said with a chuckle as I pointed at an incomplete jigsaw puzzle on the table, "you really want to spend the rest of your life doing those?"

She smiled broadly. "You're right."

We let Angie know we were going to spend some time together at Sally's. There were too many notes to haul them back to Angie's house. Once we got to her place, Sally led me to a room that appeared to have been used as an office. Stacked from floor to ceiling, taking up at least half the room were identical stenographer's notebooks, each with date ranges on the outside cover. From what I could see, they were stacked in chronological order. Each year was separated with a single sheet of loose-leaf notebook paper with the year written in black magic marker. There were more for some years than others. The most recent years had the largest number of notebooks. From what I could tell, they dated back to the 1980s.

I was overwhelmed. I surveyed the room and asked Sally, "Where did you start? How much have you covered? What have you been looking for?"

She plopped down onto a well-worn office chair. "I don't know. I started with the new ones and worked my way backward. But the cops have the one he had on him when he died. I'm sure it ain't worth a damn to them, but they have it for evidence and it could contain the answers we need to solve this."

I wish I had known that. "They have to provide a copy for us if we ask. It may take some time because someone would have to stand at the copier turning the pages, one after the other." I thought for a second. "Hey, you know what? Tina Bright owes me big time. She had no idea what Jacob Mabry was up to, and he made her look really bad today. She might just put a rush on it. I'm going to check with her." I giggled, "I also want to see if he still has a job."

My gut told me that if she started with the most recent, I should go with the oldest. The first year was 1980. My instinct was right on several levels. First of all, when Burt first started these journals, he wrote in longhand, not in code. Second, he didn't write nearly as much back in those early days, just the important things. Burt was eighteen in 1980. He wrote his first entry the night of July 4th. "The hotel burned down tonight and with it, the dreams of the Roop family. The future of the Hot Springs Resort was riding on the hotel. There was no insurance, and it burned to the ground. I have my suspicions and will track down whoever set this fire if it's the last thing I do."

I looked at Sally, who was already mired in notebooks. "So, you said they never prosecuted Tommy Pearson, right?"

She kept reading. "No. His father was some kind of big deal. Burt said it was a sham."

I looked at the number of notebooks and couldn't believe that I had promised to do this, much less that I wouldn't take any off site. I needed to sleep, eat, and basically *live* here until I found what I needed. I had to call Wanda to make sure that she could handle Tea in my absence. She answered on the third ring. I figured she must be at work.

She answered, "Marshall." She was definitely at work.

I decided to be bright and cheerful. "Hey, Wanda, what's up?"

She sounded exhausted. "Hey, Miranda. What can I do for you?"

I continued. "I might need some extended time to review evidence in this case, which would mean I won't be home for a while. Do you think you can keep Tea out of trouble?"

She laughed, "I'm not her mother, but I think I can. If things get out of control, I'll haul Mike in and scare him to death."

I chuckled, "That would be so fun to watch. I'm probably going to stay with Sally for a few days to read Burt's journals. I'll have to figure out what to do about work, but that's my cross to bear. I guess Jason had better be thanking his lucky stars that he's got such a dedicated ex-girlfriend."

She responded, "You're right about that. I hate to cut you short, but I gotta go." She hung up.

I figured I'd call Jason since I was on a roll. "Jason Wall, how can I help you?"

I hesitated. "Jason, it's Miranda."

He brightened. "Miranda, hey, how are you?"

I didn't want to get too personal. "I'm still working on your case and need to spend a few days out of town." I didn't want to tell him I'd be a couple of houses down from him. "Can you get someone to fill in for me? I've got a good lead, and I don't want to drop it."

He sounded surprised. "No, that's great. I really appreciate you continuing to work on my case while we go through whatever this is."

There were at least eighty-two things I wanted to say but I said, "No problem. I'll talk to you soon." I hung up.

Chapter 33

I spent the next four days with Sally Roop, reading, eating, talking, drinking, sleeping, laughing, crying, sometimes feeling hopeful, sometimes feeling discouraged, like there was a light at the end of the tunnel, or like the light was just an oncoming train.

I finally learned the details, reading the 1981 notebooks. It wasn't until nearly a year after the hotel burned that they concluded that it was arson. The circumstances of the arson investigation were shady. There were several other arson investigations around that same time and they all pointed to the same person, Tommy Pearson. He was never prosecuted for any of them, and they were all swept under the rug. That had everything to do with the fact that his father Thomas Pearson, Sr. was a county supervisor for Santa Clara County.

At the age of nineteen, Burt went to the Santa Clara County Sheriff's Department to file a complaint, accusing Tommy Pearson of burning down the Gilroy Hot Springs Hotel on July 4th, 1980. The case was eventually dismissed due to insufficient evidence.

I couldn't help but wonder, so I asked Sally, "Do you know if Burt had seen Tommy Pearson since school?"

She chewed on the end of her pencil. "Don't think so. He probably would of killed him."

I decided that either meant that he hadn't seen him since school, or he had seen him but hadn't told Sally about it. Burt, where are you when I need you?

I asked her a little later, "Did you see any references to meeting a Tommy or maybe TP since he likes to use initials?"

She strained to remember. "Maybe but I thought he was picking up toilet paper and wanted to remind hisself. Want me to go back and find it?"

I decided it didn't matter as long as he had referred to him at some point recently. That, to me, meant that they might have met or at least planned to meet. That was a good sign, at least for me, maybe not so much for Burt.

#

After nearly a week of reviewing the crazy world of Burt Roop, I finally called it quits. Sally and I hugged and said our goodbyes, and she headed back to Angie's house. I was convinced that I had my man, or at least I had a suspect, which was way better than not having a suspect.

On Friday afternoon, my next stop was the Santa Clara Sheriff's Department. But I called Mark before I went inside. According to Sally, Burt had a notebook in his possession, and I wasn't aware that they had given us a copy of one in the evidence transfer.

He answered on the first ring. "Hey, Miranda, you got anything?"

I replied, "Yeah, I think I do, but can you check the evidence they provided? I'm looking for a notebook that Burt had on his person when he died. They should have provided a copy."

He had a table in his suite with all the evidence they had provided. He was back in about thirty seconds. "There's not much here, so I can give you a definitive 'No' on that."

I said, "Okay, I'll get a copy from them. I'm just about to go into the police department."

He responded, "Say 'Hi' for me."

I laughed. "Yeah, I'll say 'Hi' to Jacob for sure." We hung up.

I didn't want to gloat about how Mark took Mabry apart in court, but actually, I kind of did. I stepped into the lobby with the hope that Tina Bright was free. The receptionist called her after asking me, "Who may I tell her is visiting?"

I smiled. "Tell her it's her friend Miranda Marquette."

She repeated, "It's your friend Miranda Marquette." She nodded at me. "She'll be right down."

Surprisingly, she was down in a matter of about two minutes. She stuck out her hand. "Miranda, how nice to see you again." I was impressed by how sincere she sounded.

I followed her to her office. I sat in the chair facing her desk. She wasted no time. "Miranda, I wanted to let you know that Jacob Mabry is no longer with us. He resigned." My mouth dropped open, and I had to close it to prevent myself from looking rude.

I mentally drew a big sigh of relief to learn that Jacob Mabry would no longer be a threat to me. I tried to think of something charitable to say. "Maybe he'll find work that's better suited for him."

She raised one eyebrow.

I cleared my throat. "Let me tell you why I'm here. We reviewed all the evidence, and there is a notebook that seems to be missing."

With an enigmatic smile, she pushed herself up out of her chair and took two steps over to a file cabinet where she pulled out a notebook. She held it up in front of her as she spoke. "I have it right here. Another deputy spotted it as Mabry was cleaning his locker prior to leaving for good. It seems he *completely forgot* that he had it. We owe you an apology, Miranda. There's no question that Jacob knew that what was contained in this notebook would clear you of any wrongdoing in this case, and he just couldn't seem to deal with that. He was so convinced that you had something to do with Burt Roop's murder, he couldn't accept evidence that supported any alternative resolution. Believe me, no one discouraged his resignation. The matter is in the hands of the DA's office now. There may or may not be reason for prosecution."

She handed me the notebook and walked me to the elevator. "Don't worry, we made copies. You can keep this one."

I shook her hand as I entered the elevator. "I appreciate everything you've done. I guess maybe we are on the same side after all."

She waved as the doors slid closed.

\#

I was so relieved to be going back home for the night. I hoped Tea and Wanda were both there. I'd love to spend some time with them after being away for most of the week.

I could tell they were home by the laughter emanating from the apartment when I went to put my key in the door. I felt a little jealous and tried to push it down. My feelings turned out to be unfounded and silly when I saw the "Welcome Home Miranda" banner hanging from the kitchen ceiling. They both yelled, "Welcome home!"

I hugged both of them. "How did you know I'd be coming home?"

Wanda laughed, "The truth be known, we've had it up since Wednesday, but that shows how long we've been in hopeful anticipation of your return." They clinked wine glasses.

I protested, "Hey, where's mine?" Tea brought me one.

I announced with some bravado, "In my hand, I have the key to solving this case."

They asked simultaneously, "Really?"

I smiled. "Well, I hope so. Sally and I got about all we could from Burt's notebooks, but this was the most recent one that the police were holding as evidence. I'm hoping it holds the final key. I believe that Burt had been pursuing the person who burned down the Hot Springs Hotel in 1980 and that he was closing in on him. I wonder if that's how he got himself killed."

I distributed the pages equally between us. "I stopped at the office and made a copy. If all of us work on it, we'll get done faster. Look for anything with the name: Tommy Pearson, the initials: TP, or anything similar. Or if you see anything talking about the 1980 hotel fire or something that looks like code for it, let me know. He used a lot of initials for things, so it might not be obvious." I figured it would be easier for all of us to get involved, even if I would have to pore through the whole thing again myself at some point later on.

Tea almost immediately found something. "Look at this note. 'S thinks I'm crazy for keeping this alive, but I will never let it die until TP goes down. He forgets I have the lighter, or maybe he never knew it. It didn't matter as much back then before DNA testing. And fingerprints would probably degrade over this much time with the heat and cold. I should have brought it to the police to have it tested back then but I was young and thought I knew it all. I figured with his connections they would just 'lose' it. I hope that the plastic bag is holding together in the hiding place. If I don't make it, I need to let S know where it is.'"

I grabbed the copy. "No way! Did the police even read this thing? My guess is they didn't know what it meant, so they ignored it or didn't have time to worry about it. You'd have to know that 'S' means Sally and TP means Tommy Pearson, but the lighter is a dead giveaway about the 1980 fire if you know any history about the Gilroy Hot Springs at all."

Wanda jumped up from the table. "Look at this. 'C to deliver Gs before I meet with TP. I hope to convince S to let me keep one just in case. Not sure the CP meeting is bright, but it's all I've got."

I couldn't control myself after all the frustration I faced with this case. "Oh my god, oh my god! Chenoa was to deliver the guns before Burt met with Tommy Pearson. He was hoping to convince the sheriff to let him keep one of the guns to protect himself in case the meeting went south. He wasn't sure that meeting in Coe Park was very bright, but that was where Tommy wanted to meet." I was sure we had this solved. Somehow Tommy was able to turn the tide on Burt, and when he tried to get away, Tommy shot him in the back. He then dragged the body up to where I found it."

I waved my sheets of the notebook in the air. "The sheriff's department had everything they needed to crack this case right under their noses the whole time, but Jacob was so busy concentrating on me, he never even looked at it."

This was an odd situation, sitting with a detective with the Santa Clara Police Department. They already had a built-in competition with the sheriff's department, wanting to one-up each other. But before Wanda could comment, I added one more detail. "Oh, I forgot to tell you, Jacob's no longer with the department. He resigned before they could fire him."

She shook her head. "Why they hired that creep in the first place made me wonder about their hiring practices. Good riddance."

I asked Wanda directly, "So now what do we do with this information? Do we go to Tina Bright with it?"

Wanda winced at the idea. "Um, gosh, I'd really hate to do that, at least right now." She got a devilish grin on her face. "Miranda, maybe you and I should pay this guy a visit, unofficially, of course."

Chapter 34

I was surprised that Wanda suggested meeting Tommy Pearson even though both the murder of Burt Roop and the arson of the Gilroy Hot Springs Hotel were outside of the city of Santa Clara and the police department's jurisdiction.

I asked, "Are you sure you won't get in trouble for this?" as we rode down toward Coyote Lake and Gilroy.

She patted me on the arm. "Sometimes you worry too much, Miranda. Sure, I'm a cop, but I'm also a private citizen just like you are. We are not approaching Tommy Pearson in any type of official capacity, just as concerned citizens."

To be honest, I was relieved to have a back-up, and I was pretty sure that she didn't want me heading out to a possible murderer's house with no plan, alone. I grabbed her hand as we drove down the highway. "You are a good friend."

She smiled but said nothing.

We planned to visit Sally first to see if she knew where Burt had hidden the lighter in the plastic bag. It was very likely the lighter that had started the fire that burned down the hotel in 1980. If we didn't find it, we would still use the fact that we knew of its existence to bluff Tommy if we needed to.

I was excited to get Wanda's impressions of Sally, with whom I had spent most of the last week. We had grown pretty close during that time. We pulled into Angie's driveway since Sally went back there when we finished reviewing the notebooks. I jumped out and walked to the front door.

Sally looked out Angie's kitchen window and saw my car. She yelled, "Miranda, whatcha doing back so soon? I thought I was rid of you." She laughed and threw the door open. She stopped short. "Oh my. I didn't realize you weren't alone. Who's your friend?"

Wanda stuck out her hand. "Detective Wanda Marshall of the Santa Clara Police Department, and a close friend of Miranda's." She smiled.

Sally walked right through her extended hand and hugged her. "Any friend of Miranda's is a friend of mine. You two come in and tell me what's up."

Angie poured coffee for us as we went through the kitchen to the sitting room and said, "There's been so much going on here since Sally arrived." She smiled and said to Wanda, "I'm Angie, by the way."

"Wanda Marshall of the Santa Clara Police Department, but I'm just here as a citizen. Nice to meet you, Angie." They shook hands.

Angie replied, "I'll leave the three of you to your business. I think it might be confidential." She went upstairs, waving. "You make sure you come back sometime when you can stay."

We all smiled and waved.

Once we settled with our coffees, I got right to the point. "Sally, I was able to get Burt's notebook, and I am sure without a doubt that Tommy Pearson killed Burt. Burt was meeting with him after he dropped off the guns with the sheriff's department, in Coe Park. He was going to tell him that he had DNA evidence that he burned down the hotel back in 1980. From what we could figure out, there must have been a struggle, and he killed Burt, and he left him in the park. Burt made a note that he was going to tell you where he was hiding the evidence, which was a lighter in a plastic bag. Did he ever tell you where he hid that?"

Sally concentrated hard. "So, that scumbucket's been threatening me. Time to put that slime in prison once and for all. He threw his freedom in Burt's face for thirty-one years. His connected slime father ain't here to protect him no more. If we gotta rip my house apart, we'll find that lighter. Let's head over there." We went out, hopped in my car, and were in her driveway in a matter of minutes. She led us through her kitchen and into the parlor.

I thought about Burt's notes. "Sally, think back to the day before he died. I know sometimes we don't pay full attention to our significant other. Was there anything he said that was out of the ordinary or didn't seem to make sense?"

Sally sat on the couch, wracking her brain. "There was something. He kept saying something over and over again, and I got so mad at him. Now, what was it?" She stared at the ceiling. "It's under something. It's under something. It's under the block. That's it! It's under the block." She stood up.

"What block?" Wanda and I said at the same time.

We followed her outside to the freestanding garage, about twenty feet back from the house. She flicked on the lights. In the far rear corner of the garage was a concrete block. Wanda and I lifted it off a small metal box buried in the dirt floor. I tried to pull it up, but it was firmly stuck in the packed dirt.

I searched for tools. Leaning against an adjacent wall was a small shovel. I started digging. It only took a couple of minutes to dig out the box which was about three inches deep and a six by twelve rectangle. It was locked with a small padlock, which I broke with a nearby hammer. Inside were a couple of Mad Magazines, an issue of Popular Mechanics, and a blue Bic lighter in a plastic sandwich bag. I yelled, "Eureka!" We had struck gold.

We kept everything in the box as we had found it except that we had moved the magazines to find the lighter in the heat of our excitement. At least it was still inside the plastic bag.

The three of us left the garage with our find. In the driveway, I asked both of them, "Now we have a decision to make, girls. Do we take everything we have to the sheriff's department and hope that they do the right thing, knowing they already messed it up once, or do we go rogue and hand him to them on a silver platter?"

Wanda laughed, "Well, if you put it that way, what choice do we have?" She looked at Sally. "Sally, do you know where this guy lives?"

Sally smiled. "Oh yeah. He lives in the house he grew up in. He never made nothing of himself, so he went back to his stompin' ground when his parents passed on. I ain't sure where he lived before that; I think an apartment in Gilroy somewhere. He's a hell of a looker and a smooth talker, but he doesn't have much else going for him. I think he's made a living as a womanizer, and when he'd wore out his welcome, he moved on until he found someone else to sponge off. It doesn't say much for the women, but it's kept him off the streets for thirty years."

We got in my car. Sally squeezed into the back seat and gave me instructions. "Their house is at the end of the dead end at Howell Lane. Take a left on Roop Road to Estates Drive, second right on Via Del Oro, right on Bridle Path Drive, and a right on Howell Lane. It's only a couple of minutes from here."

Before I pulled out of the driveway, I asked, "So, what's the plan when we get there?"

Wanda said, "Hey, we're women, and he's a womanizer. I don't think it'll be hard to get him to invite us in. Once we get inside, we're in control. We keep talking and keep him off balance. I'd like to get him so riled up that he turns himself in, and the only way that's going to happen is if we threaten him with something less pleasant if he doesn't."

I was a little worried about transporting him all the way back to Santa Clara. "Did you bring cuffs or anything? He might change his mind half-way back to the sheriff's department."

She reached in her pocket. "I do have some zip ties for occasions like this." She laughed.

I smiled and said with my best British accent, "Well, you are quite naughty, aren't you?"

She responded proudly. "Oh, my dear, you have no idea."

I addressed Sally, who was looking a little bit uneasy. "Sally, if this makes you uncomfortable, you can stay here. You have done so much already."

"I'm nervous, but I wouldn't miss this for anything. This guy took down Burt's family. He destroyed their dream for the Gilroy Hot Springs. He thumbed his nose at everyone around here for three decades and then, if that wasn't enough, killed my beloved husband. Oh yeah, and he threatened my life. It's time to watch him get his." She pulled something out of her pocket. "Oh, here, I have a micro-recorder just in case you need a record of what goes on there." She thought for a second. "I want to be there, but I don't think I should go in. He'd recognize me immediately and that would give us away. I'll stay in the car. If you get in trouble, just text me. I can call for backup or something."

I gave her a thumbs up and said, "Great thinking on the recorder too, Sally." Then, I looked over at Wanda in the co-pilot seat. "Are you ready?"

Wanda saluted, "Aye, aye, captain. Let's roll."

I shifted the Rover into reverse, destination: Tommy Pearson.

#

Sally was right. It was only a couple of minutes to the sprawling ranch house at the end of the cul de sac. It had a brick front and a three-car garage, and I was sure it was very expensive and extraordinary when it was built in the sixties. These days, it just looked like a ranch house with a three-car garage.

I pulled the Rover into the driveway, assuming that no vehicles would need to leave while we were here. From what I knew of his background, I figured he lived here alone since he probably wouldn't tolerate anyone sponging off him.

Wanda and I exchanged knowing glances as we headed for the front door. We shared the confidence of knowing we had this guy where we wanted him. I pressed the doorbell. Until he answered the door, I wondered how a man nearly fifty could still be called Tommy, but it fit him. His face was boyish and beautiful. He smiled broadly when he saw the two of us as if we were old friends. "Well, well, well, what can I do for you?"

"Hi. We're Miranda and Wanda. are you Tommy Pearson?" I said.

He ushered us in. "I sure am. I have no idea why a couple of gorgeous women have appeared uninvited to my front door, but I never question a blessing; I just thank God and move forward."

He sat on a love seat, and we placed ourselves on a couch facing him. We were separated by a massive mahogany coffee table lined with golf and sports-car coffee table books.

He smiled, and the dimples on his cheeks got even deeper. "So, now we know who we are, what can I do for you?"

I just had to use some of my knowledge of Gilroy Hot Springs history to toy with this guy just a touch before we put the hammer down. "We've been studying the history of the Gilroy Hot Springs, and we understand that you're quite a hero."

He looked confused, "Hero? How so?"

I continued. "Well, weren't you one of the boys who helped to put out the fire that Fourth of July night in 1980? I understood that several of the local high school boys helped the firefighters."

He squirmed a little on the loveseat. "Well, yes, I suppose I did."

I exhaled loudly. "It was such a shame, though, wasn't it?"

He suddenly seemed distracted. "Uh-huh. What was a shame?"

I sat on the edge of the couch. "It was such a shame that they never caught that—oh, I just don't know what to call him. That person who burned down the hotel."

He looked like he suddenly woke up. "Well, then. Is there something I can do for you, ladies?"

I couldn't control myself any longer. "What would be helpful would be a DNA sample."

He squinted and lost all his dimples. "What? No." He suddenly stood up. "I'm going to have to ask you to leave."

Neither of us moved. Wanda took over with her very police-like voice. "Sit down, Mr. Pearson. None of us are going anywhere." She took out her badge. "I'm afraid I didn't introduce myself properly. I'm Detective Wanda Marshall from the Santa Clara Police Department."

He bit his lip. "Do you have a warrant?"

She responded, "Of course not. We're not here on police business. We're here as concerned citizens."

He sat back down and spoke in a soft voice almost as if he'd been waiting all these years for someone to show up. "About the hotel fire?"

I commended him, "Very good, Tommy. We're here for other things too. The fire does play a part, though. We just couldn't understand why anyone would kill Burt Roop. Motive was the toughest part of this crime. He was a man everyone liked, even the Native Americans who had been trying to get control of the Hot Springs for as long as anyone could remember. Did he sometimes drive his wife crazy? Sure."

He didn't respond.

I continued. "So, after all these years, Burt finally realized he had you where he wanted you. Your parents finally died and couldn't help you anymore, and he had the lighter. The lighter that he held onto for thirty-one years. The lighter with your DNA on it.

He was a visionary. Who would have imagined there was such a thing as DNA testing back in 1980? So, he made the mistake of meeting with you in a secluded park. I have no idea why Burt thought that was a good idea. It wasn't. He had a gun. You two wrestled for it, he tried to get away, and you shot him. Then you took him and the gun further up the mountain to get away from any other DNA evidence you left behind. I'm assuming your DNA is on the gun, but I guess when they got a positive match with Jason, they didn't care who belonged to the second DNA hit. But now they can match the gun with the lighter and tie you to both crimes. Neat and tidy."

Apparently, my analysis didn't impress him as much as I'd hoped because he leaned back on the love seat with a smirk on his face. "I don't know who you women think you are, but you just blew any chance of getting a conviction for either crime. You came in here under false pretenses without a search warrant. You lied about who you were or why you were here. And when you leave here, I will disappear, never to be seen again. If you don't think I haven't been planning for this day even before I killed stupid Burt, you're even more ignorant than you look. You think he's the first person who got in my way and had to be eliminated? Come on. Give me some credit. The sad thing is that now I can't let either of you go. And now that you're on my turf, I know all the tricks and hiding places."

Just then, I heard a siren not far in the distance. It sounded like it was already in the neighborhood.

Wanda said, "Oops. I guess I hit 911."

Tommy appeared to be reaching under a cushion for something.

Before he could find whatever he was searching for, Wanda had jumped up, whipped out her service revolver, and aimed it at Tommy's head. "Freeze!"

He complied. The wide-eyed look of shock on his face was priceless. Within a few minutes, the Gilroy Police Department had cuffed him and taken him away.

\#

DNA testing accomplished something good, which had not always been the case in my experience. Tommy Pearson was convicted of Burt Roop's murder and arson in the 1980 destruction of the Gilroy Hot Springs Hotel. He was also convicted of three other murders in the Gilroy area of several significant others or husbands of women he eventually moved in with. In a fitting ending to Burt Roop's legacy, he assisted in convicting an arsonist and a serial killer but, unfortunately, paid the ultimate price for his efforts.

After the trial was over, Jason and I decided to take a weekend to talk out our differences to see if we still had any hope left for us. He accepted responsibility for the communication breakdown in our relationship and for hurting me deeply by hiding his continued texting and emailing with Chenoa. He swore that he never saw her in person after they broke up, and I chose to take him at his word despite the cryptic coding in Burt Roop's journal that appeared to say otherwise.

A couple of months after the charges were dropped against Jason, I moved back in with him. Things weren't always perfect between us, and sometimes I wondered if he always told the truth. So far, I have been able to deal with my agonizing mistrust.

Tea remained a permanent apartment mate of Wanda. They developed a very close mother-daughter relationship that appears to work for both of them. I still spent loads of time with them whenever I could.

Patricia, Toni, and baby Nate continued to be part of my life and I visited them weekly, happy had our rift healed.

And the WAIT Women's Club, Wanda, Margo, Lyanne, and I, get together at least monthly at Margo's new home on Monterey Bay, just waiting, wine in hand, with mixed feelings of anticipation and dread, for another reason to use our unique powers for solving crimes.

MIRANDA MARQUETTE MYSTERIES
BY J T KUNKEL

Secrets in Silicon Valley (Book 4)
Death in Santa Clara (Book 3)
Murder in the Extreme (Book 2)
Blood on the Bayou (Book 1)

If you have enjoyed this book, please let your friends know by sharing a review on Amazon and Goodreads. Thank you for following Miranda and be sure to watch for her continuing adventures.

Made in the USA
Middletown, DE
14 May 2023

30368618R00146